# ANARCHY FOUND

## JA HUSS

ALPHA LINCOLN

ANARCHY
FOUND

Learn more about this series here:
www.SuperAlphaSeries.com
Copyright © 2015 by JA Huss
ISBN: 978-1-936413-98-0

Edited by RJ Locksley
Cover and Interior Drawings by Ambro Jordi
Cover Design by JA Huss

# SPECIAL THANKS

To Ambro Jordi for the beautiful cover and interior sketches. Please check out his website to see all the amazing photorealistic drawings he does here: http://ambrojordiart.blogspot.com/

MOLLY GUN GIRL

## CHAPTER ONE

Today is like any other day.

If every other day was filled with hopeless abandonment

And it is. Has been. Will continue to be. For as long as we both shall live.

The wannabe writer in me thinks like this. All poetic. Stringing words together just because they sound like music when you say them out loud.

"You're crazy, Molls," I whisper to the fogged-up windshield of my brother's truck. That's what he would say. And why not channel him? Today of all days? Why not?

I'm not a writer, not in the traditional sense. I don't write sentences or paragraphs. Just lists. And today I have a long one brewing inside my head. When I get home, I'm going to write it down in my journal and then, no matter what happens after this day, I can look back and remember how it feels to save your soul by selling your past.

Hate. That's the name of the list. Or if you want the full title, *Things I Hate While Driving on a Mountain Road Pulling My Dead Brother's Bike Trailer Home from the Racetrack After Successfully Ignoring Said Bikes for Six Months*.

But Hate, for short.

1. Mountain roads.
2. Rain.
3. Foggy windows.

4. ...

A pair of motorcycles whip past on either side of me, their engines roaring, the riders' helmeted faces buried deep against the gas tanks. I slam on my brakes, my heart beating so fast it might jump out of my chest. Their red taillights disappear around a curve and I let out a long breath.

"What the fuck, you assholes?"

I scream it. And that makes me mad because there's no one to hear it. So I get out of the truck and stand in the rain and scream it again. Only this time I scream it to God.

"What the fuck? You asshole!" I think I'm crying. Not for those jerks who will probably crash on the slick roads, but for me. Because I'm angry. I'm so, so, so fucking angry.

A horn honks behind me and snaps me out of my fit.

"Sorry," I yell, a smile on my face. The good-public-servant smile I've practiced for the past six years. "Problem with my headlights. But it's OK now," I add quickly, as the older man makes to get out and help me. I wave at him. "I'm fine, all fixed." I motion for him to pass and he goes around, shaking his head at me. Feeling sorry for me.

That's what people tend to do. Generally. If they know me well enough, they feel sorry for me. That's part of the reason I moved to Cathedral City.

Which is where I really need to be right now. Home, making my hate list, feeling sorry for myself so people don't have to.

I jump back in the truck, soaking wet, and put it in gear. I move forward with the same lethargy I had before the bikers pissed me off and morph back into my normal self as I take the corner around the mountain.

The car that just passed me brakes and then swerves like it's avoiding something on the side of the road. This road is narrow, so everyone drives right down the middle unless there's another car coming. I strain my eyes through the blurry fogged-up window to see what the issue is, but before I can get a handle on it, the two bikers from before peel out from the side of the road, their red taillights flashing at me again.

"Assholes," I whisper to myself, speeding up. "You're a couple of assholes."

The trailer I'm dragging fishtails as I pass over a deep puddle, and I force myself to slow down. But I keep my eyes trained on the twin taillights ahead. The road meets the mountain and splits at a fork, and one light goes right, another left.

When I get to the fork, I go left, away from Cathedral City and towards the bike shop that wants my brother's last creations. It's the only reason I came out here to pick them up.

1. It's a way forward.
2. A way past the anger.
3. And sadness.
4. And pity.

I call that list *A New Start*.

I'm desperately in need of one. And the new job just doesn't quite cut it.

I round another corner and the biker is only a few hundred yards ahead. I brake again out of habit. He's looking down at his foot or something near his gear shift. He surges forward for a few seconds, looks up, then a sputter of smoke comes from the exhaust and he surges forward again. Only this time, the bike swerves, fishtails like my trailer did in the deep puddle, and then he's on his side, scraping along the blacktop pavement.

It all happens in slow motion. Metal grinds sparks against the asphalt, his body swings sideways, his arms fly up in the air as he lets go of the handlebars, and then the bike slides away from him and comes to a stop in a ditch.

"I told you, asshole! I told you!" I pound on the steering wheel and slow the truck down as I get closer to the rider. He lies absolutely still and that pain in my heart is back. Something like a fist grips it, twists it, and all I see is the bloody mess that used to be my brother. "No, Molly," I say, shaking my head, forcing the image from my mind. My stomach gets all queasy as I roll to a stop a few yards away.

He's dead. Dead. Dead. Dead.
1. Wrecked a bike.
2. Lying in the middle of the road.
3. Unmoving.
4. Dead.

But then the rider raises his head a little, cranes his neck, and points his black-faced helmet right at me.

I step out of the truck and walk towards him as he sits up and begins unfastening his helmet. "Are you… are you OK?" I ask, shaking uncontrollably. He's not dead, so that's good, but my heart is beating so fast I have to put my hand over it.

He whips his helmet off, throws it on the ground, and gets to his feet. "Motherfucker," he says, eyes blazing with anger. His dark hair is cropped short and he has a two-day beard that casts the perfect shadow across his hard-edged jawline. He looks down at his black leather jacket, ignoring my question, and studies the rips in the elbows. Then he holds out his black-gloved hands and studies his palms before moving on to the rips in his racing jeans. There's a gash along the thigh that took the brunt of the slide on the asphalt and I catch a glimpse of tanned skin stained with blood beneath the thick cloth.

"Do you need help?"

He looks over at the bike, the back wheel still spinning as it lies there in the ditch. "Sheila?" he calls out. "Talk to me, baby."

For a moment I think he had a passenger I didn't notice. But when I follow him over to the bike, there's no one else there.

"Sheila," he says again. "Come on, don't do this to me."

"Who's Sheila?"

His gaze darts over to me, and I catch a muttered, "Fuck," under his breath. He leans a little to the side, trying to see my truck around me. "I'm not sure if this is luck or not," he says, walking right past me, without a word or even a glance in my direction. "You got bikes in there," he calls over his shoulder after he passes. "I guess I'm gonna need a ride."

GUN GIRL

## CHAPTER TWO

"Hey!" I yell as he walks around to the back of my trailer. "What are you doing?"

He's already got the back doors open by the time I catch up with him, and he's just about to step inside when I pull my gun.

"Step away from the trailer, dirtbag." I growl it out and he stops mid-stride, chances a look over his shoulder, and grins. "I'm not going to tell you again. Step away—"

"Are you Wild Will?"

"Do I look like Wild Will?" Jesus. Just saying my brother's name out loud makes my heart ache with emptiness.

"No, but you're pulling a trailer with his name painted on it in bright orange."

"Look, I'm sorry I stopped, OK? I can see you're fine. So number one, you're gonna back away. Number two, I'm gonna get in my truck, and number three, we're gonna forget that you made an ass of yourself—"

"Hey, hey, hey," he says, holding his gloved hands up in the air as he slowly turns around. "Easy, gun girl."

"Don't patronize me. I'm not your girl."

"I'm just trying to keep you calm, that's all. You're waving a gun in my face."

"I'm not waving! I'm carefully aiming—" I take a deep breath. Because he's pressing my buttons on purpose. Trying to get a rise out of me for some reason.

He shoots me a pathetic look, complete with pouty lips and droopy eyes. "I just need a ride, OK? Help a guy out. You've got Wild Will's trailer and I've got a downed bike. If you don't help me I'll be out here for hours waiting for a friend to come save me." He smiles, releasing some hidden dimples. "Save me, gun girl. Please."

I have just enough time to blink twice before he doubles over laughing, grabbing his stomach. "What's so funny?" Jerk. He's making fun of me!

He stands up straight, still chuckling. "That look on your face. Hahaha. It was priceless."

That's it for me. I'm outta here. I put my gun away, push him aside, and close the trailer back up.

"Hey, wait," he says, grabbing my arm.

I whirl around, grab the collar of his jacket, swing my legs up, twirl my body around his neck, and drop him in a puddle on the road. "Don't," I seethe, "touch me. And don't call me gun girl. I don't need that gun, asshole. And if you think I do, then you're gonna be sorry when I beat your ass with my bare hands. The gun isn't the weapon, bike boy. I am."

I push myself up with a hand on his back, stand up, and wait for a response. He looks over his shoulder again, grinning. I'm fighting the urge to kick him in the teeth when his hand sweeps out, grabs my ankle, and pulls. I tip back, instinctively reaching to break my fall, and feel the sting when my palms crash against the asphalt. "You fucker."

And then he's on top of me. He pulls my gun out of my pants, throws it so it goes skidding under the trailer, and sits all his weight down on my stomach as he pins my hands to the road. "I said easy, girl," he growls. "Because I don't want to hurt you."

"Right." I laugh. "We'll just forget I took you down in two seconds and pretend that I'm not the one who'll hurt *you*."

He cocks his head to the side, doubling over and grimacing from the crash, or maybe considering me for a second. Then he takes a deep breath and stands up, offering me a hand. "Let's start over. Hey, gun girl." He smirks. "I'm bike boy. I crashed my bike over there and need a ride home. And since you've got this pretty trailer built for hauling bikes, I was wondering if you'd help me out?"

I eye him for a minute. He leans down and whispers, "This is when you take my hand."

I reluctantly take it since he's towering over me and I'm pretty sure if I attack him again, things will get serious. His black gloves are soft against my skin, and his palms are so warm, the heat radiates up into my chilled body. He grips my hand tightly as he pulls me to my feet and looks me up and down real fast. "OK, we're good? I'll pay you for your time. Make up for the fact that I ruined your afternoon. Just drop me off a couple miles down the road and we'll call it quits. Deal?"

I sigh heavily as the rain picks up and starts rolling down my face. I pull out my phone, check the time, realize I'm late and I have no signal up here in the mountains, and give in. "Fine. Just hurry, please. I have business today."

He's walking off towards his bike before I even finish the sentence. Asshole.

But damn if he isn't one sexy asshole in that leather jacket, the tight jeans that show the muscles in his legs, that black t-shirt clinging to his chest like it's painted on, and a face I might be thinking about when I'm alone tonight.

Jesus, what is wrong with me? *No, Molly. Asshole. He's an asshole. For too many reasons to list.*

"Hey, help me out here?" he calls from the ditch.

I roll my eyes like a teenager as I walk over to him. He's got the bike upright again and he's pointing to the rear fender. "Just lift it up a little bit while I push it up the embankment."

I slip on my way down, slide on my ass, and then sit there at the bottom of the ditch wondering if my day could possibly get any worse.

"Need another hand?" he asks, looking down at me.

"I got it, thanks." I get up, slip in the mud one more time, and then lift up on the back end when he counts down from three. He heaves hard, trying to force the machine up, but it rocks back and the rear tire settles in the mud near my feet.

"OK, this is pissing me off," he says. "This is really pissing me off." He takes off his leather jacket and throws it down on the road. His biceps are popping out of the short sleeves of his shirt like cannons, and the rain is plastering the thin fabric against his back where my eyes rest on the corded muscles.

I almost don't look away in time.

"Ready?" he asks, looking over his shoulder.

"I'm ready," I say, looking down at the tire.

"On one." He counts down again. I push harder this time, giving it all my effort. I just want to get out of this ditch and be done with this day. So I lean into it, my boots slipping in the mud. His boots slip in the mud above me, and just when I think we'll have to give up and call someone else to help, he grits his teeth, strains his muscles, and yells as the bike finally gets past some threshold and eases back up onto the road. He pushes it forward a few paces and then drops the stand and comes back to help me out of the ditch.

"Thanks," he says, pulling me up from the ditch in one smooth tug. His eyes meet mine and hold there. I squirm under his intense inspection. "I really do appreciate it."

His eyes are a striking amber brown. And he's so close I can see little flecks of gold in them. We are stuck like that for several seconds. He squints at me, like he's thinking about something. But then he shakes his head and turns away.

"No problem," I say, tugging on my light jacket and straightening it out. I don't want strange bikers thinking too hard about me. "I'm soaked though. So can we get that thing loaded and go?"

"Right," he says, walking back to the bike. "Just get inside the truck and I'll load her up."

I can't wait to get in that truck. But the thought of him sitting in there with me makes me nervous. Not because I'm scared. I can take care of myself. But because this is a very hard day for me and I don't want to share it with anyone. Least of all this douchebag of a stranger.

I go looking for my gun, find it on the road on the other side of the trailer where he kicked it, and then get in the driver's side and take my jacket off so the heater can warm me up and dry me off. The clock on the dash says four-thirty, so I only have an hour to get to the bike shop before it closes.

I look down at my hands as I think of the bikes while the rhythm of the wipers lulls me into myself. Will's bikes. The only thing I really have left of him aside from the photographs. I've put off collecting them from the racetrack, knowing that I would have to make a decision if I ever did come out here to pick them up. Knowing that I could never look at them and not think of the night he died.

So I'm selling the bikes today. And then I'm never going to think about motorcycles again for the rest of my life.

The driver's side door opens and bike boy is there, pushing me on the shoulder. "Scoot over, gun girl. I'm driving."

"You're not driving." I push back. "Get in the passenger side."

He tilts his head down and looks up at me through the drops of rain running down his face. "Look, I live off a very slick dirt road. It's dangerous and I'm really not in the mood to go crashing over the side because you can't handle the trailer."

"What the—"

"I'm not saying you're helpless, OK? I'm just saying it's tricky and I know the road. You don't. So arguing with me is just a power play on your part, and if you don't want to go over the side of a cliff, you'll let me—"

"Fine," I say, pulling my legs up so I can scramble over to the passenger's seat.

He throws his wet leather jacket in the back cab and then slides in and adjusts the seat all the way back so his long legs can stretch out. "Jesus, you're like a little midget."

I scowl at him.

He laughs at me, puts the truck in gear, and we take off down the road.

I stare out the window and enjoy the mountain scenery as we sit in silence. After ten minutes, I start wondering where the hell we're going. "How far is it?"

"Just up the road a mile or so."

But the miles come and go and we are still driving. "Come on," I say, irritated. "Just tell me where the hell your house is so I know how long this is gonna take. I have an appointment and I've got to make it there today."

"What kind of appointment?" he says as he slows to turn on a dirt road. At least we are getting closer. This must be the dirt road he was talking about.

"Never mind what kind of appointment. Just hurry up."

"So what do you do?" He glances over at me and I'm mesmerized by his amber eyes for a second before I can look away.

I huff out a long breath and cross my arms.

"Not chatty, huh?"

I look out the window.

"You don't like me, do you?"

"You seem like an arrogant prick."

"How do you figure?" he asks, turning onto another dirt road.

"How do I figure?" I laugh. "Well, let's see, number one, you were riding in the rain like you're invincible. Number two, you were cocky even after you wrecked that bike. And number three—"

"Are you listing me?"

"What?"

"Listing me."

"I don't... I don't know what that means."

"You're making a list. You did that earlier too. When you were trying to get me to back off."

"I didn't *list* you. I'm just the kind of girl who likes to keep things straight."

"Ah," he says, with a wink in my direction. "I get it. OCD and shit. You're definitely a lister."

"I'm not a lister—forget it. Just stop talking and get to your house so I can drop you off and be on my way."

He comes to a stop in front of an arched, rusty gate built into the side of the mountain. It's big enough to pull a tank through, but he puts the truck in park and sighs. "We're here. Guess you'll get your wish then, lister."

But before I can say anything, he jumps out of the truck and slams the door.

*Just ignore him, Molly. He's baiting you on purpose. Assholes do things like that. In a few minutes he's going to be gone and you'll never see him again.*

GUN GIRL

## CHAPTER THREE

I scoot back over to the driver's seat and place my hands on the steering wheel, gripping it tightly. How did I get myself into this? I listen as he clunks things around in the back of the trailer, and then he backs his bike down the ramp and engages the stand.

A few more seconds—a loud clank as the ramp is maneuvered back into place—and I'll be outta here.

Finally, he closes the doors and bangs on the back three times. He disengages the stand on the bike and wheels it forward. "Good," I whisper to myself as I look at the clock.

Another bang makes me jump, so I look over at the window. It's raining harder than ever now, and he's dripping. "What?" I say, unwilling to lower the window and let that cold water in.

He points to the back cab and yells over the pounding rain, "My jacket!"

"Oh," I say back, fingering the button to unlock the back. "Sorry," I mumble, as he opens the door and shrugs his wet jacket on over his t-shirt.

"No, problem, lister. Thanks for the ride." He slams the door and begins to push his bike towards the giant gate in the side of the mountain.

What the hell is going on here?

"Don't," I warn myself. Whatever he's doing, wherever he's going, it's none of my business.

But then he brings out his phone and tabs a few things to make the gate in the mountain begin to lift up. There's nothing beyond but a very dark tunnel.

Yeah, he's a creeper. Probably a criminal. Most likely a deviant, and a freak, and that just goes perfectly with the fact that he's an asshole.

I put the truck in reverse just as he disappears inside. I back up, forgetting that I have a fucking trailer hitched, and immediately make a mistake.

My foot slams down on the brake and I put the truck back in park. *Just calm down, Molly. You know how to pull a trailer. You could do this blindfolded.*

I check both mirrors, memorize the road behind me, and close my eyes.

The whole world floats away as I put the truck back in reverse and fix my mistake.

I'm Molly Masters. Daughter of Crazy Bill and sister to Wild Will, world-famous stunt riders. I grew up on a dirt bike and I can back a trailer up blindfolded.

I open my eyes, calm again.

Now back to the business at hand. Putting my dead brother's bikes to rest. I back the trailer up a little more, then angle it into a small turnout and pull forward to head back the way I came.

I get about ten feet before the wheels start spinning. So I shift into four-wheel drive and try again. This time I get about five feet before I slip and slide a little over to the edge of the road.

Bike boy wasn't kidding. His road is tricky.

Asshole.

I try again and again and again. I put it into two-wheel drive, four-wheel drive, get out, find some pine branches and stuff them under the wheels, get back in, try it again.

And the only thing I accomplish is getting even more stuck in the mud.

I hate my life. My life sucks because…

1. I'm stuck in the mud.
2. I'm sad.
3. My brother is dead.
4. My father is dead.
5. My mother is insane.
6. I will never make this appointment.
7. This will not be the first day of the rest of my life.
8. I might die out here in the mountains.
9. My only hope is some crazy asshole who lives in a tunnel.

I sit there for several seconds trying to think of a number ten because my particular brand of OCD likes to round things when it has a chance. And ten is a perfect list, right? But I'm grateful and hopeful about the new job. So I'm out of bad stuff to complain about.

I feel better though. So I get out and follow bike boy's tracks into the darkness.

Little red lights line the tunnel. It sorta reminds me of an airport runway. The mud turns to concrete about twenty feet in and there's a small light up ahead. I'm really not sure what to expect, so I get my gun out just in case.

A few paces on and the tunnel turns sharply to the left where the light is brighter. I can hear yelling. Bike boy is yelling.

Someone is talking back to him, but he's laughing too. I let out my breath and relax a little as I creep forward into the chamber. The first thing I see is the wrecked bike mounted on a red mechanic's lift. Then toolboxes, some weird contraption that looks like a… robot, rolling around? A computer, then another, and another. A whole wall of computers, actually. Food wrappers and half-empty protein shake containers. Parts. A black muscle car. A long table lined with shit that looks like pieces from a chemistry lab. And a massive aquarium-sized tank holding luminescent jellyfish.

All this time bike boy is yelling and waving those black-gloved hands in the air, splashing a protein drink all over the floor.

"What the fuck, Case? I told you not to mess with my bike, you asshole."

"I didn't touch your bike, Lincoln."

"Stay the fuck out of my business. I crashed the goddamned bike and had to hitch a ride home and Sheila is somehow offline. Offline! You motherfucker!"

"Calm down," Case says. "She's not gonna miss anything being offline for a few minutes. In fact, if I were you I'd be asking how it's possible she got knocked off so easy. Doesn't that strike you as weird?" It comes from a giant face on a wall-sized flat screen mounted on the side of a… cave? What the fuck? "And you lost your right to work alone months ago, so don't get all self-righteous about me being around today."

"What's that supposed to—"

"Hey, asshole," the guy on the screen says over bike boy's tantrum, cutting him off.

"I didn't need this complication—" Bike boy stops talking. Because the guy on the screen is waggling his eyebrows at me. "What the fuck are you doing?" bike boy asks. "Stop making stupid faces—"

"We have *com-pan-eee.*" The guy on the giant screen nods his head at me.

Bike boy whirls around, shoots me a dirty look, and then growls, "I'll call you back," as the giant screen goes black.

We stare at each other for a few moments, our eyes locked. "Oh, my—"

"You're still here," he says over me.

"—God." I look around one more time.

1. Cave filled with...

2. Super bike.

3. Souped-up muscle car.

4. Giant flatscreen phone chat.

5. Computers everywhere.

6. Robot?

7. Some kind of science lab.

A few loud beeps interrupt my list. "Online," a female voice says from the ceiling. A pause, and then, "There has been a breach and we have a visitor." A hologram in the form of a woman appears in the middle of the cave and I can only assume this is...

8. Sheila, apparently back online.

I look around a little more and spy... not a cape, thank God, but a... a...

9. Helicopter, parked at the far end of the enormous cavern.

And then I get the perfect list after all, because I see...

10. Guns.

No, they are more than mere guns. I know my way around a gun and these are—

"What the fuck are you doing here, gun girl? I thought we parted back in the forest."

"Oh, my God," I repeat. "You're Batman."

## CHAPTER FOUR

I force a smile as I set my protein shake down, but inside I'm pissed as hell. She is not supposed to be here. "How the fuck did you get in?"

She's shaking her head, gun in hand, and backing up the way she came. But I can't just let her walk out. Not after she's seen all *this*. Not after she's seen *me*. Jesus Christ, she might be able to identify me. I really need to do something.

"The gate in front of the tunnel was open and I just followed your cave running lights."

"*That's* what happens when Sheila goes down." I curse under my breath at Case.

"And I can tell by your reaction"—gun girl is still backing up—"that you're not one of the good guys, are you?"

"Good guys?" This actually makes me laugh. "There's such a thing?" I lunge at her, trying to cut her off before she backs herself into the entrance, but she dodges me and skirts to the right, kicking over an oilcan as she moves. "Why are you running, gun girl?"

"Why are you chasing me, bike boy?"

"Not Batman then, huh?"

She shakes her head, her eyes are darting around like she's looking for an escape route.

"Sheila," I call out. When I look over, Sheila's got a little smirk on her face. Like she's feeling vindicated about this whole fuckup.

"How can I help—"

"Uh…" I cut Sheila off before she says my name out loud. "Secure the perimeter and the tunnel."

"Perimeter and tunnel secure," she says as soon as I'm done.

"That's clever," gun girl says. "What are you, some diabolical mad scientist?"

"Something like that."

"I'm gonna get out of here. You can't keep me here. And if you think I'll surrender and let you—"

"Hey," I say, putting my hands up, palms out in front of me. "Take it easy, OK? I'm not keeping you here. I just need to make sure the place is buttoned up. I have a lot of expensive stuff happening in this room."

She stops backing up, and that's enough for me at the moment. "Who are you?"

I shake my head. "You don't need to know that."

"I'm afraid I do. I brought you here. You made me bring you here. And now I see those wheels turning in your head. You can't let me go. Not after I've seen all this stuff you have. Do you have permits for this place? Hell, do you even own this land?"

I scrub my gloved hand down my unshaven face and sigh. *Think, Lincoln. Think.* How the fuck do I get out of this? There's probably six different ways I can handle this, but most of them would be difficult, involve a lot of talking and explaining, and I'm not in the mood for that shit right now.

"I just want to go, OK? But my truck is stuck in the mud. So if you help me get it back on the road, I'll leave and never come back."

I shoot her a grin, the one that disarms all the girls I never bring home. It's big, with dimples, and makes my eyes soften so people trust me. "No problem. Let's go do that." I shoot her a little wink.

Gun girl recoils a little. She starts shaking her head again. "You're lying. You're lying and I'm not falling for it."

"I'm not lying, I'm gonna help you." *Just not the way you think.* I take a few steps towards her, but she takes off running to the right, trips over a floor mat, barely catches herself before she faceplants, recovers, and stops on the other side of my black muscle car.

"You wanna play the kiddy chase game, gun girl?" I laugh a little at the thought. She's tough, and scared, and holding a weapon aimed at my chest. So the whole idea is a little ridiculous. But she's very cute in her I've-got-a-gun-and-I-know-how-to-use-it way. "I can play, but I always win."

"Well," she says, a little out of breath and with one of her hands on the hood of my car, like she's trying to calm down. I take a few steps forward, and she eases away. "I always win as well. So we're an even match for this game."

She's in bolt mode. One wrong move and she runs. And even though I could catch her easily under normal conditions, I don't have the energy to catch her right *now*. My body is more fucked up than it looks from that crash. I need to eat and recover or I'm gonna pass out.

Her feet are not sure which way to go until I make a move one way or another, so I need to play this smart. "There's no need for such fierce competition," I say, taking a few steps towards the front of the car. She sprints to the rear end, keeping the car between us. "I might not be a good guy, as you put it. But I'm really not gonna hurt you." Especially after what happened out there on the road when I grabbed her foot and took her down. I want to think a little harder about that, but she starts to move, interrupting my thoughts.

"Right," she says, moving two steps away with each one of mine. "I pegged you for some kind of deviant criminal the moment I saw you fly past me on that bike. Careless, reckless, and so sure you're invincible, the safety of other people on the road is of no concern."

"What are you, some do-gooder crossing guard? It's a deserted mountain road. That's what we do up here."

"It wasn't deserted, I was on it!"

"Yeah, but we went around you."

"That's not the point. You could've hurt me. What if I had swerved into—"

"OK, fine," I say, getting bored with this quick. This was not how I planned to spend this day and I'm already getting a migraine. "I'm the bad guy, you're the good girl. I give up. Now do you want help with that trailer or not? Because I'm still soaking wet here, and I'd like to change."

And that's when I make my move.

I reach down and grab the edge of my dripping wet t-shirt and pull it up over my stomach. I catch her eyes going wide just as I tug it over my head. And by the time I'm tossing it aside, she's staring at my abs.

I almost can't tuck down the laugh.

"I d-d-don't trust you," she stammers, fixated on my bare chest.

"What's not to trust, gun girl? I'm sure you'd like to get out of your wet clothes too. Hey, I got an idea. How about I take you upstairs and give you some dry ones. We can have coffee, warm up a bit, and by then the rain will have stopped and we can go see about your trailer."

The whole time I'm talking, my feet are inching away from her, making her drop her guard. And that's when I make my second move.

I drop to a crouch and start crawling along the side of the car. Not the direction she thinks. Because she thinks I'm gonna take the shortest distance. But she's wrong.

"What the fuck are you doing?" She's unsettled. Maybe even frightened. I can't say I blame her. But a guy's gotta do what a guy's gotta do to protect his man cave. "Oh my God," she whispers. "Where the—"

And that's when I get around to the front of the car again. I'm watching the shadow of her feet as she moves, unsure of which way to go. But she fucks up just like I knew she would. A moment later she takes a chance and loses when she rounds the car and comes right to me.

I spring forward, grab her by the legs, take her down to the floor, sit on her stomach, and pin her hands above her head. The nausea hits me again, only this time it's so strong, I might actually throw up.

She writhes underneath me, still gripping the gun, but her finger's not on the trigger. So before she can even think about shooting me, I drag that arm down, place my full weight on her wrist with my knee, and then grab the gun from her hand.

"Now stop," I growl, as the saliva pools in my mouth. I might heave and my head is aching even worse than before. I need her to give in right now so I can stop this fight. "It's over. You're gonna cooperate, I'm gonna get you out of here, and we're gonna forget this day ever happened."

"Get off me," she says, kicking her legs up, trying to unseat me. My head spins. *Hold it together, man. Hold it together.*

I lie down across her chest, almost smothering her with my weight. "Stop," I say, leaning down to whisper in her ear. She shakes her head like it tickles, but I touch my lips to her soft skin and breathe, "I don't want to hurt you, but you're gonna have bruises if you keep struggling."

"Let me go."

"I will, but not until you're still."

She tries to take a deep breath to calm herself, but I'm too heavy so she can't get enough air. I ease up a little and she draws in air through her teeth. My head clears and the sick feeling starts to subside.

Yeah, she's still pissed and yeah, that sure the fuck was something I haven't felt in fifteen years. I'm gonna have to get out the big guns for this one and put a stop to this before it goes too far. So I lean back down and kiss her.

She twists her head back and forth a few times, but I don't give up. My lips lock with hers and then I'm probing with my tongue, trying to get her to submit.

"Stop," she says with a little desperation.

But it's a chance to kiss her deeper. I slip my tongue into her mouth and she goes still. A moment later her lips soften and she's kissing me back. I let go of her wrist and ease my knee up off her arm to see if she's gonna fight. But her hands go right to my hard muscled shoulders and she digs her nails in.

Fuck. That feels good. Good enough to make me close my eyes and almost make me change my mind about getting rid of her. I pull away and now we both need to catch our breath. "That's more like it." She turns her head away from me, unwilling to accept the fact she kissed me back. "Do you want to come upstairs?" I ask. "Get some coffee? Dry off and calm down?"

She's very fucking cute. Little dimples in her cheeks, even when the frown is there. Her hair has a bit of wave to it and drapes over her shoulders. Something between blonde and brown. Her eyes are hazel. Swirls of brown and green and blue.

"I don't know," she says, interrupting my moment. "I really just…" Her body relaxes more as she gives in to me. "I really need to go."

And fuck if I don't like that little bit of giving in. Because what the hell… I can feel myself getting hard.

Well, I'm sure as fuck not giving her *that* power over me. So I get up and extend my gloved hand to her for the third time today.

She takes it, squeaking out a little, "Thank you." She stands there, looking at the ground, like she can't believe this is where we're at.

No one is more surprised than me. "Just let me get my keys, OK, gun girl? And then we'll go talk about this like grown-ups." I walk over to one of my big red toolboxes, open the top drawer, fish around a little and come up with what I need.

I walk back over to her. She's still in the same place, but now her arms are wrapped around herself, like she's freezing. She probably is. She's soaking wet and covered in mud.

"Cold?" I ask, smiling down at her so she gets a little lost in my eyes. She nods and I pull her close to my bare chest, knocking her off her guard even further. I lean into her ear and whisper, "Sorry, gun girl. But I have no choice." She tries to turn her head to look at me, but I've already bitten the cap off a hypodermic needle.

I stick it right into the fleshy part of her shoulder.

"Stop," she says with a little desperation.
But it's a chance to kiss her deeper. I slip my
tongue into her mouth and she goes still. A
moment later her lips soften and she's kissing
me back. I let go of her wrist and ease my
knee up off her arm to see if she's gonna fight.
But her hands go right to my hard muscled
shoulders and she digs her nails in.
Fuck. That feels good. Good enough to make me
close my eyes and almost make me change my
mind about getting rid of her.

35

**LINCOLN 4**
*BIKE BOY*

## CHAPTER FIVE

The static hum of a police scanner fills my car as I ease my way through the dark, wet streets of Cathedral City. Sheila is commenting endlessly on the scanner though the computer in the dash, but I'm only half listening. Case is waiting for me and I'm late. I had to turn my phone off last night to stop worrying about his incessant calling, but everyone has to face the music eventually and my time is now.

The darkness of the city streets mimics my mood, but that's not unusual. My mood has been dark for many years now. Too many to count. And looking back, was there ever a time when things looked bright?

If so, I've blocked it out.

What else can you do? I mean, why bother wishing for something you can't have? Why bother with hope that will fail you over and over again, when you can count on revenge and retribution to deliver every single time?

It fills the holes. Maybe those holes aren't overflowing with satisfaction yet, but that's OK. Being filled up with indifference is better than being empty.

I pass one of the cathedral ruins that stand guard at the entrance to the Merchant District and look up for a moment. There was a time back in school when I was obsessed with them. I studied each of the thirteen cathedrals like a historian looking for the meaning of life. This one is barely standing. Three walls are gone, the stones hauled away centuries ago after the old city fell during a long-forgotten war, the treasures inside pillaged, the stained glass broken. There's not one scrap of glass left. Not one shard, not one sliver of color remains.

And we're back to the darkness.

Cathedral City has its fair share of darkness. Every metropolis has problems. But the recent downturn in the economy has taken a toll on the lower classes. Unemployment is at an all-time high. The crime is so bad on this side of town, most goes unreported. Education is failing. The kids drop out at an alarming rate. The streets, especially here on the south side, are packed with the homeless, the drug dealers, the criminals, and the morally bankrupt.

Public services are inadequate, politicians are corrupt, and the police are in the pockets of the tech industry that floods this town with wealth. Blue Corp is a giant among giants. They own almost everything. All the public utilities, even the mobile phone service. My jaw clenches just thinking of the insane power they wield. Law means nothing when you have fuck-you money. And Blue Corp definitely has fuck-you money.

People have no respect for good and evil anymore.

*Easy, Lincoln. Just get this meeting over with and then you can get on with the night business.* Just the thought calms me, and I take in a long draw of air as I slide up next to M-Street Bar and cut the engine. There are no drug dealers eking out a living on M Street. Even they know enough to find a safer place to squat.

This is my little piece of the pie. This is my one place to feel safe when I'm here. One square block.

I get out of the car and the rain immediately starts pelting me, so I flip up the hood on the jacket I wear under my leather and jog over to the entrance where the unmarked door swings open before I even have to knock.

"Good evening, Mr. Wade."

"Hey, man," I say back as amicably as I can. I don't need to be nice to him. It's his job to be nice to me. But I am anyway. Maybe we're not friends—I don't have many of those—but I'm on good terms with Mac's guys and I make a point to be amicable when I can muster it up.

I spy Case over at the bar talking to Mac, the bartender and owner of M-Street. Case looks over his shoulder when the cold, damp wind from outside makes its way over to him and gives me a disapproving shake of his head.

I ease into the barstool next to him. "Whiskey," I tell Mac. He nods, and then disappears to give us privacy as he pours my drink.

"Where the fuck have you been?" Case seethes through his teeth. "I called you all last night after that monumental fuckup and Sheila said you were out."

"I *was* out," I say, catching the glass of whiskey Mac slides down the bar. I take a gulp and let the dark liquid burn my throat. "And now I'm here, so what do you want?"

Case stares at me, his blue eyes squinting down into slits as he looks me straight on. I might scare a lot of people in this town, but Case Reider is not one of them. We go back way too far. We've done too much, seen too much, and owe each other our lives many times over.

He's wearing a suit tonight, and his fancy trenchcoat is draped over the back of his stool. His shoes are high-end leather. Unlike the biker boots I wear. And I know he's got a knife strapped to his calf under those expensive trousers. It's one more thing that sets us apart because I don't bother with knives.

I prefer weapons that shoot shit. Anything. Bullets, cartridges, grappling hooks, grenades, rockets, and spears.

If you can blast it out of a barrel and use it to climb, kill, escape, maim, or poison, I've got a way to shoot it. Ballistics weapons are my best friends. I live, eat, breathe, and dream of ways to use them.

I don't use them. Not yet. Don't have to. My methods right now are discreet and untraceable. The guns are being saved for something special.

And of course, I have Sheila to make sure my aim is true. Because every gun I make is coded with her AI program for accuracy. Just like the car. Just like the bike—before I crashed it, anyway. I need to fix that thing because the new prototype isn't ready yet.

"You're gonna fuck this all up, I just know it," Case says, taking a sip of his own drink. He prefers a nicely aged Scotch, while I like domestic whiskey. The mountains flanking Cathedral City on all sides are home to some of the oldest distilleries in the country and I like to take advantage of that. "And that's why—"

His words are cut off by another blast of cold air from the door. I reach for my gun under my coat, and I'm pointing it at the shadowed figure in the doorway before the wind dies.

But I lower it just as quickly and snarl, "What the fuck is he doing here?"

Thomas Brooks' gaze wanders down to my black leather gloves before he stuffs his own pair into the pocket of his dark gray trenchcoat. He walks towards me as Case stands.

"I was invited," Brooks says simply, sliding his coat over the back of the barstool on the other side of me. "Because you don't seem to be very dependable these days. You're going off the rails, brother. And Case thinks you need a little intervention." He sends me a snarled grin. "Isn't that right, Case?"

I turn to Case and he's already shaking his head, knowing I'm about to protest. "Don't bother, Linc. He's right. I told him everything. You can't go off-script like this. You can't just start killing whoever you want and call it justice. We're not on board with the way you're handling things." He pauses to stare me down. "You need to remember what the hell we're doing here, man. That's all this is."

"That's fucking classic coming from the two of you."

"Martini," Brooks says to Mac, who, when I look over at him, is looking like he might bolt out the back door any second. "And relax, Mac, it's me. He's not doing anything stupid tonight because we all know who's in charge when I'm in the room."

"You prick—"

"Lincoln," Case says, grabbing my shoulder and turning me around to face him. "Shut the fuck up and listen. Because he's back and when he's back, he's the boss. There's nothing you can do to stop that aside from killing him, and we all know you won't do that."

"We have history," Thomas says, talking more to Mac than me. "And if you want a fight, Lincoln, I'll give you one. But don't expect me to pull any punches for old times' sake." He shoots me a semblance of a smile before turning his head to hide it. "Besides, we're on the same side. We've always been on the same side, Lincoln. You just require regular convincing."

My anger peaks, and maybe I can't kill him. But that doesn't mean I don't get to have my say. "And why do you think I require regular convincing? Where the fuck have you been for the past fifteen years? Huh? You just pack up and leave, no big deal. Case and I were the ones to put shit back together. You're nothing but a corporate sellout. A pig in a sty filled with filth just like all the others." I sneer it at him, seething with anger. "You know what Case and I call you behind your back?"

"Come on, Lincoln—"

"No, fuck you, Case. You get all paranoid because I go missing for a few hours—"

"A whole fucking day, you asshole. A night *and* a day, actually. Where the hell did you go? And what's the deal with the girl?"

"It's been taken care of."

"I hope you did it right," Thomas says, taking his martini from Mac, who makes another quick escape down to the other end of the bar. "Because you're fucking up a lot of plans right now." He glares at me from the corner of his eye. "And we never gave you authority to start killing people."

"We? What is this *we* shit? You're so sure we're on the same team, Thomas?" I laugh, it's so absurd. "Maybe we were way back, but you haven't been one of *us* for a very long time, brother. Way too long to just start talking about bygones. So why don't you put your fancy black gloves back on, take your coat off that stool, walk back the way you came, and go fuck yourself."

"Shit," Case says with a grunted laugh. "You're an idiot, Lincoln." Case grabs my gun hand and points it at Thomas. "Shoot him, then. If he's not one of us, then shoot the fucker and prove it."

I can't shoot him. The three of us know this. And it's not that I've got some sentimental affection for the old days. Some long-ago sense of loyalty. No. I simply *cannot* shoot him.

My hand trembles and I'm not even aiming, Case is. My whole body starts to sweat and my hands heat up. Perspiration collects on my forehead in drops and then it's rolling down my face. The shakes start and I'm ready to double over from the nausea. Another second and I'll collapse to the floor.

I wrench my gun hand away from Case, lower it to the ground, and the symptoms of inhibition poisoning ease back. But it takes many more seconds to recover than it does to be affected.

"I guess I am one of you," Thomas says with a satisfied smile as he takes another sip of his martini. "Now be a good boy, Lincoln, and do your job like we planned it. Stop this madness before you get us all killed." He gulps the rest of his drink, places his glass on the bar, and then reaches for his wallet, throwing down a twenty. "I'll see you both Friday night at my new headquarters for the SkyEye party. And feel free to bring your date, Lincoln. I'd love to see her."

"It's sick what you did over there," I say.

"So you saw it?" Thomas asks, one eyebrow raised. "I think it's quite spectacular."

"Yeah, if you want to be reminded of death."

"You're so dramatic, Lincoln. Grow a pair, will you? This is the big leagues and I'm not going to let you mess this shit up over petty vengeance."

"Says the kettle to the pot."

"My plans are a lifetime in the making. A legacy. I'm only taking what's owed to me. And don't you ever forget that I'm the one who saved you, Lincoln. I could've walked out and never looked back."

"I thought that's what you did," I growl.

Thomas looks over at Case. "You better get him on a leash," he says, turning his back to us and walking out. "Or I'll step in and do it myself."

There's a lingering silence as the door whooshes shut after Thomas makes his exit and when I finally look over at Case, he's got lots of questions. "What?" I ask.

"What did you do to the girl?"

"I took care of it." And I did. But damn if she hasn't been on my mind ever since. Everything about her has been on my mind since the minutes we wanted to fight out on the road. And she had a badge in her purse issued from the CCPD.

Detective Molly Masters.

Why didn't I know she was the new detective?

"What if she…" Case stops, maybe choosing his words carefully. "What if she becomes a problem?"

"I told you," I growl, giving him a look from the corner of my eye. "It's taken care of. She *won't* be a problem."

I leave Case at the bar, all his questions unanswered. If I wasn't offered answers about why Thomas is here, then why should Case get answers about me?

"You better go home tonight, Linc. I'm fucking serious."

I shoot him the finger over my shoulder as I walk out the door.

GUN GIRL

## CHAPTER SIX

"Hello?" I croak out, my voice raspy and my throat so dry it feels like sandpaper.

"Goddammit, Masters. You're still sleeping? What, two days isn't long enough for you? You think you're special, need three-day weekends? What fucking day do you think it is, sweetheart?"

I pull my phone away from my ear and look at it with blurred vision. "Who is this?"

"Who is this?" He's screaming now. I can almost picture a blood vessel popping out from his fleshy neck. "You goddamned better know who is this, Masters. And if you're not at work in thirty minutes, you'll be unemployed."

*Beep, beep, beep.*

Oh, shit. My mind clears up in an instant and I jump out of bed. I totally fail at that and fall face-first on the pink chenille rug where my pink stilettos are parked, ready for... what the fuck happened?

happened?

1. It looks like...

2. I got really drunk. Because there's empty wine and whiskey bottles everywhere. And...

3. There must've been a whole lot of people here, because I don't drink. One or two, every now and then. But this? This looks like...

4. I had a rager and there might even have been drugs involved from the look of the...

5. Ashtray?

Jesus fuck.

6. It's a good thing pot is legal in Cathedral City, or I'd be out of a job.

I get to my knees and realize I am going to hurl. So I throw every instinct I have out the window, get to my feet, peel out, making the pink chenille rug slide on the polished wood floors, and dive for the bathroom. I land face first on the white field floor a few feet through the doorway and crawl the rest of the way to the porcelain god, where I hike myself up, flip the lid open, and spew.

Oh, God.

I'm disgusting.

I sit like that for a few minutes, just hugging the toilet like we're best friends. And then I remember my boss' threat and crawl to the shower. It takes me another minute to stand up and turn the water on. And that's when I notice...

7. I'm wearing lingerie. And not just any lingerie, but...

8. Sexy shit I don't even own. It's light pink with cream-colored lace. And the bra has a wire in it to lift my girls up towards my chin.

I look around at my ass and nope. My cheeks are not covered. It's just a strip of fancy pink lace riding up my butt crack.

What the fuck? And who the fuck wears this shit to bed? No one, that's who. Unless you're getting...

9. Oh. My God.

I bolt out of the bathroom and cringe as I scan my bed covers. They are all rumpled up into a pile on one side and I hold my breath as I jerk them off the bed in one swoop.

No one. Empty, as usual.

I sigh and start laughing. "Right, Molls. Like you'd be getting laid." *Good one,* I think, walking back to the shower holding my head.

But where the hell did this lingerie come from?

I check the clock and realize I've used up twenty minutes and start to panic. I can't go in without a shower, so I'm totally late. My ass is getting chewed out good when I finally make it in. But I don't have time to wonder about my dubious choices right now.

So I whip the pink lace cami over my head and shimmy out of the panties I would never—ever, ever, ever—wear. And get in the shower.

More than an hour later—I had to stop for coffee—I walk into the Cathedral City Police Department headquarters wearing my best work suit and my brown and white saddle shoes, wishing I was back in bed and trying my best to avoid Chief O'Neil. It's not hard at the moment, because the place is jumping like the circus. There's four sets of couples, each with a woman crying her eyes out, in the front lobby. The men with them, probably their husbands, look like they are all about to punch someone.

"Welcome back, Sleeping Beauty," Roger, the intern at the front desk, says as he buzzes me through to the back offices. "Chief says you need to see him as soon as you get in."

"What's going on?" I ask, nodding my head to the couples.

"Kids ran away over the weekend. A whole group of them. And the parents are making a big scene about it."

"Oh, that sucks." I study the faces of the crying women again, this time with a new appreciation for the grief. It's got to be the worst thing that can happen to a parent. But I need to get to work. I walk through the security door and start weaving my way through the maze of desks. I really need to sit down and nurse this hangover.

"Masters!"

Shit. "Coming, Chief!" I yell over the commotion. There are suspects everywhere. Some are handcuffed to benches, some to desks. When I pass the intake door, a whole line of them are chained together waiting to be processed. I've only been here two weeks but I've never seen it like this.

Something definitely happened over the weekend.

"Shut the door behind you, Masters," Chief says when I enter his office. He's got one of those stereotypical fishbowls with windows on three sides, but only one of them looks out onto the city. The other two face the main work stations so he can keep an eye on things. And so everyone can watch when someone gets their ass chewed out, because he never lowers the shades when he does that.

Today I am the one about to get an ass-chewing.

I sigh and close the door, then walk over in front of his desk and wait for him as he shuffles papers around.

"Do you have any idea how short-handed I am right now, Masters?"

"No, sir."

He looks up from his paper-shuffling and stares lightning bolts into me. "Why not? Isn't it your job to notice things, Masters? Isn't that why I hired you? Military cred. Spying undercover. It's all impressive on paper, but in the field, you're a major disappointment. Worked with some of the biggest hush-hush cases in the country for the past three years, your resume said. And now you're telling me you don't even have the intuition to figure out I'm severely short-handed?"

"Sorry, sir. Yes, I can see we're busy—"

"We're not *busy*, Masters. This is the Monday after Cathedral Festival Weekend. And you have the nerve to be late?"

"I forgot, sir. I'm sorry, it won't happen—"

"And I heard all about that party you threw at your house, Masters. Do you think I don't know that the police were called seven times?"

"No!" That's not even possible.

"Oh, yeah, honey. And I'm going to ream your ass good for that. But you're lucky I need you today and don't have the time."

"I saw the parents out in the lobby. I'll get right on finding those missing juveniles, sir."

"Kids? What do we look like, babysitters? No, Masters, you're not working on the runaways. I had a very angry Atticus Montgomery in my office this morning."

Shit. Montgomery is the town billionaire. His family owns… well, I could make a very long list of what he owns, but it would take far more internal monologue time than I have right now.

"One of his employees killed himself in his office over the weekend."

Double shit.

"And it's the second one in a month. So you're gonna get your pretty ass over there"—he does not miss a beat even though calling my ass pretty is against policy—"and figure out what the fuck is going on. You got me?"

"Yes, sir," I say, adding a salute. "I'm on it." I turn on my heel and make for the door before he can say anything else.

"And Masters?"

Triple shit.

"Don't salute me. You're not in the military anymore."

"Right," I say, pulling the door open quickly and making my escape.

That—I sigh—is crystal clear.

I don't talk to anyone as I pass through the desks, the other cops, the suspects chained to anything that's bolted down, and make my way back out to the lobby. Alone.

I had a partner. Sort of. He retired last week, which is why I'm now a detective for Cathedral City Police Department instead of just a cop. He was on short-timers the whole two weeks he trained me. But at least he was a friendly face in the midst of animosity.

There were quite a few men in the department who wanted to be promoted to detective. But the chief hired me. Begged me to come out of retirement, actually. Filled my head with promises and all that crap about public service.

And I believed him.

Because, well. I believe in public service. I get most of my satisfaction in life out of helping people these days.

I take one more look at the group of overwhelmed and sad parents before I make my escape, feeling like I'm letting them down. So it sucks that I'm on the chief's leash and I've been ordered to sort out a suicide. There's been a rash of them, I hear. People desperate over the bad economy. Crime is up a hundred and twenty percent from five years ago. People are ready for a change. And those juveniles are among them, I guess. But they're just kids. They should be protected and if they go missing, someone should notice. It pisses me off that the CCPD can just ignore them like that.

*But you need this job, Molls,* I remind myself. *You need it because:*

*1. You haven't had a job since Will died.*

*2. You got depressed and… yeah.*

*3. You can't hide from the world forever.*

*4. People need to pay their dues and this is how you will pay yours.*

Maybe there's another detective in our department who's familiar with these kids? I wouldn't know. I'm too new. So maybe the chief is doing the best job he can with the people he's got. And I just happen to be new, with no cases, since my last partner closed them all out. Maybe the chief wants me to contain the backlash the city's biggest corporation might encounter if the public finds out they are a hotbed for suicides?

I'm gonna go with that. Chief O'Neil knows what he's doing and I need to focus on the task I was given.

## CHAPTER SEVEN

Blue Corp is in a very modern thirtysomething-story building on the far west side of Cathedral City, right up next to the foothills. It's not called a headquarters, it's called a campus, that's how many acres this place needs to house all the employees working here.

There are a few entrance gates since it's so sprawling, but the main one, the one where visitors enter, is on the south side of the campus and it's heavily manned with armed guards.

I stop at the guard house and roll my window down to talk to a very hard-looking man dressed in a black uniform with the Blue Corp logo on it.

"State your business," he demands.

I flash him my badge. "Detective Molly Masters. I have an appointment to talk with Mr. Montgomery."

The guard looks me up and down, then studies my badge for a moment. "Hold it steady," he says as he waves a piece of tech blazing a blue light over it. "Let me scan the image in and I'll be right back after your identity is authenticated."

I sigh as he walks away, then roll my window up to keep the light drizzle from blowing in.

Thoughts of the weekend run through my head. I threw a party. Which is very unlike me. Especially since the only people I know are from the department. Not to mention I got drunk enough to pass out and there might've been a man involved since I woke up in lingerie.

*Lingerie you don't own, Molly*, my inner voice reminds me.

Well, I own it now. Did I meet someone fabulous who likes to spend money on stupid things like pretty underwear that's supposed to be ripped off—or ripped apart, I snicker—during sex? I wonder what he looks like. I wonder if I had sex with him. I wonder if I liked it.

I consider my love life for a moment and what bad luck that I might've had sex for the first time in over a year and I drank too much to remember the best parts. I sure hope we used protection.

Jesus.

The full consequences of what I did over the weekend come crashing down on me. I'm gonna need to go to the doctor if I don't start remembering who my date was.

The guard appears again, so I roll the window down and let the drizzle accost me as it blows in my face.

"You're set, Miss Masters. Mr. Montgomery's assistant will meet you in the lobby and take you to his office."

He walks off before I can finish saying, "Thanks!"

Whatever. I buzz the control for the window and pull away as the gate lifts up to allow me entrance to the campus. The road is long, deserted, and flanked on either side with towering Ponderosa pines. After a mile or so, I finally come to the main building parking lot. There's a number at the head of each space, so I find one near the entrance marked, *Visitors*, and park my unmarked police car.

I look in the mirror, wish I had put on more concealer under my eyes this morning, then thank my lucky stars that I wore my best professional suit. I got it for Will's funeral.

God, I'm so sad. I have a moment where I feel nothing but defeat and surrender. The depression I suffered after Will died was so debilitating, I had to leave the military with a medical discharge. It was honorable, so there's that. But I loved the military. I loved the order and the way things needed to be done just so. I don't think I have OCD, like as a diagnosis. But orderly things make me feel good. They make me feel in control.

*Stop, Molly. Stop going backwards.*

The whole point of taking this job was to move forward. Every day I tell myself that I won't think about it, but I always find a way.

So I steel myself for another day, grab my raincoat, get out, tug it on, and then make a dash for the lobby doors. Inside there is soothing classical music being piped through the hidden sound system and a row of half a dozen immaculate blonde women quietly talking on phones behind the main reception desk.

There is no one else here but me and them. But at least a dozen security cameras pan as I walk across the black marble floors. I can spot them anywhere. No matter how well hidden, I can tell. It's like I have some sixth sense when it comes to surveillance.

The building, while new and shiny, mimics the old-world architecture that Cathedral City is famous for. On the outside the building looks like a collection of massive blue crystals, something you might find growing up from the floor of a cave.

I pause for a moment as the word *cave* rolls around in my brain like it's been there recently, but then shake myself out of my subconscious and concentrate on what I'm doing.

The lobby feels like a church, if a church was made of polished black stone and glass. It even has a pitched ceiling, like the interior of a spire, and mimicking the outside architecture. The walls are made of bluish glass. Probably bulletproof.

"Miss Masters," a soothing voice says from behind me.

I turn to find a woman about my age and my height, dressed in a cream-colored skirt suit with a tan piping outline down the front. Her legs are long and end at a pair of matching stilettos. I wonder how she walks in those things all day long.

My hand extends automatically. "Yes, I'm Detective Masters. And you are?"

"Miss Veti," she says in a low, calm voice. It borders on seductive. "Valentine Veti. But everyone calls me Val."

"Nice to meet you, Miss Veti. I'm here to talk to Mr. Montgomery about the issue he had over the weekend."

"Yes," Val Veti says, leaning into my ear. "Thank you for coming. He's very unhappy about this, Detective. And I'm afraid you will bear the brunt of his anger today. So please don't judge him too harshly."

"Great," I say sarcastically as she turns and beckons me to follow her with a flick of her finger. This is going to be fun.

The elevator ride is long and silent, with only Miss Veti's fake smile to keep me company. I massage my temples and if I had one wish, it would be to go home and go back to bed. The doors finally open when we get to the thirty-third floor, and Miss Veti leads me out into a posh receiving area with the same polished black marble floors and glass everywhere I look. It's clear glass up here and I suppose no one needs bulletproof glass this high up in the sky.

"This is Mr. Montgomery's office. Please wait here while I see if he's available."

"He better be available," I mutter under my breath. But she either doesn't hear me or chooses to ignore my remark, because she walks off down a long hallway off to my right.

Mr. Montgomery's office is one entire floor of a multi-million-dollar building. Pretentious much? Well, what did I expect? His first name is Atticus. I do believe he's the first Atticus I've ever encountered outside of fiction.

There are no chairs and no desk. Just a wide-open room with floor-to-ceiling windows and an expansive view of Cathedral City draped with an eerie mist.

I walk over and gaze out. The day is gray and cloudy, as per usual in this part of the country in the late winter. And the drizzle has turned into rain in the past few minutes since I left my car. I can count all thirteen cathedrals that the city is named for from this view. I wonder if this building counts as one? Probably not, I decide. The cathedrals down there are old. A hundred years at least. Most of them are ruins. Only the largest one, used for public events and religious holidays, and the second largest, both of which flank the town square, are in good repair. And the second tallest was just refurbished by some out-of-town corporate billionaire, I hear. I guess he plans on giving Blue Corp a run for their money.

"Detective Masters?" A deep voice from behind makes me turn.

"Yes," I say, putting on my public servant smile. "The chief wanted me to come and look into the… issue you had over the weekend." I look around, unsure if anyone else is listening and trying to be discreet since Miss Veti was low-talking when she mentioned it downstairs.

"Please," Mr. Montgomery says with a wave of his hand and a furrow of his brow. "Speak freely here. My offices are completely private. Come, let's talk in my inner chambers."

I smile again after realizing I'm squinting at him, and move ahead as he waits for me to go first. I try not to gawk as I walk down the long hallway. Pictures of him on the walls capture my attention. In one he is skydiving, another he's climbing a mountain that requires an oxygen mask. A few more flash by as I proceed and I am unable to get a good look at them, but the last one makes me stop.

"Ah," Mr. Montgomery says with a small chuckle. "Do you like it?"

I study the photo for a moment. He's very handsome now and I'd peg him to be in his early thirties. But he was young in this picture. Early twenties, maybe. The hair was blonder, the eyes brighter, and the smile wider. There are no worry lines on his forehead on that day, just pure joy. It's actually a series of pictures, four of them lined up horizontally along the wall, but contained within one expansive frame.

He's surfing a giant wave in the second of the series and the caption says *Monsoon Beach—wave height, forty feet*. I'm no expert in surfing but that's a big fucking wave.

"It wasn't even close to the biggest wave ever surfed, but it was a record for me. And I can tell you this, Detective, my heart was pounding so fast, I thought I might pass out before it was over."

I look up at him and he's smiling. He almost looks like the young man holding a trophy in the third image. "I bet," I say, knowing what it's like to put your life on the line for sport, "your mother was pissed."

He laughs heartily. "Oh, you have no idea." He puts a hand on my back and guides me forward into his private office. When we get inside there are more pictures of him. Snowboarding competitions, skiing down pristine, virgin mountains. Rock-climbing sheer cliff faces. Sailing. I pause on that one, trying to find the connection.

"Solo trip around the world," Montgomery says, like he's reading my mind. "I was seventeen and that boat was nothing but a twenty-four-foot sloop."

"So it bit you early, huh?" I turn to look at him as he smiles at his younger self.

"What?" he asks, dragging his eyes away from the memory of that day.

"The X-bug." He gives me a confused look. "That's what I call it. My father was a stunt rider. I grew up in the circus. My brother and I followed in his footsteps until the unthinkable happened."

Montgomery's smile falters. He understands better than most, I bet. "I'm sorry."

He probably is. He's probably one of the few who know what it's like to lose people in the game of daring. "The X-gene. The X-factor. The life of an extreme addict. It must've been difficult to settle down in this..." I look around at his office. "Prison."

His laugh is uneasy, like I hit the nail on the head. "Well, you're certainly perceptive, Detective Masters. Which is why I'm glad you're here. I'm hoping you'll be able to figure out if the last two suicides are related. And whether it's something internal we need to deal with, or just a coincidence."

"Well, I'm here to find the truth and nothing more, so take that any way you want." It's unnecessary to make an enemy out of him, but there's this chip on my shoulder. It's not easy being a woman in a world filled with men. It was difficult in the military, but they had discipline. And I'm starting to get the impression that the CCPD doesn't give one fuck about discipline. But at least Montgomery isn't the pretentious asshole I imagined him being on the way over.

"Good," he says, back to business. "Have a seat, Miss Masters."

Ah, they always do that eventually. It was all Detective this and Detective that until I didn't play along with the illusion that I'm at his beck and call. "Thank you, Atticus."

His eyebrow shoots up but he keeps his mouth shut. Perhaps realizing he needs my services just as much as I need his cooperation.

"Why don't you start from the beginning so we can get started?" I sit down and get my tablet out to take notes. "Who found the body?"

This is how it starts. This is why I do this job. I've always had this keen interest in figuring things out. Puzzles, the best way to do a trick on the bikes, and then later, security details to keep people safe. I was good at it. Very good. So good I was promoted after noticing something strange about a man during a highbrow politician's inaugural speech a few years back. I saved the politician's life and found a new passion at the same time. And this one simple question is the first step down the path of truth.

I live for it. I'd die for it, that's how much I love getting to the bottom of things. I have never been tolerant of mysteries. I need answers and I need them immediately. But I force myself to be patient when I'm working. Force myself to be calm, and still, and quiet as I listen for lies, or missing truths, or wasted opportunities.

And Atticus Montgomery gives me all that and more. Because the first thing out of his mouth is, "We might have a problem."

"How so?" I ask, leaning in.

"These two men started working for the company at the same time. Fifteen years ago, to be precise. And they were working on the same project."

"What project is that?"

"I can't tell you specifics, as it's highly secret. But it's enough of a coincidence that I'm worried."

"Well, tell me everything you can and I'll try to figure it out."

He tells me some, but it's mostly corporate double-talk. I might as well be a member of the press. So I leave there with no idea what's going on and with no possibilities rambling around in my brain.

But I did get a name, and after a visit to the wife of the last suicide victim, an inkling. Top-secret project was all she knew. No specifics, so that was a dead end. But she did say the job was weighing on him and he had been feeling out of sorts. Irritability and loss of interest in her and their children. Hopelessness and insomnia. All typical signs of severe depression. This is something I have firsthand knowledge of.

But she also said he was talking about moving away. Getting out of science and retiring early. And when I pressed her, asking if he was doing this in secret or if she felt he was trying to set her up to go on after he killed himself, she said no. They were making plans to buy a small bed-and-breakfast business in the tropics.

It's possible she misread him and he was setting her up for after he was gone. Giving her a head start on a new life that didn't include him. But it didn't feel that way. It felt like... she was describing an escape.

It's not much. Hardly anything at all. But it's always the small things that solve a mystery. So I tuck it away and head back to the department.

GUN GIRL

## CHAPTER EIGHT

Chief is yelling my name the moment I walk through the front security doors at CCPD and I wince. "In my office. Now!" he bellows across the room.

Jesus. Can this day get any worse?

1. I woke up drunk.

2. Wearing strange lingerie.

3. Was late for work.

4. Blue Corp has some serious internal issues, but I'm never gonna be able to solve a case when everything is top secret.

"I said now, Masters!"

I leash the internal list and make the walk of shame to the boss' office.

"Do you know who I just got off the phone with, Detective?"

"Um—"

"Close the goddamned door. Do I look like I want an audience?"

Holy fuck. Please make this day end. I turn and tap the door so it swings closed with a loud click, and then turn back to the chief. "Was it Mr. Montgomery?" I take a wild guess.

"It was, Masters. It was. And do you know what he told me?"

"I'm a shitty detective?"

Chief screws up his face at me. "No, Masters," he says in his almost-never-present I'm-a-human voice. "He says you were the epitome of professionalism and the department is lucky to have such a competent detective on the case." Chief sneers at me like he's taking that as a personal assault on his character. "And he wants to have breakfast with you tomorrow because he talked his father into giving you more clearance. Be there at six AM."

"Great," I mutter under my breath.

"Oh, and Masters? There's a party this Friday at the Thirteenth Cathedral in honor of some new rich fuck moving his business here. You're the new man in town, so you're in charge of security. My other detectives all have real cases. Wear a dress. And"—he looks down at my shoes—"get rid of those."

Thirty minutes later I'm pulling into my driveway across town. I don't live in a city condo like most of the other cops in the department. I like my space and since I practically grew up a gypsy in a circus tent that allowed me unprecedented freedom as a child, I got used to my space.

So it's a suburban two-bedroom townhouse in a quiet neighborhood for me. I have a lot of neighbors, but it's mainly older people who grew deaf to the call of the city a long time ago.

I get out of my car, curse the never-ending rain, and jump when my neighbor yells out from across the street. "I hope you don't plan on playing loud music like that every weekend. This is a nice, quiet, orderly neighborhood, *Detective*." The old woman practically snarls the word.

"I don't," I say back, as amicably as I can. Then I turn and walk up my front porch steps.

The party. I forgot how trashed my house was. I open the door and wince at the sight. The liquor bottles, the paper plates. There's even food. Several pizza boxes, hamburger wrappers, old French fries, and at least a dozen protein shakes. Jesus Christ. What the hell was I thinking?

"Well, Molls," I say, channeling my brother. "You made this mess, now you have to clean it up."

*Yes, Will. Yes, I do.*

It takes me hours. And all I wanted to do when I got home was soak in the tub. But no. OCD-ish Molly can't relax with a house filled with garbage. So I pick up bags of trash. I clean the kitchen counters, which are so sticky from food and booze, I have to break out the bleach. I vacuum, I dust, I even wax the wood furniture to make sure there's no lingering rings.

Then I go upstairs and tackle the bedroom. Sheets— eew—first. I still have no idea if I had sex or not. And that bothers me. Enough for me to call my doctor out in Wolf Valley and leave a message for a referral to another primary care doctor here in town.

I lather, rinse, repeat all the cleaning I did downstairs and when I'm finally done, four hours later, I am looking at three full trash bags.

Three. I cannot even remember the last time I filled up three bags with trash.

I grab a bag, open the door that leads to the garage, flick on the light and stop dead.

Will's truck and trailer are parked neatly in my garage. One vehicle in each of my two parking spots.

I have a flash of rain and a mountain road. Another flash of a bike on the asphalt. Then Will's accident cycles through my brain like I'm reliving it in slow motion.

I drop the bag and slam the door.

*That's a just a memory, Molly.*

Right. But a memory of what? Will didn't crash on a mountain road, he crashed during a race. So some of that was real.

What the fuck happened to me this weekend?

BIKE BOY

## CHAPTER NINE

I rewind the footage of the detective as she stalks down my outer tunnel and makes her way into my cave. What must she have been thinking? *Batman.* That makes me laugh. Molly Masters. Detective Molly Masters. I'm impressed.

I was so tired last night after trashing her house all day, that impromptu meeting with Case and Thomas, and the… extracurricular activity… I just came upstairs to the little house I rebuilt over the ruins of the mansion I have no memory of, and fell onto my bed.

But today I can't get her out of my mind. I was thinking about her all day. Even Sheila noticed I was distracted. This is why I'm upstairs again. Normally I like to sleep down in the workshop. I have a bedroom of sorts down there. Bathroom and kitchen. And it's a lot nicer than it is up here, that's for sure. This little house is nothing but an afterthought left over from my stolen childhood.

But Sheila is everywhere down there. I have no privacy. Normally I don't require much, but I don't want to share this girl with anyone until I sort things out. So many nagging feelings about this Molly Masters. So many familiar things too.

I have doubts, but not enough to stop myself from drawing the only conclusion I can.

So I stretch my legs out on the bed and rewind the security footage again.

Molly is a strange combination of emotions as she walks through the tunnel. Afraid? Maybe. But she has that gun out and she's trained in mixed martial arts. That was obvious with the takedown move she used on me back on the road. Plus, she's pretty young to be a detective, which means she's got something. Some skill, or some brainpower, or something that marks her as exceptional.

But does that surprise me? I shake my head.

Her expression, even in the grainy night-vision footage, is one of curiosity and determination. There is no point during this trip down the tunnel where I get the feeling she wants to turn back.

If life is a mystery then Molly isn't afraid to go looking for the answers. And that does not fit into my current plans.

Her face is soft and round. Her cheekbones high. Her eyes are wide and bright. Hazel, I remember from seeing her out on the road. And her hair is long and light, but not blonde. It's up in a ponytail in the footage, but not a neat one. Long, wet, twisting strands fall down and frame her face. And her clothes are what most athletic women would wear. Jeans, a sweatshirt, and a canvas jacket that says she likes the outdoors. They are nothing but mud.

I type in a web address and pull up the cameras I placed in her house—just to keep my eye on her, I told myself. Just to keep tabs on her as the drugs worked their way through her system.

But it's a lie. I watched her last night and it wasn't out of concern.

The style of her house is minimal, but not modern. Her couches are old and comfortable. I tried them both out. Her bedroom furniture is rustic and unpainted, her sheets a soft blue and her walls a bright white.

And her body. Jesus. I fast-forward the footage until we disappear from view when I put her in the shower. I know it was creepy as fuck to take off her clothes, but she was covered in mud. And going out to buy that lingerie, well, that was stupid. So fucking stupid. I told myself it was a joke and I'm even fighting down a laugh as I watch her wake up and try to figure it all out. But it was really stupid. It was almost like I wanted her to remember me. Make those drugs wear off.

And that is not the best way forward at this point. It comes with a whole lot of problems.

So what is she thinking right now, practically crawling to her bathroom to hurl?

I flick a tab on the screen and bring back the live feed just as she goes into her bathroom to change. Does she always change in the bathroom? Or can she feel my eyes on her?

She comes out wearing shorts and a tank top, her full breasts pressing her peaked nipples up against the fabric of her shirt.

She makes me hard.

And then she bends over, allowing me a good look at her ass.

I unzip my jeans.

She slips into bed, her long legs stretching out on the new white sheets.

I shove my hand into my boxer briefs and fist my cock. It grows in my hand and I have a moment of longing. A moment when I wish that was her hand. That she was the one pumping me up and down in long, even strokes. I sigh, wishing her mouth was coming towards me and we were together.

Together. It's a weird thought, but I try it on for size.

*Don't go there, Lincoln. You can't.*

She leans over and turns the light out, and then her face illuminates as a reading device comes on.

I imagine her face in the dark next to me, lit up by the computer on my lap as she sleeps by my side. I imagine slipping my arm underneath her toned body, grabbing her breasts, and pulling her ass up against my hard cock.

Fuck.

I stop masturbating and close the computer. I'm not the kind of guy who needs a dream to get off. I'm the kind of guy who likes the real thing.

But this girl is off limits. Detective Molly Masters comes with a great big off-limits sign flashing in my head.

*She's a fucking cop*, the inner voice says. *A cop and a girl who will bring up more problems than you can deal with right now.*

She comes out wearing shorts and a tank top,
her full breasts pressing her peaked nipples up
against the fabric of her shirt.
She makes me hard.
And then she bends over, allowing me a good
look at her ass.
I unzip my jeans.
She slips into bed, her long legs stretching out
on the new white sheets.
I shove my hand into my boxer briefs and fist
my cock. It grows in my hand and I have a
moment of longing.

GUN GIRL

## CHAPTER TEN

I toss and turn all night on my clean sheets while wearing my tank top and shortie-shorts. You know, what I *usually* wear to bed. No prissy pink lingerie.

Tanks tops and shorts are:

1. Comfy.
2. Comfy.
3. And comfy.

That's the easiest list I ever made and I made it back when I was eight. No second thoughts necessary. So how the hell did I end up in clothes I'd never in a million years choose for myself?

My alarm goes off on my phone, letting me know it's four-thirty AM. It's a half-hour drive over to the Blue Castle, and I really need a shower before I start a day that will undoubtedly be long, stressful enough to induce a marathon of list-making, and sad. It's been a while since I investigated a murder and after talking to the victim's wife yesterday afternoon after leaving Blue Corp and Atticus Montgomery, that's what I think it is. She said he got a call late the night before. That he was told to report to work for an emergency.

I throw my covers off and pad over to the shower and get the water started. My head starts spinning and I grab hold of a handrail to steady myself. But a vision of me standing out in the rain yelling at the sky flashes through my mind.

What?

I shake my head again, but I get even more dizzy. And then another vision pops into my mind. Will's trailer. Me sitting behind the wheel as someone loads a bike in the back.

*What?*

I bend over, sure I'm going to hurl like I did yesterday morning, and press my face to my knees, hoping for some clarity.

*Breathe, Molly. Just breathe.* It's probably an anxiety attack. I mean, wasn't I just thinking about suicide and murder? And the fact that I never sold Will's bikes and got drunk instead—hey. Wait a minute. That's why I had a party. I must've gotten drunk to take my mind off selling the bikes.

I breathe again. Then again. And things start to become clear. So I stand up and wait for another wave of dizziness.

But it passes.

And I'm late again.

So I do the only thing I know how to do.

I push it away and go on.


The Blue Castle is way south of my neighborhood, but luckily the traffic is heading the opposite direction and I'll take any luck I can get at this point, so I sip my coffee and try to prepare for the inquisition at the front gate.

It never comes.

Oh, Mr. Who-the-fuck-are-you is still manning the guardhouse. But he's out of the building and waving me through the opening gate before I even get close enough to think about rolling down my window.

When I get to the visitors' parking lot I pull into the same spot I did yesterday. But the plaque at the head of the spot bears my name.

Detective Molly Masters.

What the? Life in Cathedral City isn't as simple as I first thought it might be. First case is a murder made to look like a suicide and I've already slipped into some old drinking habits that I thought were long behind me. Now Atticus Montgomery is passive-aggressively insinuating he's got me on his payroll?

I am gonna go in there and…

1. Be sweet as hell and not mention the parking plaque.

2. Do everything Montgomery asks and answer his questions like a professional.

3. And then get the fuck out so I can go interview the other suicide's wife.

Sounds like a plan.

I get out of the car and walk to the lobby. This time a doorman is waiting and Val is chatting with the ladies manning the phones. She smiles when she sees me.

"Oh, hi, Detective Masters!" She beams, breaking it off with her co-workers and walking over to me in her stiletto heels. This time her suit is a light pink and her shoes are taupe. She's one of those summer people, I guess. And she does look pretty in the pastels. "Mr. Montgomery is waiting for you upstairs." She links her arm in mine as we walk towards the elevator. I bet we are a sight. She is polished perfection and I'm back to my regular plainclothes. A white blouse, a trenchcoat, and tan wide-legged slacks that end at my favorite two-toned oxfords. It's sort of the detective uniform, right?

She towers over me because—*you're like a little midget*—*What?* Where the hell did that come from?

*Not now, Molly. Not now. Just ignore the weird shit. You are not crazy like your mother. You're not hearing things, or making things up, or losing time. It was a binge, the first one in a long time, and it does not mean you're having a relapse. You are not crazy, you are not hearing things—*

"Detective?" Val stares at me. "Are you OK?"

I let out a laugh and then shake my head. "Sorry, I was wondering if I left my garage door open at home."

"Oh, I'll have someone go check on that for you so you can stop worrying." I start to protest, but the elevator doors open and she waves me in. "All set! See you later."

And before I can come up with a reason why she should not go snooping at my house, the doors begin to close.

I lean back against the far wall and watch the numbers light up above the door as I ascend. Please, dear God of circus people everywhere, let Mr. Montgomery be quick today.

The doors open and there he is in all his six-foot-something, blue-eyed, blond-haired splendor. "Good morning, Detective. Did you sleep well?"

This is probably a trick question. I'll say yeah and he'll snap off some snide remark about his dead employees like it's my fault. So I say, "No, not really."

He shoots me what might be a genuine sympathetic look. "Oh, I'm sorry. If there's anything I can do to help with that—massage, relaxation music, a soothing book— please let me know. We have a wellness center on campus and I can arrange for you to go see one of the homeopathic consultants."

"That won't be necessary. I'm sure it will be better tonight when we get a handle on this case and figure out what happened."

"You don't think it was a suicide?"

*Jesus Christ, Masters! Keep your fucking mouth shut!*

"Just protocol," I say with a smile. "We have to look at all angles." He looks at me for a moment and then nods and turns away. I follow him down the hallway and into his office.

"I don't have much time, so this briefing will have to be quick."

"Perfect," I say, taking a slurp of my now-cold coffee. I make a face and force myself to swallow.

"Oh," he says, noticing my grimace. "But let's have breakfast. You haven't eaten yet?"

"No," I say. "I don't eat in the mornings. It makes me sick."

"Mmm," he mutters. He wraps my hands around his forearm like he's my chaperone. "Humor me for a little while, will you?"

Great. I'll probably end up here all morning. But I go along because I have no other choice. This is the real world and after a lifetime in the circus and years in the military, I'm once again a part of it.

We don't walk back to the elevator the way we came, instead he pushes a button on his watch, and a panel slides up on the far wall revealing an elevator. "Private," he says, like he knows the questions popping into my mind.

"You like things private, don't you, Mr. Montgomery."

"That I do," he says, waving me towards the opening doors.

I enter, he follows, and we ride it up one floor. And when the doors open we find ourselves in a small dining room that has soft music playing and one table with one man sitting at it. The view is amazing—not that Atticus Montgomery's office view wasn't, but this view is through windows two stories tall that slant up into the pitched glass roof of the crystal spire.

"It's amazing at night," Montgomery says. I look over at him and his smile disarms me for a moment. "I'll have to have you up for drinks some time so you can see it. This spire is the executive dining room. But there's another one my father calls his office over there."

I look out the window to my right, spy the other spire he's referring to, and raise my eyebrows, unsure what to make of this man. Surely he's not flirting with me. *Dear circus god, please, please, please do not let this man make a move on me today.* I just don't have the energy for it.

He places a hand on the small of my back, forcing me to move forward into the room to avoid his touch. But before I can get over that little maneuver, he's wrapping my hand around his arm again, leading me towards a table. We stop in front of the older gentleman eating eggs Benedict and reading the stock report on a tablet.

"Detective Masters, my father, Alastair Montgomery."

Alastair Montgomery does not look up or greet me with anything more than an uninterested grunt. Atticus pulls out a chair and I force myself to take a seat. *Be sweet, Molly. You'll get out of here much faster by playing along.* "Thank you, Mr. Montgomery."

"It's my pleasure," he says, taking his own seat next to me. "But my father is Mr. Montgomery and I am just Atticus."

Before I can reply, Montgomery senior barks, "Did you find out what that mess down on twenty-one was all about?" Still, he does not look up. Like I am not even worthy of his gaze.

"No, sir," I say as politely as I can. "I'm afraid this case will require a little more effort than one afternoon of questioning."

"Then why are you here?" He looks up. And his anger is as ugly as his indifference. It lingers on me and then focuses on his son.

Atticus might be a powerful snob just like his father, but his demeanor is one of patience. To my horror, I find myself leaning in his direction, seeking some sign that he's not going to throw me to his wolf of a father.

"Don't mind the old man, Detective," Atticus says, breaking the silence left by my speechlessness. "He has no use for manners these days."

"I don't need manners," Montgomery senior barks at his son. "Two dead bodies were found in my building, Atticus. So it's only natural that I expect answers. What I don't expect is to be breakfasting with the CCPD's rookie detective in my private dining room."

"OK," I say, pushing back from the table and looking at Atticus. "I'm going back to work. Your father is right. Thank you for the offer, but I—"

"I'll join you. I've already eaten."

"But—"

He cuts me off with a look. Something in his eyes that says, *Quiet*. He mutters a half-hearted goodbye and leads me back to the elevator.

When the doors close, sealing us off, I shake my head. "Well, that was awkward."

"Awkward doesn't even come close, Detective Masters. But now you know." He stares down at me with an intensity that makes my heart skip a beat.

"Now I know what?"

"What you're up against." A small smile forms as the elevator car descends. Floors fly by. "How high the stakes are," he continues. "And maybe a minute of rude conversation isn't enough for most people to make a decision about a person, but I think it was enough for you. Detective Molly Masters is not most people, is she?" He cocks his head at me and drops the pretense of a smile just as the elevator stops and the doors open to the lobby. "I'll get in touch with you about the date."

"Date?" I ask, stepping out of the elevator and turning back to look at him.

"The stars, Masters." He points upward. "You can't say no to that. Every woman deserves to see the stars from the top of a castle."

And then the doors close and he disappears from view.

LINCOLN 4
BIKE BOY

## CHAPTER ELEVEN

"Goddammit."

"How can I assist, Mr. Wade?" Sheila is hovering over me, a worried expression on her semi-transparent face. "What do you need? I hate seeing you so upset."

"I'm not upset, and I don't appreciate that whole Mr. Wade routine," I say. "You're pissed off about my decisions, but it's not up to you, Sheila. And I know what I'm doing. So no more passive-aggressive bullshit, OK? I'm busy."

She's silent after that and I'm left feeling like a class-A prick. I'm frustrated. Sexually frustrated. That detective has been on my mind non-stop since last night. But taking it out on Sheila is the wrong way to handle it. "Sorry," I say. "You can't help, Sheils, you know that."

I wish she could. At least with the engineering stuff and the lab work. I have a few robots in the labs, but they have no intelligence. They just do what you tell them to do. Sheila has intelligence but she has no physical body.

For a genius, I sure didn't think that one through. But I never figured on being in this position, did I? It's been a dream for fifteen years. Something Case and I talked about, but never thought we'd see. And then Thomas appears—not physically at first, just in email—and he offers us everything we need to do what we always said we would.

I don't care what Sheila thinks about it, I'm on board. And maybe Thomas is a dick and I don't like him, but I don't have to like him to take what he's offering.

"It's to the left," Sheila says as I blindly search for the wrench I'm looking for on the ground. I find it with my gloved fingers. My hands are sweating like crazy.

It's the stress. It's the job. It's the girl.

I really do need to make Sheila some kind of solid body when I get the time. Something with hands so she can expand her duties. Right now she's perfection when it comes to computers and weapons. She runs all the automated systems in the cave. And I have several small robots used for cleaning that she's wired into, so they are busy all hours of the day and night. She runs the bikes, and the car, and the helicopter.

But she cannot hand me tools. And the biology bot I call Hammer, despite his name, can't do shit in that department either. He's the largest robot I own at the moment. But he's contained inside the inner labs. Stationary and mounted to a bench. He's really just an arm with half a brain.

I sigh to stop myself from cursing too much as I try to fix the bike that Case fucked up last weekend. I had to take the whole engine apart and rebuild, and that's just the mechanical damage. The body work is something else altogether. If Hammer was mobile… if Sheila was solid…

But wishing aside, there's no one here but me and these bits of computer code. So I go it alone. As usual.

"Why not just build a new one?" Sheila asks, still hovering over me like a mother. "The prototype is ready for engineering."

"I don't have time," I growl through a wrench between my teeth.

"You need an automatic engineering system."

"No shit."

"That way we can work harder for you."

Fucking Sheila. I stop what I'm doing and look up at her. She smiles. And goddamned if she isn't the perfect replica of a human woman in her holographic form. I'd never be able to assemble something like that. It pains me to think of reducing her to a tin can of nuts and bolts like Hammer. "You work plenty hard, Sheils. I'd be sued for violation of labor laws if you were human."

"I'm not human. And I enjoy working. I can't work enough. What is rest to me but time spent being idle?" She cocks her head at me.

"Well, one day. When things quiet down, I'll have time to build more. But right now I just need to make do with what I have."

"We have all the parts, Lincoln. I inventoried everything in stock at the moment, and your new prototype could be assembled in seven days if you gave me control of your engineering lab."

"Control how?" I growl, still trying to concentrate on the task at hand.

"If you gave me owner access to the entire lab, I'd recode the cleaning bots to build parts. Then I'd recode the AI program in this bike and transfer it to that bike." She stands and points to the holographic image of my dream. The perfect motorcycle. Sleek, aerodynamic, powerful, and well-equipped.

Weaponized, is the word I'm looking for. This bike, the one I'm working on, has no built-in weapons. But if Sheila could...

"I can do it," she says, like she's reading my mind. "Just give me access and I will get to work. Then you can stop spending so much time in here and get out a little more. Mr. Reider sent me a reminder earlier that you're expected at a party tonight in the city."

"He's out of his mind," I snap. "I'm not going to a party being held by Thomas. I'm not his fucking dog. I'm not at his beck and call. I'm not—"

"Detective Masters is going. I found her name on the guest list."

"What?" I stop messing with the bike again and look at her. "Why would I care about that?"

"Because," Sheila says in that superior I'm-a-genius-AI voice, "you've watched the footage of her in the cave at least seven different times since last Saturday. And I don't have access to the house upstairs, but I'm not an idiot, Lincoln. You're obsessed with her."

"Fuck." I laugh. "No. It's a sign of paranoia. I was trying to gauge how much she saw just in case her memory comes back."

"Hmph," Sheila says. "That's a lie. I can detect an increase in your heart rate and a sheen of sweat forming on your brow. You *like* Detective Masters."

"No—"

"In fact, it's my duty to see to your well-being. So I think we should call her up and ask her out on a date."

Beeps sound off on her speaker system. "What the fuck are you doing?"

"Calling Detective Masters."

"Sheila, this isn't funny. She's a fucking cop, for Christ's sake. Hang up."

"Only if you go to the party."

"You can't disobey me."

"Health override. You're stressed, which affects your moods. Moods are part of my wellness recognition protocols. And I have decided you need a date."

"Sheila, I will turn you off."

"Oh, look, it's ringing."

"OK, fine! Just hang up!"

"Promise me with a pinky swear."

"I don't pinky—"

"Hello?" I stop mid-sentence at the sound of Molly Masters' voice. "Hello?" she asks again.

I look up at Sheila and mouth, *I swear*, as I wiggle my pinky finger at her.

"Good evening," Sheila says in her fake automated computer tone. "You are the lucky winner of a free trip to—"

*Beep, beep, beep.*

"Oh, darn, she hung up."

"You're a bitch," I say. But I say it through a laugh.

"I am," Sheila says with a smile on her transparent face. "Every good woman has a little bitch inside her. I'll have the cleaning bots press your tux before I morph them into my engineering minions. Now please accept my request to run your life so I can make sure you get laid sometime in the next century. People can go months, but you're straddling that line between frustrated and desperate."

Fucking Sheila. She's been around Case too much.

But I get out from under the bike and walk over to the main computer terminal so I can accept the request. Because women, right? Every man wants one. Even me. And maybe Sheila's not real and she's more like a mother than I'd like to admit, but she's all I've got.

GUN GIRL

## CHAPTER TWELVE

I hang up the phone and look at it for a moment. The voice sounded familiar. *It was a computer, Molly*, the rational person inside me says. But it did… feel… familiar.

My phone rings again and I snatch it up and tab the answer button. "Hello?"

"Ah, Miss Masters."

Fuck. Atticus Montgomery. I spent all week avoiding the Blue Castle, but I should have known better than to think I'd slipped under his radar.

"Mr. Montgomery. How nice to hear from you again. I'm sorry, but I have no news about the case just yet. I'm—"

"It's a personal call."

Shit. "Oh. Well, how can I help you?"

"Our date, remember? To see the stars."

"Mr. Montgomery—"

"Atticus."

Whatever. I roll my eyes. "Atticus, I'm afraid I have plans tonight."

"I know. Big party for the new kid in town."

I laugh. "Surely you're not trying to tell me you're going?"

"Why wouldn't I be?"

I sigh. He's not going to make this simple. And what did I expect? He's the son of a billionaire. It's easy to make snap judgments about people and see them as ridiculous, or snide, or lacking in manners. But people at the top like Atticus Montgomery are where they are for a reason. And silver spoon aside, he's well-educated, fearless, and persistent. "Well, it's a party for the new satellite company—"

"SkyEye."

"Right. SkyEye. They're something of a direct competitor, aren't they?"

"Satellites," Atticus says with a pfffft. "Expensive tech built for the super-rich. It's just not practical. So no, we're really not competitors. And we were invited."

"Oh, God, is your father going to be there too?"

"You're going then?"

"Oh, I have to. I'm in charge of security. So yes. But I'm afraid if you think we can use it as our date, I have to decline. Duty, right?"

"Right." I can almost hear the smile and it sends a shiver up my spine. I'm not sure why he's sorta creepy to me, but he is. That tower. I really don't want to see the stars from that thing. It's just weird. "But you're dressing for the occasion, I hope? I'd like to see you cleaned up. No offense to your everyday wear. But the tan slacks and white blouses are kind of... ordinary. You're definitely not ordinary."

I huff out a breath. "Well, no offense taken. I do my best to be as ordinary as possible. I'm afraid it suits me."

"All pretenses. No ordinary woman wears saddle shoes." He chuckles on the other end of the line. "It says fearless nine-year-old. But in all the right ways."

I burst out laughing. "Jesus, Atticus. You have a way with words. I'm not sure how to take that, but—"

"Some children just naturally feel invincible and immortal. Like the world is at their beck and call. Like it owes them nothing but a challenge and no wall is too high, no obstacle too large, and no enemy too close."

I stand there in silence for a moment, thinking about how right he is. Or was. "Well," I say after several long seconds. "I might've been that way once. But today, they're just comfortable shoes."

"Hmm," he says thoughtfully. "We'll have to agree to disagree on that. And even though you're working, I'm sure you'll be able to spare a moment to say hello when I seek you out. Have a nice morning, Miss Masters."

The line goes dead.

I press the end tab just to make sure the call disconnected and slump down in a chair near the front window as I think about what he said. He's been checking up on me, obviously. And why not? I'm the detective in charge of a major case that involves his billion-dollar business. It's only logical that he went looking.

But I respect the fact that he didn't bring it up. Not directly. And that he could read so much into my scant history available online. I *was* a fearless nine-year-old. And that lasted through ten, eleven, twelve. All the way up to sixteen.

But sixteen… I look down at my saddle shoes. The two-tone brown leather is scuffed and the soles are worn down just right. I wear them every day without fail. They remind me of happier times. Back when motorcycles were fun and I was fearless. Back when my family was whole and even though the people who raised me were transient—we moved from town to town and only stopped when we had to—their love was limitless. Back when living meant something more than military duty or solving crimes.

I kick my shoes off and pick them up, then take them into my bedroom and throw them in the closet. I don't like people to see through me like that. And it's not that I think Montgomery is being mean or facetious. I think he is genuinely interested in figuring me out. But I don't want to be figured out. And I certainly don't want to walk around with clues on my feet.

A chime announces an incoming text, so I walk out of my room to get my phone. It's the chief. *You better be on time today.*

Well, duty calls. One more day and then some downtime this weekend. I really do need to get rid of Will's bikes. I hate seeing that trailer every time I have to take the garbage out. This weekend I'll—

"I'll what?" I say out loud. The thought was there and then it wasn't. It feels like a hole in my memory. "What did I do last Saturday? I got the bikes. I drove…"

And this is where it gets fuzzy. I drove home, obviously. But I don't remember any of it.

"I drove—"

But another text from the chief comes in and jars me back to the present. *Acknowledge me when I message you, Masters!*

I text back, *Leaving now.* There's no time to start wondering what I might've done last weekend.

I check the ammo in my gun, holster it under my arm, slip my feet into some hideous loafers in the coat closet, grab my jacket and purse and walk out the door.

They had a saying about me back when I was a fearless nine-year-old. Everyone from my father to the ringmaster used to sing it in my ear whenever I'd get lost in a daydream about life outside the business.

*If wishes were horses,* they'd say.

*If wishes were horses, beggars would ride.*

*If turnips were watches, I'd wear one by my side.*

*If 'ifs' and 'ands' were pots and pans, there'd be no work for tinkers' hands.*

That was the song, anyway. But that's not what they'd say.

*If wishes were horses, you'd ride forever.*

But they were wrong. Wishes were motorcycles.

I left the business behind years ago and all my dreams went with it.

GUN GIRL

## CHAPTER THIRTEEN

Cathedral Thirteen is on the far east side of town and when you stand on the top step, just in front of the grand arched double doors, the view of the mountains is magnificent. I know. I'm standing there now and I've got horses, and wishes, and motorcycles on my mind.

"Detective Masters?" A gruff voice pulls me out of the daydream and a tall, dark man ascends the steps two at a time like he's late.

Which he is. Four minutes. I'm typically punctual when I'm not waking up drunk with a head filled with questions, but I'm not a stickler over four minutes. He extends his hand to me and a ring gleams with a bright red stone set in what is most surely platinum on his ring finger. It's his right hand, so not a wedding ring.

Don't judge me, he's very attractive.

"I apologize," he says, grasping my hand firmly and giving it a gentle squeeze. Handshakes intrigue me. Mostly because I like to compare them. And the gentle squeeze from Thomas Brooks comes off as seductive. "The complexities of this day are almost beyond description."

"Interesting," I say, letting go of his hand without squeezing it back. My handshake responses are almost as intriguing as the offers. I shake a lot of hands as a detective. And I shook a lot more as a special agent in the military. Very high-level hands.

But Thomas Brooks' attention on me is fleeting. His mind is on his party tonight as SkyEye Inc. opens its new headquarters in the rehabbed ruin I'm standing in front of.

"But you don't need to worry about security," I say. "You asked for four dozen officers this afternoon, and we've called everyone to accommodate this request. Your party will come off without a hitch."

"Perfect," he says, opening one of the grand doors and stepping aside to wave me in.

"Wow," I say, as my eyes are drawn up towards the panels of colored glass depicting the constellations. "That... is..."

He laughs as I search for the words. "Nice, isn't it. We've got all eighty-eight original constellations up there. And the spire is Polaris."

"The North Pole."

"Yes." He smiles for the first time. He's dark, that's for sure. And probably broody. Much like I thought Atticus would be, but isn't. But the smile breaks the clouds from his face and exposes the possibility of sunlight. "The stars under the spires. It's poetic, don't you think?"

"Hmmm, funny you should say that. I was at Blue Corp all this week." I notice a slight twitch in his smile before he stops himself, and make a note of that. "And Atticus Montgomery has something very similar under his pitched ceiling. Only they're the real deal."

It's sort of an insult, right? Comparing headquarters of these two men, when they must surely be rivals.

"Ah." He laughs it off. "But he has no claim to the sky, Detective. We've got all the eyes up there." He smiles again and this time I don't find the stress, but I do get a little chill up the back of my neck.

"Satellites. Yes. Very interesting. And I'm as curious as anyone what your purpose here in Cathedral City is."

"I grew up here." He waves me forward down the center of the cathedral. There are dozens of people setting things up, and we glide right through the fray like chaos must part for us, until we reach the back of the room and start down a long hallway to the offices. "And I'm a sentimental guy. There's nothing quite like returning home as the Prodigal Son."

"You're hardly destitute and begging." I laugh. "I'm not sure the parable fits."

"Oh," he says, "but it does. I left long ago and spent many a night dining with the swine of corporate culture and have finally come home to make good."

"Huh," I say, for lack of a better response. "So this party tonight is…?"

"Exactly what I said. Giving back and coming home." He stops in front of a doorway and nods at it. "This is the control room and I want two men assigned to it as soon as they start bringing the equipment in. There's an entrance in front, plus four on each side of what used to be the altar—two in front, two in back—and the back doors at the top of the old altar. Out back there's a delivery entrance that will be closed and locked, manned by my own security. Your men will patrol all the exits and you will be in charge of the main hall."

"Oh, yes, of course," I say, caught off guard with the sudden switch back to business. "It's your dime, Mr. Brooks. Your wish is my command."

"I expected no less, Detective Masters. I hope you bring your dancing shoes tonight. I put on a helluva party. Now if you'll excuse me, I've got a million things to do."

And with that he takes my hand one more time, gives it a gentle squeeze as he bows, ever so slightly, and turns to walk away.

"Mr. Brooks?" I call after him. "What will this room hold?"

He tsks his tongue and calls over his shoulder. "A good detective should be able to figure that out."

I stand there and watch him disappear into a crowd of men who want things. Answers to questions, signatures on tablets, and an ear for whatever important bits of information corporate billionaires are subjected to throughout the course of a normal business day.

Jesus Christ. This town is filled with eccentrics. It's a regular hotspot of intellectual oddballs. I turn to walk myself back out to go find Sergeant Seville, who will be running the off-duty officers we've got scheduled for today. Normally a lieutenant would handle my job, but since it's private—Mr. Brooks is paying dearly for our services today—and we've got crime coming out our ears, I'm in charge.

It's a punishment for being late on Monday, I realize that. But it's an honor, really. Security is what I do best. And it's an opportunity to meet some of the most prominent leaders in the community.

The next few hours pass quickly as Seville and I assign duty stations and place the requested officers in strategic locations around the exits. My curiosity about what Brooks is setting up in here is killing me, but no one seems to have any inclination to let me in on it. Hired help. That's all I am to these people.

My phone rings in my pocket. The chief. So I bring it out and tab answer. "Masters," I say in my professional voice.

"We've got another one."

"Another what?" I say, annoyed.

"Suicide. At Blue Corp. They found him this morning, same as the last one. Alastair Montgomery is waiting for you."

"Fuck," I say under my breath.

"He's pissed, Masters. This is not good for business and he says his tech department detects interference in the security cameras."

"What? But they didn't say anything when I was there on Tuesday."

"Well, they're saying it now. So get your ass down there and make that old man happy. He's a major contributor to this city's social programs—"

*And the mayor's reelection campaign,* I don't say.

"—and he deserves answers."

I get the hang-up beeps and look down at the blank screen as I process this. Murders. I suspected it and I've looked for more clues, but there were no signs in the deceased's home. And the first suspected suicide was contaminated weeks ago after the case was closed. The second wife didn't have anything useful to say when I questioned her. Dead end.

But something bad is definitely happening here in Cathedral City. Someone is killing people connected to Blue Corp. And someone wants us to know that.

It feels like a game. The kind of game a serial killer might play with a detective.

The kind of game that can quickly become personal.

Atticus is waiting for me in the lobby this time. In fact, he's pacing. The place is filled with cops and an ambulance is waiting outside, doors open, like all it needs is a body to be complete.

"I have something to show you—"

"Detective Masters?" A voice bellows from across the lobby, and when I turn, old man Montgomery walks briskly towards me. "I need answers and I need them now. That's three dead employees, Detective. And all of them occurred on these premises."

I have an urge to point out it's a private campus and while the outcome is certainly my problem, the fact that the deaths happened here is not.

But Atticus shoots me a look and I take that as a warning. So I rein it in. "I've already assigned a team of computer forensic specialists to look at your security footage, Mr. Montgomery. We don't have an answer yet, but this is the department's top priority. We will have beat cops on campus until we figure out what's happening, all we need is clearance from you."

I really don't know if that's true or not, but after Chief's call, I'm betting this is the direction he wants to go. I might as well make the promises.

Montgomery senior stops mid-tirade and stares me down. "You have it," he says. "But I expect results. This case should not be difficult for you, Detective." He practically sneers my title. "You should be making better progress. In fact, you're quite disappointing professionally. So if another incident happens on Blue Corp campus, you'll be out of a job."

I rein in my sigh as well. As if any of this is my fault. But thankfully Montgomery senior walks off, leaving me standing there with Atticus. I look up at him and he nods.

"Right," he says. "You need to see this."

I follow him to the elevators and we go up to the twenty-first floor. It's the same one the last employee was found on, so I'm betting they did very similar things in their top-secret research and development duties. When the elevator doors open Atticus leads me over to the secure door to the inner labs. The corridor is small and narrow, and there are about fifteen people crammed up here, including the first responders.

"We've kept them all out until you arrived," Atticus explains. That's hush-hush speak for, *We have a clue that might need to stay secret.* He palms his hand over the biosecurity, waits for the lock to release, and then opens the door with a whoosh that says this lab has an internal air circulation system. I follow him in and the door slams closed behind me.

The body is immediately visible. He's at the very back of the lab, slumped over a small desk. His right cheek is pressed flat against a black soapstone tabletop, and his eyes are open. A gun lies on the floor, directly below his drooping arm.

I squat down to inspect his hand, but Atticus's fingertips lightly touch my shoulder. "Never mind looking for powder burns, Molly. This is what I need you to look at."

I stand back up so I can look at what he's pointing to and then my head goes fuzzy.

"Molly?" Atticus' voice is far away. "Molly?"

The last thing I see is the red anarchy symbol carved into the man's forehead before I collapse.

"Molly!" Atticus catches me before I hit the tiled floor. "Hell, are you OK?"

"I don't know," I breathe. "I don't know what happened. I just felt dizzy all of a sudden."

He leads me out of the lab and down a corridor where there is a dark break room. The lights flip on as we enter and he helps me sit in a chair.

I let out a long breath. "Thanks. I don't know why that happened. I've seen worse, believe me."

Atticus takes a seat across the table and lifts up one eyebrow. "It's a clue, Molly."

"Obviously, Atticus," I sneer. He opens his mouth to say something more, but then closes it and remains silent. "We're going to need to keep this quiet. Does your father know?"

"No," Atticus says. "No. He has no interest in the details. He just wants this to stop."

I can't say that I blame him. "OK, well, thank you for your help and the heads-up. I have to get back to security, but I'll be working on this today."

"There's going to be more." It comes out at a statement. "There's going to be more and there's no way to stop them."

I don't even have time to ask what the hell that means, because he walks out the door and a few seconds later the outer lab door opens and the first responders come inside and begin cataloging the scene.

## CHAPTER FOURTEEN

"This is a mistake," I say to my reflection in the mirror. I flatten down my hair, trying to make the unruly mess conform into some semblance of respectability. Then I scrub my hand across my newly clean-shaven chin, already missing the days-old stubble I usually find there. "She's a cop. She's been with Blue Corp all week for an investigation. She's gonna figure me out if we play this wrong."

"You need to get out of this cave," Sheila says from the main cavern. This is my room and there are no optics in here for Sheila to project herself into her holographic form. I did that on purpose. No one wants a hovering nag in their bedroom. So she stands just outside, ready with an answer for my misgivings. "And you're a partner."

"A silent partner," I growl, still pissed off I had to shave. "Which means I don't have to show up for shit like this. I don't have to play nice, or pretend to care, or any of those other things that Case has to do. That's why he takes an extra five percent. I pay that fucker to do this shit for me."

"The detective will be useful once things start happening, Lincoln. You need to make her acquaintance tonight."

"And what if she recognizes me?" I walk out and stare her in the face. "What then? What if the drugs didn't work? What if they wore off? What if—"

"Then it would be optimal for you to be there when that recognition happens, don't you agree? If she wakes in the night and remembers what happened, what do you think she will do the next day?"

"If she sees me tonight and starts to remember, we get the same ending, Sheila. She'll get on the phone to her boss and have me arrested. I'll be in jail and then the whole fucking thing is blown. Someone will have to come bail me out. And you certainly can't do it. You're a fucking lightshow. Case can't do it, he'll be implicated. Thomas…" I laugh. "Well, fucking Thomas *wouldn't* do it. So who the fuck is gonna bail me out if she catches on? This is so beyond stupid."

"I think," Sheila says, turning her back to me and walking over to the engineering lab door, "you just proved my point. How useful would another friend be? And a detective, at that?" She turns back to me and smiles. "And don't insult me with the remarks about the lights. I'm working on it."

"Working on what? And since when is calling you a lightshow an insult? That's what a hologram is."

"I'm not a hologram, Lincoln." She lifts her chin and crosses her arms. A gesture that resembles defiance and hurt.

I sigh. "I know that better than anyone, Sheila. Remember?" She tries not to smile, but she can't help herself. "I built you first."

"You did," she concedes. "And it's a good thing too. Because if it wasn't for me you'd be all alone in this world."

I nod in understanding. She's right. But I'm right too. "She's gonna figure this stuff out, Sheila. I have a bad feeling about things tonight. I've been running on luck for fifteen years and now that everything is starting to happen, that luck is about to run out."

"Then make friends with her, Lincoln. You don't really have a choice, anyway. She has a place in all this. You know that. Molly is the missing piece you've been waiting for."

She's not though. She's the one piece I've been counting on never coming back. And now that she is... well, my days are numbered. "I'm taking the bike tonight. The old bike."

"It will mess up your hair."

I laugh. "Like I care." The old bike isn't the one I wrecked last weekend. The old bike is the one my dad used to ride. Nothing flashy on it. And it's not ever been connected to Sheila. So it's a punishment of sorts. For her making me go in the first place. I know she's interested in Molly and was probably hoping she could eavesdrop, if only from the periphery. *But not gonna happen, you bossy little lightshow.*

I'll go, because I do need to figure out if Molly Masters is getting some of her memory back. And I could use another friend, although how Sheila thinks Molly will forgive me after what I did to her is beyond me. But... if Molly *is* going to remember, it's better that I be there for it. Talk her down. Calm her down. Manipulate her into staying quiet, and maybe, if I'm lucky, into seeing the big picture.

Thomas is Thomas. And whatever his reasons for coming back with a bang are, they're not anything I can control. He does what he does, when he does it. He's always been that way.

But everything else feels a little too much like luck running out.

And if she does remember what I did to her... well, I don't want to think about that yet.

Maybe I'm just paranoid. I've used the drugs on other people. They've always held. I've gotten away with a lot worse things than what I did to Molly Masters.

"Luck," I mumble, walking back through my bedroom, grabbing my keys from a drawer in a small table, opening a door that leads to a long tunnel, and stepping through. "Stay with me tonight. Just one more night and I swear, I won't ever ask for anything again."

It's a child's prayer. One I've muttered for decades. And luck has always held up its end of the bargain. But I feel like a liar. I feel like I've been asking for luck my whole life, always coming out the other end whole, yet unsatisfied with my gift.

Because I always come out just as empty as I went in.

I feel like Molly Masters will be my downfall. She is the opposite of everything I stand against. She will make me weak. Make me fail. Make me lose.

And isn't that her job?

Right.

I come to a stairwell at the end of the tunnel and start climbing. When I get to the top I press my palm against the pad and a laser swipes across my print, granting me access to the house.

I end up in the garage, looking at the heap covered by a thick canvas tarp, stained and weathered by age.

Maybe the bike won't even start? It's been a while since I took it out. And I can't go into town using the car. Not for something with so many witnesses. And my truck has been decommissioned for... personal stuff.

I rip the tarp off with a whoosh, dust filling the air and probably settling on my robot-starched white shirt, and get on.

But it starts right up. And I can't help but wonder, as I give it some throttle and pull out of the garage, if that means my luck is still holding… or if it just ran out?

GUN GIRL

## CHAPTER FIFTEEN

My dress is old, but still nice. I was in charge of security for a high-level foreign official a couple years back. The ballroom was extravagant, the finest chefs were flown in, and the china cost more than everything I owned at the time, including my car. I imagine tonight to be much of the same, minus the dinner.

I chose a long gown last time to hide my weapon in a thigh holster which can be accessed through a slit in the well-hidden pocket on the right side. There's a pocket on the left too. Both are almost invisible and just in front of my hips, so anything concealed within can be hidden in the layers of the skirt. It's strapless and intricately beaded from the top of the bodice to the tops of my thighs. It looks, to my dismay then and now, too much like a wedding dress for my comfort level. But at least it's not white. It's a subdued cream color.

And it hides my gun. So mission accomplished.

I actually put on makeup too. And my hair is up off my shoulders in a twist I did myself. I might not pass muster with tonight's fashionistas, but I don't have to.

I'm security. It's a ruse. A costume.

"Blah," I say to my reflection in the mirror. I turn away towards my bed where my gun is waiting. I check the barrel, make sure it's loaded, then hike my skirts up and snap it into the holster. There are two extra magazines, just in case. But there has been no chatter at all about this party. Why Brooks feels the need for such heightened security is beyond me.

I slip my badge into my other pocket and then my feet into my shoes. They are flats, made to go with the dress, with rubber soles for silence and traction, and the same pretty beads that match the dress for appearances.

"OK, Masters," I say, looking at my reflection one more time. "Let's go."

Atticus Montgomery has sent a car. It's been waiting outside my house for the better part of an hour. When the chauffeur knocked on the door I was only mildly surprised. Montgomery is a control freak. One of those alpha males who likes to keep the illusion of superiority. And he wants everyone to know that I'm working with him. Maybe even that I'm working *for* him.

I don't mind the ride. The idea of slipping behind the wheel of my five-year-old department sedan and driving to the party in a ball gown is ridiculous.

I'm thankful for the car. And Atticus Montgomery can make people think whatever they want. I'm not in his pocket. He can't buy my cooperation with a ride.

So I walk downstairs, grab my house keys off the foyer table, stuff them in my pocket, drape the matching shrug over my shoulders, and walk outside to the limo. The driver is waiting at the passenger door and I wonder for a second if he's been standing there the whole time, or he's just so good at his job, he noticed me getting ready to exit and took up the position.

"Thank you," I say as he opens it for me and I slip inside. It closes with a soft whoosh one only hears from a luxury vehicle, and then he walks around to get in.

We drive to the cathedral and get in line behind all the other cars waiting to drop off important people. When it's our turn, the driver turns his head and says, "Mr.

Montgomery said he might be a little late tonight. But he will find you later."

"Noted," I reply back, as he slips out of the car to get my door. That's good luck. Gives me plenty of time to chat people up and find out who Thomas Brooks really is. I'm at a disadvantage here because I'm new in town. I don't have the history of these people. And like most places, Cathedral City has prominent citizens whose families date back generations. They know their own history and they will be talking, even if it is in hushed whispers. If there's some sort of past relationship between Blue Corp executives and Thomas Brooks, it will be gossiped about tonight.

The driver offers me a hand after he opens my door and I take it so I can ease out of the car with some dignity. Fucking ball gowns.

Immediately cameras start flashing in my face and I have to cover my eyes. The flash lingers in my vision as bright spots, but I bustle past and make my way up the cathedral stairs without comment.

Sergeant Seville greets me at the door and offers me his arm. He's dressed in his formal uniform and smiles warmly. "You clean up well." He shoots me a wink and I scowl.

"Thank you," comes out automatically though. Men. They tell me to fuck off and don't give me a second glance at work, but put me in a pretty dress and they turn into gentlemen. "Is everybody in place?"

"We are, Detective," he says, his professionalism back. "Just as you asked. But there's nothing to report. Quiet and dignified, that's what this crowd is."

When we get inside I let go of his arm and turn away, scanning the main room for faces I might recognize.

The mayor is here. Herbert Rothschild is not the first in his family to be mayor of Cathedral City. But so far the only other thing I've had time to learn about him is the fact that he went to law school and never ended up practicing law.

Also here is a judge I know by name, Peter Livingston, and several I know by face, but haven't had the time to meet yet. Livingston and I had an unfortunate encounter my first day on the job. I was shadowing Detective Rollins that day, and he was due to testify. It didn't go well for him. And the judge was pretty upset that the suspect on trial was found not guilty a few days later.

It bugged me then that Livingston seemed to take it personally and it still bugs me now. But again, I have no history with these people. And I never did have time to look up that suspect's records to make sense of it.

"You look lost," a gruff voice says from my left.

I turn to find a tall man with light blond hair grinning at me like a wolf. "I'm not," I say, "just getting my bearings."

"You're the new detective, right? I'm Case Reider."

He extends his hand and I reciprocate but instead of shaking it, he bows a little and touches his lips to the back of my hand. "So very nice to see you," he says, standing up tall again.

I squint at him for a moment, almost in a trance, and then shake myself out of it. "You look familiar. Have we met before?"

He smiles and lets out a soft laugh. "No, not really. But I run ToyBox Inc. We're based over on the west side of town. You probably saw my picture in *Cathedral Reports* last week."

"Oh," I say, smiling. "One of those Peter Pan guys, huh? You never quite grew out of the video-game phase and decided to make your fortune by selling good times to other perpetual children?"

He chuckles again, this time heartier. "Something like that."

"Well, it's a pleasure—"

"Let's dance, Detective Masters. Do you waltz?"

"Um," I say, hesitating.

"I'm sure you do. I can see many days of dance lessons in your past." And with that he takes my hand, pulls me towards him, and begins to lead.

"I do waltz," I say, my feet reluctantly following along. "But I'm here on business tonight."

"The dress is a ruse, then?" He smiles, making his blue eyes light up. "But you can't let it go to waste." He looks down for a moment as we glide across the stone floor together, like we've been partners for ages instead of seconds. "You're very good at it. Where did you learn?"

"Yeah, well…" I sigh. "It's a long story."

"I have time."

"Where did you learn?" I ask, changing the subject.

"Oh, my life has been one long boring string of charm school classes."

"Oh, has it?" I can't help myself, I laugh for real this time.

"Have you ever seen the debutante ball they have each year in the main cathedral?"

"No, but I imagine that is some affair."

"You have no idea. I was roped into being someone's date back in the day. And let me tell you, if she had warned me about the rehearsal time, I might've never agreed." He says the words but I can immediately tell he's not sincere. We glide past a few other waltzing couples as his eyes glaze over a little. "Close your eyes, Detective. And let me help you imagine it for a moment."

"Close my—"

"Just do it. I promise it's worth the few moments of trust you'll have to give me to lead you around this room."

Jesus. Another alpha. What is it with the men in this town? They are all handsome, rich control freaks.

"Come on, it's a vision you'll enjoy. Women love shit like this."

"Well, you certainly have the gift of persuasion," I say through a chuckle. But when I glance up at him again, he looks... nostalgic. And maybe a little sad. Possibly a bit regretful.

I close my eyes. Because I would never turn down the opportunity to get a story that can cause so much emotion a decade later.

"Picture this, Molly," he says, leaning down into my neck. I breathe in deeply as he whispers my name across the sensitive skin. "Hundreds of girls dressed in white gowns, much like the one you're wearing tonight. And hundreds of escorts, dressed in a tux, much like mine. We filed into the grand cathedral, four abreast. Girl, boy, girl, boy. Black, white, black, white. Each escort holding the hand of his beautiful partner up, like he'd won the lottery.

"The stained glass was glowing from the interior lights. The music was lively. And nothing but proud faces beamed from the perimeter. My heart was beating fast that night. We'd been practicing the dances for months. Each one was coordinated to show us off. Each one classically choreographed to stun the families who sat in the boxed seats above. And when I watched the video days later, I felt like we were spinning for Heaven. Like every move that night was synchronized for God's pleasure."

"It sounds lovely," I whisper, lost in his dream.

"It was a moment of peace in a life overflowing with chaos."

"So what happened to her?"

"What?" he asks, breaking the spell he's put me under and stopping our dance.

I open my eyes. "Where is she? It sounds like the night of your life."

His smile is gone and his eyes are no longer bright. "I was a few years older than her, already in my third year of college by that time. And she was still in high school. But she never finished because there was a family emergency a few days later and she left town. I never saw her again."

"Oh, I'm sorry. It sounds like she meant a lot to you. Did you ever go looking for her?"

"No." He sighs. "I couldn't. I—" He stops talking abruptly and his gaze fixes on something across the room. "Sorry, I have to go," he says, letting go of my hands and bowing slightly. "Maybe we can dance again later?"

I nod as he forces a smile, and then turns and walks off, leaving me there in the middle of the floor.

I try to follow him with my gaze as he makes his way through the throngs of dancers, but there are too many people. So I start after him, unwilling to let go of the fantasy that he put in my head and the implied tragedy he left there.

I search, pushing past the other dancers, my detective instincts on full alert for some reason. I think back to the moment I saw his face. There was something there. That bit of recognition might've been more.

And then I see the back of his head. He waves his hands as he talks to another man in a tux about his same height. It almost looks as if they are arguing, so I keep walking. Slower now. Taking it all in. The cathedral, the dancers, the music, the stained glass. I have that vision in my head of the debutante ball he put there, still clouding my senses. It all seems rather too romantic, considering what has happened today. Someone peeks out around Case Reider and I stop dead.

That face. I know that face. And this time it's more than just a slight bit of intuition. It's...

1. A soft kiss across my neck.
2. A dark place with lights and technology.
3. A muddy road and rain.

He looks me straight in the eyes, looks away, but his lips move and then Case Reider turns around and looks at me too. An instant later the other man turns and walks out the open back door of the cathedral, where two of Thomas Brooks' doormen stand watch in their matching outfits. They seem militaristic in their uniforms, almost Secret Service in the way their attention focuses on the events before them.

But they ignore the stranger. Case makes his way towards me and I towards him, and when we meet a few feet apart, he's stuttering excuses. "I'm sorry, I just—"

"Excuse me," I say, pushing past him. "I need to talk to someone."

I walk through the doors, the men on either side giving me only a brief glance, and when I check over my shoulder to see if Case Reider is following, he's disappeared.

"Hmm," I say to myself as I lift my elaborate skirts and descend the stone stairs that lead out to an expansive garden with tall hedges. It's a cool night, and there are only a few couples milling about, but I hear laughter coming from the other side of the hedges and stop in front of a sign explaining what it is.

A maze.

I look around for the stranger I instinctively recognized, but he's nowhere to be found. The back garden has a stone wall around it twelve feet high, at least. And the gate is locked, per instructions. So there is only one possible place he might be hiding.

I find the entrance and head into the maze.

## CHAPTER SIXTEEN

"Dancing with her, Case? Really? What are you trying to do, undo fifteen fucking years of luck in the span of three minutes?"

"Hey, relax. I was just trying to feel her out. See how much she knows."

I lean to the side a little and give her a quick check. "Fuck, she's coming."

"Just play it cool, man. And call me tonight and tell me how it goes."

"Right," I say, as Case chuckles. "Asshole." We're in a lot of trouble. I can feel it. All the shit I've been pushing away is about to knock me back on my ass.

I turn and rub my temple as I head out the back door, willing the headache that's building to go away. There's no way out from the garden. I know this place better than Thomas. I was the one who designed it back when we were still in school. I didn't know what they were gonna use it for until it was too late.

I think that was the moment I turned. Walking back through the quad after finals. The maze was supposed to be used for animals. A test, that's what they told me. For animals, they said. But they ran *us* through the maze. We were the animals. More than a dozen went in and only three came out.

Me, Thomas, and Case in that order.

Thomas brushed past my shoulder as we walked through the Prodigy School doors, damaged even more at the end than we were going in, trying our best to pretend that shit didn't just happen.

"It was a good design," he said. "And hey, you knew it better than the rest of us. So good job on being first. But brothers don't let brothers die in the maze, Lincoln. A little heads-up next time, eh?"

It was the first time he ever called me Lincoln and it changed everything for me.

How he got his hands on those old plans, I have no idea. I don't really care either, I'm just glad he did. Because the only way to stop a public scene now is to get Molly Masters inside the hedge maze where we can at least have some privacy. Not many people want to wander around a dark maze at night.

I duck in through the opening in the hedges, then check behind me, and yeah, sure enough, her feet are flying down the stone steps. She's looking everywhere for me.

How much does she remember? I guess I'll start there first. It's possible she's just getting little hints. And maybe my face triggered a memory, or maybe she just knows she recognizes me and can't place it. Either way, I've got her attention.

That makes me smile a little more than I'd like to admit. Because... well, Sheila was right. I like her. I more than like her. I crave her.

Laughter pulls me out of my introspection and a few young couples go running by, probably thankful that they found the exit. There's another exit on the far side, but once you make it to the middle most people don't want to push their luck. They go out the same way they came in.

I walk up around a corner, then double back though a cut in the hedge to an alcove that has a window cut through, so I can watch the detective pass by.

The sound of soft footsteps on the large flat stones make me duck back into the darkness. A few seconds later, she walks past the window. Her eyes dart around. She looks right at me, but she's unable to see past the shadows.

Can I turn her? It's a good question. One Case and I discussed at length this week after I told him the whole story. He came by the cave earlier and watched the footage with Sheila and me, and then we pulled up the tracking map from the transponder I magnetically attached to the undercarriage of her work car.

She was at Blue Corp all week. Which, as Case pointed out, might be useful to us. If we can get her to cooperate. Everyone—I do mean everyone—knows why she was put on that Blue case and it wasn't because they're short-staffed.

It was because she's new. She's got no history. No context. No memory.

I wait until her footsteps fade and I walk to my left, deeper into the maze. It's not the right path, and eventually it will dead-end on the far side of the garden after twisting and turning so much, a person unfamiliar with this puzzle might feel dizzy.

But it goes in the right direction and meets up with another side path that will take me back to the main one. So I continue. I hear her a few times. And she hears me too. Because she stops, like she's listening.

I pause for several seconds and let her get ahead, and then, as silently as I can, weave my way through the heavily shadowed corridors until I'm back on the main path that takes you to the center. Thomas spared no expense building this place and rehabbing the cathedral. And I wonder why? Why spend all that money just to relive what we left behind? I've spent the past fifteen years trying to forget that place. Don't get me wrong, I remember the important parts. The drugs. The doctors. The manipulation. The end.

But the maze? And the cathedral? No. That's not shit I need to keep.

"I know you're here," Detective Masters says from a hedge or two away.

"Come find me," I whisper back.

Her feet whirl on the stone path and she's closer than I first thought. Sneaky thing, isn't she?

"I remember you."

"Yeah?" I ask, easing into another alcove. She's gonna pass by me if she goes towards the center of the maze, so all I have to do is stay put now.

"It was raining."

"It was snowing, gun girl."

"And you crashed a bike in front of me."

"I pushed you out a window."

"What?" she asks. I walk forward a little, and then slip across the stone path and into another corridor where I make a turn that will bring me back towards her, but on another side of the hedge. "You drugged me."

"You drugged yourself that night. I was just the supplier."

She's silent. And then, "I was with you last weekend, wasn't I?"

"I thought you remembered?" I can hear her breathing, that's how close she is. I can see bits and pieces of her cream-colored gown through small breaks in the hedge. "What do you think I did?"

"Took me home—"

"I sent you away, remember?"

She hesitates. So she doesn't remember all of it.

"I didn't have a party last Saturday."

"You sound unsure. Like parties are your thing. Are you a party girl, Molly?"

She starts walking without answering.

"That's the wrong way."

"Why should I believe you?" She's breathing hard now, like she's scared. And she should be. Because she's alone out here with me. She's the last person on earth who should be alone with me.

"Because I have the maze memorized. I designed it. Many, many years ago."

"Liar," she whispers.

"Keep walking then," I say, following her on the other side of the hedge. "You'll come to a fork—"

"A fork in the road. You went left and he went right."

"You ran one way and I ran the other."

"There was a dirt road. And you were driving my brother's truck."

"You got a nice new brother out of that deal, eh? I should've never trusted him."

"I don't know what that even means, but…" She lets out a long sigh.

"Found the fork, did you?"

"Why are you here?"

"I'm here for you. Why else would I bother to show my face?"

She stays silent for a few moments, and then I hear laughter from the start of the maze as more people enter. I wonder if she'll scream?

I decide no when she stands her ground. She wants to talk. Wants answers. And she wants to follow my lead.

She might not realize it yet, but she wants me to take over. Be alpha again. "Go left at the fork," I say.

"Just like I did last weekend."

"Just like that, gun girl."

There's a long silence after that, and then she draws in a deep breath, lets it out slowly. "Bike boy," she whispers.

"The one and only. Now do as I say and then we can talk."

"What if I don't want to talk? What if I want to arrest you for rape?"

"Rape?" I laugh. "Come on."

"I woke up wearing lingerie."

"What's so bad about that?" I say, walking towards her voice. I have to go the other way to get to the middle, but I don't think she's ready to see me yet, so I stay close, but not too close.

"Girls don't wear shit like that to bed when they're sleeping alone."

"Some girls do."

"Not this girl. And this girl doesn't drink."

"Doesn't drink anymore?"

"Right."

"Hmmm," I say. "But that lingerie was pretty. And you looked pretty wearing it."

"You took my clothes off," she growls.

"You were very muddy and wet. I needed to clean you up. So why not make you look pretty after?"

"You fucking pervert." She's breathing harder now and I start to get a little worried.

"We didn't sleep together, if that's what you're worried about. You were stoned, man."

"You're the one who got me stoned."

"I had to."

"Why?" she demands. "Why—" And then the rest must come rushing back. Because she stops and stays silent for more than a minute. We stand there, just a few feet apart but separated by more than a tall hedge. We're separated by fifteen years. By a night in the snow and an eternity of regrets. By choices that pulled us apart, and fate or bad luck that will bring us back together.

"Do you want to talk or not?" I finally ask, breaking the silence. "Because I have a secret to tell you."

"I want to arrest you."

"Meet me in the middle and see if you still feel the same way after."

"I will. You're not going to get away with what you did."

"You can believe what you want, and I might be an asshole for last weekend. But it's the things I did fifteen years ago that count. And I did keep you safe. I never raped you. And I never wanted to hurt you."

"No? So coerced drugging isn't hurting someone? What if I was allergic to that drug? What if I was—"

"You're not."

"Don't interrupt me, asshole. You don't know anything about me."

"Go left," I growl back. "Then take the first right, go past the second alcove, and then turn right again. I'll meet you there."

## CHAPTER SEVENTEEN

I stand absolutely still, listening to his fading footsteps as he walks away. He's crazy. Insane. What to do?

1. Run. Any man who would drug a woman, take her home, wash her off in the shower and then dress her up like some doll—well, I don't have a strong enough word for how goddamned creepy that is.

2. Go meet him. Because any man who does all those things just to keep a secret… yeah. That's some secret he has.

3. That fucking cave.

It's all coming back to me. The gate in the side of the mountain. The dark tunnel with the red running lights. The… lab? Holographic woman? Guns.

I swallow hard. I'm not new to danger. Hell, I cut my teeth on things far more dangerous than standing in a hedge maze at night with a creep. But… he's so very, *very* creepy. Serial killer kind of creepy.

I shudder and look down at my gun. I do have this. And if I don't go meet him then I'll have to try to backtrack my way out of this damn maze. I can still hear voices—people might be in the maze. But will they find me and let me follow them out? It's a lot larger than I originally thought. I counted the longest path and it was forty-two steps. And that wasn't even the entire length of one side.

I could scream and someone would come rescue me. But how the hell would I show my face at work tomorrow?

So… I walk forward and take the first right, go past the second alcove, and then turn right again.

And simple as you please, there I am. Standing in the center of the maze.

"What a letdown, huh?" bike boy says from the other side of a huge statue of a satellite dish. It's fifteen feet in diameter and mounted on a pedestal ten feet high. Spotlights on the ground point up at it, highlighting the greenish copper patina.

"I expected more from Thomas. A Greek god or something. A fucking minotaur, maybe. But this piece of shit?" He stops looking at the disappointing sculpture and drags his gaze to meet mine. "He's let me down before, though. So what's new?"

"You know Mr. Brooks?" Brooks doesn't look like the kind of guy who hangs around serial killers. But then again… I have no idea. God, I wish I knew the people of this town better. Having no history sucks.

"Damn," bike boy says. "I didn't get a chance to look at you inside." And then he looks me up and down like he's a wolf and wants to eat me up.

I swallow down the apprehension I have about being alone with this man in the middle of a giant puzzle and start with the basics. "What's your name? And why did you… do all those terrible things to me?"

He gives me half a smile. And when I say half a smile, I mean only half there. Like he's at war with himself and good and evil are the same thing. "How much do you remember?"

"Most of it leading up to the…" I was just about to say kiss. I grunt and shake my head. "Drugs. What were they? Memory inhibitors, obviously. But what exactly? So I know whether you've damaged me permanently in some way."

"Well, *obviously*"—he laughs, repeating my own word—"I'm not telling you that. I'm not telling you anything, in fact. If you want to know, well, Detective, you're gonna have to put in a little more effort. Come find me. You made me that promise and I'm gonna hold you to it."

"I did find you," I remind him, spreading my arms wide. "And what makes you think you're going anywhere but jail tonight?"

"Jail for what? You have evidence?" He takes a step forward and I have to force myself not to instinctively step back at his approach.

"I'm sure I could muster some up."

"Aha," he says, tsking his tongue and pointing a black-gloved finger at me. "I see you're catching on already. If the CCPD doesn't have any evidence that's what they generally do. Just muster some up. Well, I've got a pretty good lawyer, gun girl. So take your best shot."

*Gun girl.* "In this case it would be true. I don't need to fake it."

All this time he's still inching closer and everything in my body says to run. Run, run, run. As far away from this man as I can get. But the fight in me doesn't give up so easy. The fight in me likes to stand and give it my best. The fight in me can be stupid at times.

"So arrest me, gun girl. Is that who you are? Their gun girl?" He winks. "Or mine?"

"I'm no one's girl."

He smiles a charming smile, his eyes bright with possibilities. "You sure about that?"

127

"Why come here tonight? Feeling guilty? You're some kind of psycho who wants to play a game? Am I your opponent? Do you really want to play with me? Because I assure you—"

And then here he is. Right in front of me. Standing so tall and ominous, I have to look up and take a gulp of air.

"Who says I'm playing?" His face is shadowed, but I can picture his features. That unruly dark hair, wet from the rain. The cold wind whipping it up around his face. His equally dark eyes with that spark of amber in them. His lips, brushing against my neck in that cave. His breath, tickling me and fooling me into thinking he wasn't going to hurt me.

Scary, creepy fucking guy. Yeah, he's got serial killer written all over him. *So why are you still standing here talking to him?*

He's tall, and I feel so small looking up at him, so I lower my eyes. His suit is tailored to perfection so that the white shirt under his jacket pulls across his chest, revealing hard muscles underneath.

He reaches up and I flinch, look back up at his face. This makes him smile. I force myself to stand absolutely still as he rests the back of his gloved knuckles against my cheek and then sweeps them downward. "I love the dress, Molly."

Jesus Christ. He's coming on to me. "Why did you come here?"

"And I love what's underneath it too."

I grab his wrist and twist my body, ready to throw him over my shoulder, but he grabs me by the waist and twirls me around—pressing his chest into my back, holding me close as he whispers in my ear. I freeze. The memory of that kiss back in his cave is the only thing on my mind.

"I've missed you more than you will ever know."

"Let go of me," I snarl, turning my body. But he grabs both of my wrists and pins them to my stomach.

"Tell me what happened that night."

"You drugged me!"

"No, gun girl. That *other* night."

"What other night?" Jesus. Has he done this to me before?

He lets go of my hands, twirls me around again, and then pushes me up against the cold stone pedestal, repositioning his hands on either side of my head and boxing me in. I can smell the leather from his gloves. I can feel the beat of his heart as he presses his chest against mine. I can hear the soft in-and-out breath of air as he maintains control.

I could get away right now if I wanted. I could knee him in the balls, grab his head and bang it down on my knee, and run back into the maze, screaming for help.

The problem is, I stay right where he puts me.

His hand glides down the curve of my neck and then he plays with a wisp of hair that fell down. "Why are you doing this?" I ask.

"I didn't fuck you last weekend, but I wanted to. I really, *really* wanted to."

I push him back with a two-handed shove to his chest and slap his face. Hard. The crack of my hand against his cheek echoes, and a girl laughs from somewhere in the maze. "Don't talk to me that way, asshole."

He just smiles, even as a red handprint forms on his face. "Never say never."

"And if you call me gun girl one more time—"

"You'll what?" he challenges, staring down into my eyes with such a glare, I have to look away.

"Just tell me what you want," I say. My heart is beating so fast now.

"I just did," he whispers, leaning down into my neck and tickling me with his breath as his words travel across my skin. "I want to fuck you. And I want to do it right now. Before we go any further. Before I tell you anything else. Before you have a chance to change your mind."

"You are some piece of work," I say, dragging my eyes back to meet his. His gaze is so intense, it makes me want to hide. "You're crazy if you think I'm even considering it."

"You're right. You're not considering it. You've already agreed or you'd be out of here. You'd be running away as fast as your pretty feet could take you. You'd be screaming for those people in the maze to help you. You'd be *gone*, Molly Masters."

He tugs the skirts of my dress up my thigh.

I swallow hard again, and a moan comes out of my mouth.

"Give in tonight, Molly. And I'll give in tomorrow."

"What's that mean? Why do you have to talk in riddles? Just tell me what the fuck is going on." My words come out as a hoarse whisper and I look at the ground. And I'd be lying if I said he wasn't turning me on. This alpha shit. I should hate it. I should rail against it. Slap him again and walk off. Walk straight the fuck out of here with my head up.

But I can't say that's how I feel, because I don't.

"Hold your skirts up and find out."

I force myself to look up. His eyes are not bright with mischief. They are dark, and cold, and commanding. And his lips aren't curled up in some playful smile. They are straight, slightly parted. And I can see his tongue doing a little dance inside his mouth, like he's thinking very hard about something. His hand leaves the wall and he drops the soft fabric of my silk skirts so he can place both leather-clad palms on my cheeks. Gently. And this is the only gentle thing about him right now. Because he scares the fuck out of me.

"Do it," he says, his mouth finding mine. His lips pressing into an unbreakable kiss. His hands caressing my skin. His body moving forward, his knee taking position between my legs. "Lift those skirts, Molly," he says, his words tumbling against my tongue. "Let me slip my hand between your legs and play a little. Let's have a good time tonight and forget that it's all gonna come crashing down tomorrow."

"I don't—"

"Please," he says. The word is so soft. So filled with longing, and regret, and emotion. It reminds me of that friend of his while we were dancing. His plea makes me want to obey. Against my will, I try to convince myself. But it's a lie. There is something on the tip of my tongue. Like my brain has been keeping secrets and they're about to explode out of me. So I reach down, grab a fistful of silk tulle and I give him what he needs.

Permission.

His mouth is suddenly hungry and crushing. His tongue dances inside me. One hand leaves my face and goes to his belt and I hike my skirts up even more, exposing the bare skin of my leg. The brisk air flows upward, making my pussy tingle with anticipation. His belt buckle drops away, and he tugs on his zipper just before he presses his hard cock against my hip.

I push forward, making him groan with the pressure against his hard-on. "Do it, then," I whisper. "Just do it. Before someone comes." The voices of other couples in the maze are louder, but there's no way for me to tell how close they are to finding the center. Or finding me here, doing this with him.

He grabs my skirts, the sudden force enough to make me gasp with surprise, and then he reaches between my legs and pulls my panties aside, just enough to slip a gloved finger inside me. "Open your legs wider, Molly."

Just hearing his gruff voice say my name sends my mind spinning. Why? Why is he making me feel this way?

But that thought disappears as soon as the pressure inside me turns to pleasure. I obey his last command like I'm that computer thing in his cave. Forced to do his bidding. At his beck and call and under his spell.

Just as that thought crosses my mind, his cock—full, and hard, and throbbing just like my pussy—replaces his finger and I moan. Loudly. "Oh, God."

"Shhh." He laughs. And that laugh twists the whole thing around from forbidden and terrifying to reckless and tantalizing.

"I want to fuck you in the open," he says. "Right here under these spotlights. With all those high-society fucks two hundred feet away, oblivious to what's coming. All paranoid and pathetic, wondering what we're going to do next. And if you make noise, Molly, I'll have to drag your trembling and aching body over into the shadows and that would ruin *everything*."

"Oh, God," I say again.

"You don't want me to ruin everything, do you?"

I shake my head as I stare up into his eyes. He grips my waist like he never wants to let go. He rocks against me, pressing me so hard up against the cold pedestal, I can feel the roughness of the stones embedded in the concrete.

"Wrap your legs around me," he says, fisting my hair with one hand until my head jerks up. "And look at me when I fuck you."

I lift my leg and his other hand is there helping. I wrap myself up against the hard, defined muscles of his stomach and around his hips just as he thrusts inside me.

"Fuck," he growls, biting my earlobe. "They're getting closer. Two more right turns and they're gonna find us. And if you think I'll stop, you don't know me very well. So come for me, Molly. Come for me and say my name in my ear as you do it."

"What—"

"Lincoln," he whispers. "My name is Lincoln. Say it. I need to hear you say it."

He pounds against me. A hand finds my breast, squeezing it like we are on the verge of something. His mouth finds my neck, and he takes the soft skin between his teeth and gives it a sharp nip. I gasp and he releases, sucking replacing the bite, until I have to give in and just let it happen.

I moan his name in his ear. "Lincoln," I say.

"Again," he commands. "Say it again."

"Lincoln," I breathe. "I'm coming."

"Again," he says, over and over. "I want to do this again."

"Oh, shit," I say, waves of pleasure rolling through my body like a tsunami. My back arches, my head pushing against the hard concrete behind me, his hands roaming all over my body, like he's desperate for more.

He pulls out, just as I realize he never got off.

"But—"

"They're here. Ten steps away," he says, dropping my skirts and backing off. I want to cling to him now. Cling and never let go.

But he tucks his cock away and buckles his belt as he makes a hasty backwards retreat. "Go that way," he says, pointing to an opening in the hedge. "Right, left, two rights, and then two lefts. Find me, gun girl. I have a lot to tell you." He turns, then turns back, grabs me by the waist and pulls me into his chest. "And Molly," he says, his soft words and his intense stare doing amazing things to my still trembling body. "When you find me, Molly"— he hesitates and draws in a breath—"when you *really* find me, I'll dress you up in pretty lingerie every night and fuck you senseless until the end comes and takes you away."

I feel like I might faint.

He releases me and takes off into the shadows.

The laughing couples make it into the center, but they are on the other side of the statue, so I slip into the hedge the way he pointed.

I run on the stone pavers, lifting my skirts, my lungs desperate for air as my heart pounds with each footfall. After a few minutes I find myself on the far side of the maze.

I gulp down air, wondering what the fuck just happened. And then I make myself walk slowly so I can catch my breath. Try to process. Come to terms with what I did.

I look for him out in the courtyard in front of the maze, but he's nowhere to be found. Not inside either, after I climb the stairs and rejoin the party. I'm just about to go find Seville and tell him to take over so I can go home, because I feel like I might collapse, when I spy Atticus Montgomery. He's been looking for me, I can tell by his expression. He smiles and walks over, his hand outstretched.

*Pull yourself together, Molly.*

"Detective Masters. For a while there I thought you ditched me."

"No, sorry," I say, placing my hand over my still pounding heart. "I was out in the maze and got turned around."

"Ah," he says, eyeing me for a moment. "Well, let me calm you down with a drink. Come." He takes my hand and leads me over to the bar where there are tables set up. "I have something to show you."

It seems to be a recurring theme. But I let him lead me. The alpha males of Cathedral City have definitely overpowered me tonight. And I don't have a speck of fight left in me at the moment.

Once we're settled with drinks, Atticus leans in and says, "There's another clue I didn't give you."

"What?" I look around to see if anyone is listening. "What do you mean?"

"I found something on the desk of the first suicide and I didn't want the wrong people to see it."

"Define the wrong people," I say, weary of riddles and unable to think straight.

He doesn't answer that question, just pulls out a slip of paper and places it on the table between us.

"What is it?"

"A red letter A?" he says, as if unsure.

"Right. I can see that." I look up at him. "But what's it mean? Do you think it's an unfinished anarchy sign? Like the symbol carved on the last body?"

Atticus smiles at me and it comes off a little sad. Like he's disappointed in me for some reason. "I'm not sure," he replies. "I didn't think it meant anything when I took it. But I thought you should know."

"Just tell me what you want," I say. My heart is beating so fast now.

"I just did," he whispers, leaning down into my neck and tickling me with his breath as his words travel across my skin. "I want to fuck you. And I want to do it right now. Before we go any further. Before I tell you anything else. Before you have a chance to change your mind."

## CHAPTER EIGHTEEN

*Molly.* I think it was her name that started it.

"Lincoln?" Sheila asks outside my bedroom doorway. "Are you OK?"

It's an obsession. I realize this.

"Did you meet with her?"

Unhealthy for sure. And not gonna end well.

"Lincoln?"

I'm lying naked on the end of the bed with only my black leather gloves on. I can smell her lust on them. My bare feet are kicked up on the headboard, my hands behind my neck, and I'm staring up at the cave ceiling. The lights are on but the darkness surrounds me. I can see Sheila in her holographic dress from the corner of my eye and picture the day I coded her image. That day I finally stumbled down the overgrown driveway and came to terms with what was left of my life before Prodigy School. That day when my vow to get even, no matter what it took, finally coalesced into action.

Sheila's raw personality was the only thing I took from school besides the clothes I was wearing. I don't know why I took her. She belonged to them and she wasn't near as intelligent then as she is now, so she didn't give one fuck about me or my motivations. She could've ruined everything and Case was beyond pissed when I told him about her. But she was the only inheritance I had aside from the charred remains of the house above the cave. And that connection was enough to risk it, I guess.

The trip inside the maze tonight brought back memories I never wanted in the first place. But it was definitely Molly's name that started it.

"She was wearing a nightgown the last time I saw her, you know. I gave her a coat and some boots and I told her to run like hell before I killed her."

"Lincoln?" Sheila repeats, a bit of sadness in her voice. When did she acquire so many different emotions? When I first loaded her down here in the lab she only had one. I'd have called it indifference, if pressed.

Now she has so many it's hard to keep track.

They say humans only have six emotions, sometimes only four, depending on who you talk to. Happy, surprised, afraid, disgusted, angry, and sad. But those people never had to develop a computer language and program a machine to take the place of a mother.

I did. And I know there's a lot more going on inside Sheila than those six things.

For one, those scientists left out confused. That's what I am right now. Or maybe I'm conflicted?

Is Molly someone I want in my life? That's confusion.

Should I let Molly in my life? That's the conflict.

The answer to the first is yes and the second is no.

"Lincoln, talk to me."

Everything about Molly points to danger for me. She's a cop, I'm a criminal. She's good and I'm bad. She's the end and I'm the beginning.

"You have to—"

"It was a mistake," I finally say. "It was a mistake to see her tonight." I look over at Sheila and she's frowning. "Before last weekend I was fine, you know? I was alone and I was fine with that. But now…" My words trail off.

"But now what?"

I shake my head. "Now I want her. Now I can't imagine letting her go and the only answer to my problem is to push her away."

"Stay home tonight. Don't go back out. It's too dangerous. You can't keep this up."

I let out a long sigh, and then bark, "Lights out." The room goes dark, only the ambient light from the computers and aquarium tank in the main cave leaking in to spoil the blackness. "I won't push her away. But it's the wrong decision, Sheila. I can feel it in my bones. My luck ran out when I wasn't looking. I thought it was luck that got me out of that crash last week, but it wasn't. It was life catching up to me. It was my past, my present, and my future all rolled up into ten minutes on a mountain road with Molly Masters."

That's all it takes. A few minutes with a girl I care about. One girl who means something to me. One girl who will bring up all the things I've been pushing down.

"It's over, I guess. But I had a good run."

The next time I look over at the doorway Sheila is gone.

But my dark thoughts are still here. And there are names etched into my memories that come out to play in the night. I recite them in my mind as I get up off the bed and start tugging on my jeans and boots. I slip a t-shirt over my head and then shrug on the hoodie.

Detective Molly Masters is on to me. I can feel it. She's on to me and she's gonna find me again and ask lots of questions. So why not get one more in before she comes? Why not take one more pathetic piece of shit down before I am stopped?

Why not?

I walk out of my room and spy my leather jacket hanging off the back of a chair, the red symbol on the sleeve practically calling my name through the green glow of digital haze.

I slip my arms in the sleeves and become Cathedral City's worst nightmare.

I am mayhem, I am anarchy, and I am found.

But most of all, I am Alpha.

GUN GIRL

## CHAPTER NINETEEN

I'm standing in my garage trying to put the final pieces together. *Find me*, Lincoln commanded. And this should not be so hard. I'm a detective, for Christ's sake.

Last night's clue from Atticus has left me drained and I can't think straight. It has to be part of the anarchy symbol. But why leave it unfinished?

My head hurts.

I also stopped by headquarters last night to pick up a fingerprint kit and I was up until four AM dusting things in my house.

No luck. Because I cleaned up after him. I bleached the hell out of this place. Wiped every smudge on every surface. Which means even if I wanted to arrest him—and I'm not sure I can after letting him publicly fuck me last night during the party—I have no evidence.

Yet. But if I can find him, I might get some.

I let out a long breath of air as I study my brother's trailer and then I walk around to the back door, unlatch the locks, and pull them open.

Will's bikes are state-of-the-art. His buddy down at the track has been taking care of them. Even raced them a couple times, he said. But he felt bad using them to win and just kept them in good working order until I was ready to pick them up and move on.

Which was supposed to be last weekend, but here they still are.

*I have no prints. No last name.*

I could go looking in the criminal database for Lincoln's face, but that would arouse suspicion.

*So? You should be shouting it out to everyone, Molly. Telling anyone who will listen there is a creepy pervert on the loose who lives in a Batcave up in the mountains.*

But just thinking about that makes my stomach feel funny.

He intrigues me, sure. I have some personal fantasies that might involve his face between my legs and his hard chest crushing me to a bed.

But he planted a seed last night. *Give in tonight, Molly. And I'll give in tomorrow.*

I shove a helmet on my head, walk into the trailer, release the ties that secure the street-legal bike to the walls of the trailer, then back it down the ramp and get on.

Lincoln said to come find him. And that's exactly what I plan on doing. Only this time, I'm going prepared. I pat the pocket of my leather jacket where my gun is stashed. And I'm not coming back until I've checked every last dirt road on Wolf Pass Highway.

BIKE BOY

## CHAPTER TWENTY

A modified servo robot goes whizzing by, barely missing my head as I lie next to the bike, messing with the brake line.

"I'm not falling for your passive-aggressive bullshit, Sheila. And I don't think you're gonna run me over with one of those monstabots." I do think that, actually. She's been programmed to act like a woman and that automatically makes her cunning, vengeful, and able to carry a grudge until she wins.

But she's not going to win. She wants details about last night. She wants for me to hear her out. She wants me to stop. And no. That's not happening. None of it is on the table. I'm too far in. I've risked too much. I've... changed, and those changes can't be undone.

Another servo goes by, clipping me on my bare shoulder. "Goddammit, you bitch."

Sheila manifests into her holographic form in the center of the room. She wears the same clothes as always, but today, she's got her hair different.

Am I supposed to notice that?

I roll my eyes and ignore her. Fucking women—even fake women—are beyond comprehension.

She walks over to me and stands there, silently waiting, and tapping her foot. It even has a sound effect. A tiny pat, pat, pat against the polished concrete floors.

"Can I help you?" I ask.

"You can't keep doing this."

"I can and I will. Until someone stops me."

"Just what exactly are you trying to prove by murdering people?"

"That I'm capable. That I'm inhuman. That I'm perfect. That I'm Alpha." I snort out a small laugh. "Even you know that can't be changed. So why bother fighting it?"

"Because you deserve a future that's not dependent on the past. I only want you to be happy, Lincoln. I want you to find a nice girl before you waste your youth on this plan filled with hate, and darkness, and revenge."

"I can't deal with this shit right now, Sheila. Just go away."

"I think this Molly woman is the one." She says 'the one' in a whisper like it's a secret.

"Would you leave me alone? All I want to do is work on my bike in peace. And that means you need to go—"

*Eeeeent, eeeent, eeent*—the perimeter alarm goes off. I look at Sheila and she disappears to go investigate. Two seconds later she's back, smiling.

"What was it?"

She crosses her arms and looks smug.

"What the fuck was—"

"I think you better go check the tunnel, Lincoln. You have a visitor."

"Shit," I say, throwing down a wrench with a clang that echoes through the cave. "That girl found me." I get up off the ground and wipe my greasy hands on my jeans as I walk over to the security room and see Molly fucking Masters on all sixteen monitors as Sheila traces her movements from the moment she crossed onto the secured property. I own more than six hundred acres in all directions from the center of the cave. But not all of it is secure. Only the parts I don't want people to find.

Detective Masters is on a street-legal dirt bike. I recognize it from her trailer last weekend. It's a high-end motocross model that looks like it could kick some serious ass. Also, very powerful. So Miss Masters must be a rider. Since her brother was Wild Will—infamous dirt racer who viewed death as a viable alternative to losing— I have no doubt Molly Masters knows exactly what she's doing on that thing. It gives her confidence.

But maybe she needs a little run for her money? Because even though she gave in to me last night, I'm damn sure that she's regretting it today. Looking for revenge, maybe? Counting on the fact that I never got off and might be wishing I had? Thinking she might reel me in and I might be the final piece of the puzzle she needs?

I grab my leather off the back of a desk chair as I head to the tunnel entrance and make a promise to myself to deliver exactly what she came for.

Answers.

And she's not going to like them one bit.

I can hear her yelling my name before I even get a quarter way to the gate.

"Lincoln, I know you're in there! I know you can hear me! Show your face in the light, you coward! You wanna drug a girl, take advantage of her? Erase her mind? Well, I've got—"

"Keep your fucking voice down. I'm right here," I say, walking into the hazy light coming from the gate entrance. Molly has her fists wrapped around the bars like she's trying to get out instead of in.

"Well, finally. I've been standing out here for twenty minutes. You told me to find you, so I did. Now I want to know what the fuck your deal is."

I walk up to her, stop less than a foot away from the rusted steel gate, and stare into her eyes. She recoils and I know why. The coldness inside of me pours out. The thirst for revenge, now that it's so damn close, bleeds from me as if through an open wound. "How can I help you?" I growl through my gritted teeth.

"I want to know what you've been doing at night."

"Do you now?" I sneer. "You sure about that, Detective? Because you're not gonna like it."

"There's been some murders up at Blue Corp."

"Sucks to be them, I guess."

"And the murderer has been leaving calling cards. And that anarchy patch on your shoulder makes me wonder."

I lean into the bars, pressing my head against them so I'm only a few inches from her face. "Is that right?"

She swallows and then sucks in a breath. My eyes drop to her chest as it rises and falls underneath a black leather moto jacket. "Who are you?"

"You don't want to know that. And I'm gonna need you to go before you get hurt. I don't want to hurt you."

"But you'll fuck me in public? That's OK?"

"You wanted it."

"*You* wanted it, asshole."

"I'm not the one who got off."

Her face turns red, her hazel eyes blazing with shame, or regret, or both. "I'm gonna look up this tract of land you've got here. I'm gonna find out who you are, what you're doing, and I'm gonna stop it. Because anyone who does what you did to me last weekend is an evil motherfucker. And I don't need to be a detective to know you're connected to those murders. I can feel it. You're gonna regret ever meeting me, Lincoln."

"Well, you got that last part right," I say, a cold wind whipping past my face and making my jacket open to reveal my bare chest.

She looks.

I shake my head when she meets my eyes again. This time I catch embarrassment. "Shy much, gun girl?"

She stays silent.

"You want me to save you the trouble of all that pesky sleuthing? Give you what you came for? Well, get out your phone, Molly Masters, and look up the name Lincoln Wade."

She huffs out some incredulous air through her teeth.

"Go on," I encourage her. "I'll wait."

"Fine," she says, setting her jaw and tipping her chin up. And then she grabs her phone from her jeans pocket and types my name in Blue Search. I can see the little earth logo in the top corner of her screen.

Ironic.

Her brow furrows and her eyes squint down as they race across the screen, taking it all in.

"Well?" I ask a few seconds later. "There you are." I point to the search page. "And now you know."

"I don't understand," she says, looking up from underneath her hair. "What's this mean?"

"What's it mean?" I laugh. "I've searched my name before and I know what comes up first. So just open it up, gun girl. Read the fucking paper that doctor wrote. It's spelled out clear as day for anyone who knows what to look for."

She gives her head a little shake and then begins to read out loud. "'Lincoln Wade, the only remaining member of the Wade family, was abducted as a ten-year-old child, along with several dozen other children from the Cathedral City area. The Wade family offered rewards for years, before dying in a fire that destroyed the family home. Lincoln Wade and Case Reider were found wandering along Wolf Pass Highway in the dead of winter when they were fifteen. After many months of questioning and therapy in the Cathedral City Psychiatric Hospital for Children brought forth no answers, the Reider family adopted Wade and the boys went home.'"

She stops reading, but I continue for her. I know that report by heart. "'Both Reider and Wade exhibited strange behaviors and were monitored by local mental health authorities until they turned eighteen. But no kidnapper was ever found and no reason for their long disappearance was ever offered by either boy or the Reider family. Reider went to a local university and graduated with a degree in computer engineering, while Wade faded from public record.'"

"But…" she stutters. "You're here. You came back?"

"I never left. They just figured it was better to leave me out here alone in the dark than get in my face after I gave them an ultimatum."

She swallows hard, wanting to ask, but forcing herself not to.

"I broke into the psychiatrist's house the night before I turned eighteen and told her if she didn't close our case I'd come back for her."

"Come back… and do what?"

"Use your imagination, Molly."

She's silent for a moment and then her expression goes from confused to angry. "Then what the fuck is going on? Why did you come find me last night? Why did you tell me to find you?"

I shrug. "A moment of weakness. Now, if you have everything you came for, then—"

"No. You're not getting off that easy. You tell me some sob story about your childhood—"

I reach through the bars and grab her coat, scaring the living fuck out of her, and then pull her into the cold metal gate. "Watch. Your. Mouth. Detective. And don't even pretend like you know my *sob story*. Because what they said in that paper was the scrubbed version of events. The court put a gag order on the really fucked-up shit."

## CHAPTER TWENTY-ONE

"Wait," I say, as he lets go of my coat and starts to turn away. "Just wait a minute, OK?"

"Why?" he asks, giving me a sidelong glare. "You didn't get the message? I'm a danger to society, Masters. And your job is to protect it. We can't be friends. We're enemies—then, now and forever."

What does that even mean? Then? Now? Forever? But I let it go, trying my best to stay focused even though every time he's around, I lose my head. "You're killing those scientists, aren't you? You're setting them up to look like suicides and then you're killing them." As soon as the words come out I know I've made a mistake, because any bit of softness in his expression is immediately gone.

"I never touched them, Detective." He laughs. But that laugh, holy shit, it sends a chill down my spine. "And no matter where you're looking or how much you think you've got figured out, you're still in the dark."

"How would you know? You said you didn't do it."

"It's not about *who* did it, Masters. It's about *why* they did it."

He's toying with me.

We watch each other for a few moments. The only sound is the wind passing through the pine trees and the birds. It's a nice day. The sun is out, the sky is blue, and the temperature is mild.

But down that tunnel he so badly wants to retreat to, it's black. That's his world, I tell myself. He's darkness and he's giving me a chance to leave.

I should take it.

So I turn away and begin to walk.

"I know who you are," he calls out after me. It comes out desperate. Like he can't let me walk away. A ploy to keep this interaction going. "I felt it back there out on that highway. I know more about you than you know about yourself."

My heart skips as I think of all the possible ways he could be keeping track of me. Cameras in my house? Tracking on my phone? I whirl around and face him again.

"Don't hate me, Molly," he says, pulling out his phone and pressing a tab on the screen that makes the rusty gate begin to lift up. "I want you to walk away, I really do. But not before I get my say. Because I never asked for this. I never asked for you to come find me. That was all you. That part was always you."

"No," I say, backing up and never taking my eyes off him. "You *told* me to come find you, Lincoln."

"You're wrong. I told you to run. I told you to never look back. I saved you and you don't even know it. But then there you were out there on the road. Saving me back. And once I accepted the fact that you were really here, I did my best, Molly. I did my best."

He takes a step out of the tunnel, and my gun is out, pointed at his chest in an instant. But a wave of revulsion hits me in my stomach, enough to make me double over and start to retch.

"Sorry about the inhibition sickness. But fair is fair, right? It's only temporary, anyway. Not like mine."

He walks forward, grabs the gun out of my hand and throws it on the ground. The waves of revulsion in my stomach ease.

"What the hell?" I ask, righting myself to look at him through my hair.

"What the *hell*? What the fucking *hell*, Molly?" He grabs me by the coat again and gives me a good shake. My head is still spinning and this just makes it worse. "You owe me everything. You owe me your life."

"Fuck you," I say, gaining back some control. "Just fuck you, you crazy vagrant. Living in a tunnel. All that weird shit you have in there. Is that hologram your wife?"

He shoves me so hard I stumble backwards and hit a tree, knocking the wind out of me. Now it's his turn to double over. I can almost feel his pain. I imagine it to be like the revulsion that receded from my own gut seconds before. "You were only eight back then," he says, spitting on the ground and regaining his composure so he can look up at me from under the hair that drapes over his eyes. "I was fifteen. I had all the power then. You were never gonna live through it, Molly. Not without my help. You were never going to make it. *Never.*"

"Shut up!" I don't even know why I'm so mad. But I don't want to hear anymore. I need to get the hell out of here.

"And when Thomas said, 'You need to kill her, Lincoln. You need to kill her or she will come back and kill us,' I didn't. But I should've, Molly. I fucking should've done it. And if I was as smart as they say, I *would've* done it."

I bolt to the left, but he grabs my arm and throws me down on the ground. He straddles me, one foot on either side of my hips, looking down at me like a wolf might look at prey.

A memory flashes through my mind. *Fire, everywhere. Explosions.*

Lincoln kneels down with me between his legs and shakes his head, grimacing like he's still in pain, but that only makes him clutch me tighter. I feel fear. Real, honest-to-God fear. "I set you free that night. I told you to run, you stupid girl. I saved you even though your only purpose in life was to hurt me."

"What the fuck are you talking about?" He's insane. And I'm dead. He is the killer and he's gonna get me next.

He grabs both my shoulders and gives me another shake. "Remember me, Molly? Remember me? I was your only friend even though you did everything they told you."

"No, I don't know you. I don't know you!" I say, desperate to make everything stop. My head hurts so bad. My vision blurs and my heart is beating so fast it sounds like the thunder created by a galloping horse. "I'm Molly Masters. You're confusing me with someone else. You're crazy. You're a criminal. You hate the world and you want to make me crazy with you."

He kisses me on the mouth.

Hard and soft at the same time. His hands wrap around my face, pulling me towards him. And then he withdraws and I am so stunned, I cannot move.

"I saved you, Molly," he whispers into my mouth, trying to kiss me and talk at the same time, grabbing my face like he can't bear to let me go. "I saved you even though you'll kill me if you ever have the chance."

"Stop," I say, pushing him away, tears streaming down my face. "Stop!" I scream it this time. I kick my feet up and even though I'm trained to take down men twice my size, I am powerless as he looms over me.

"You can't make me stop, Molly. But don't worry. I can't really hurt you. It's how they made us."

"No," I say. "No. Everything you're saying right now is a lie. I want you to get off me. I want you to let me go. I want to go home, Lincoln. I want to go home—"

## CHAPTER TWENTY-TWO

Alpha #3
Prodigy School
Fifteen years ago

*"Tell me what to do, Alpha."*

*The little girl looks at me with her wide hazel eyes and swallows down her fear. She is one of only a handful of people I should be afraid of. But I love her more than anything. She is the only good thing in my life. Even in this place filled with hate, and greed, and cruelty she makes me feel love.*

*If I were following orders she'd be dead right now. Lying in her bed in a pool of her own blood. The other Alphas have already finished. They are waiting for me so we can escape. But the other Alphas don't have little girls as their Omega. The other Alphas don't feel the way I do.*

*"You have to run, Omega." I wish she had a name. I wish so much I could give her a real name. But it's too late now. She's leaving my life—dead or alive. One way or another, the time for naming is over.*

*"Don't leave me, Alpha," she pleads in that little-girl voice that makes me love her even more. "Don't leave me here." She whispers the last part, a tear trickling down her cheek. Her face is so pale in the bright moonlight shining through her bedroom window.*

*"I have to. But listen," I say, pulling her up, so she's sitting on the side of her bed. "Listen to me, OK?" She nods as I shove her boots on her feet and thrust a coat in her hands. "You have to run. And you have to do it alone."*

*"No," she whimpers as quietly as she can. She's still afraid of being heard at night. She doesn't realize we've already killed everyone but her.*

*There's a loud bang from the floor below, and we both go still as the dead and look each other in the eyes.*

*The seriousness of the situation is written all over my face. She understands now.*

*I take her hand and pull her up so she's standing, then hold her coat open. She slips her arms in automatically and pulls it tight around her chest.*

*"Run," I say, leading her over to the window and lifting the sash up. It's cold, windy, and it's snowing. And if the other Alphas see her footprints, they will hunt her like a rabbit. But the wind is strong enough to cover up her tracks and I think she can get away. "You go that way," I say, pointing into the woods. The opposite direction to where I know we will be going. "You go that way, Omega, and you never look back. You run until you find someone. And you never, ever tell them about this place. About me or the other Alphas. Or what we did here."*

*She starts to cry again. And what did I expect? She's eight years old.*

*"You can never talk about this place again or they will kill you."*

*I wait for her to acknowledge my order. She should be the one ordering me, but she's always looked to me for guidance. The administration would've figured it out soon. They'd have figured out she'd never be able to control me and had her eliminated.*

*That's why I agreed to escape tonight. To save her.*

*She finally nods, giving in, or giving up, or both. So I lift her up until she can swing her legs over the side of the windowsill, and then I push her and she plops down into a snowdrift.*

*She looks up at me one more time, the tears on her cheeks already freezing. And she says, "I'll find you, Alpha. I will. One day I'll find you."*

*Then she turns and instincts kick in. She runs and she never looks back.*

*I take a deep breath because her words mean more than she knows. They are the words of my killer. My death. My demise. Because that little girl is the only person left in the world who can hurt me.*

*And I just let her go.*

GUN GIRL

## CHAPTER TWENTY-THREE

*I do as I'm told. I start running and I never look back. And every time my feet crunch into the deep snow, my long flannel nightgown gets pushed further up my legs. It gets wetter and wetter. And so heavy I feel like I'm dragging a dead weight.*

*I pump my arms, pleading with my legs to take me under the cover of the trees before someone from school sees me outlined against the stark whiteness of the valley.*

*I expect to be shot in the back with every passing moment. I expect a yell, telling me to, "Get your ass back here," and then the sharp crack of a rifle and the scream of a bullet into my spine.*

*But I gather up all my strength and leap from the deep snow into the scant dusting under the pines. I slip, skid, and fall down on my knees.*

*The air is rushing in and out of my mouth in long heaves. My chest is burning, my throat is burning. I feel like I might die right here and now. Of fear, or exhaustion, or sadness.*

*I grab fistfuls of snow because there is nothing else to cling to, and the burning from exposure winds its way from the tips of my fingers to my palms. In a few minutes it will pass my wrists and run up my arms.*

*I shove my hands into my coat pockets, desperately wishing I had Alpha's gloves and the heat of his hands to keep me warm.*

*But I don't get either of those things from my pocket. My fingertips bump into a slender tube of plastic. A chill of fear runs through me, because I know what this is. Every time Alpha had to use it, he showed it to me first. He said, "I'm not the one hurting you, Omega. This"—he'd hold the syringe up—"this is what hurts you. Not me. They make me do this, Omega. I have to do it. But what happens after?" His face was always calm and his words were always soft. "Tell me," he'd say.*

*And I'd say, "You take care of me."*

*Every time I said those words he'd smile and say, "That's right. I have to give you the drug, but I always take care of you after. I will never leave you, Omega. You're mine and I'm yours. And we take care of each other."*

But he made me leave him, and that's the same thing as leaving me.

*I'd always nod. Because as soon as I was better, after he'd cared for me for days, and sometimes weeks, as I pushed the drug through my blood, I'd have to hurt him too. And they never let me take care of him. They only made me watch him writhe in pain, alone, on the other side of a glass window that he couldn't see through.*

*The syringe in my pocket comes with a note. It's wet from the snow and a little bit smeared. But I rub my wet hands on the inside of my coat, smooth out the piece of paper, and the words form in my head. I hear them in his voice.*

My Omega, *it says.* This is the last time, I promise. It's not what you think. It's a new start and a way to forget the past.

*I bend my head until my chin bumps up against my coat collar, and I cry.*

My Alpha.

*I cry for him. I cry because of him. I cry for the times he hurt me and I cry for the times he didn't. I cry because I'm an Omega and the only reason I exist is to hurt him back. I cry because if I do what my Alpha says, if I leave this place and use that drug, I will never be his Omega again.*

*I will stop. Everything will stop. And even though each time he drugged me in school I begged God to make the pain go away, I never want it to stop.*

GUN GIRL

## CHAPTER TWENTY-FOUR

I wake up surrounded by darkness, with his name on my tongue. Not Lincoln. *Alpha.*

"Shhh," he whispers into my neck. His hush is a wave of warmth that floats across my skin and then pools in my belly. His arms are wrapped tightly around me and we are lying on a bed, somewhere in the dark.

"Where did you go?" he asks.

"Back to that day in the snow."

"No. Where did you go when you left me?"

"I didn't leave you. You made me go."

"It was let you go or kill you dead, Molly."

"Omega," I say, a sob coming out with my name. "And I died anyway."

I see it in my head. I feel the cold freezing my body from the tips of my toes on up. It burned so bad. And maybe I wasn't old enough to understand what frostbite was, but I knew if I did not get somewhere warm soon, I would fall down and stop existing.

"I found a town." It wasn't really a town, but the modern-day version of gypsies. "Of circus people. They had a collection of trailers and one was unlocked. It had all these dirty blankets. Thick, quilted cotton blankets. And they smelled like engine oil and transmission fluid. But once I stacked half a dozen over top of me, they were warm."

"Did anyone see you use it?"

He doesn't say what he's talking about, but I know. "No. I was all alone when I pricked the needle into my neck, the same way you pricked me dozens of times before. And when I woke up, I was nobody."

## CHAPTER TWENTY-FIVE

I have never let myself imagine this moment. I have never pretended that there was anything in my future but revenge and death. Warm summer days filled with planning. Cold winter nights filled with stalking. No matter what day it was, no matter what time it was, no matter how many times I wished things could be different, I have never let myself imagine this moment.

Molly starts trembling so I squeeze her tighter. She's crying, but trying hard not to. And if I give in, if I stop being Lincoln for just one second, I might break too. "I missed you the second you turned your back to run."

"You have no idea how that felt for me. How terrified I was."

"I don't know what it was like to be you. But I know what it was like to be me. I know what it felt like to inject you with those drugs at school and watch you go insane. Watch you try to scratch the skin off your body because you were hallucinating. I know what it was like to be the reason you banged your head against a wall until you were bloody. I know what it was like to hold you tight, have you spit in my face, call me evil, call me monster, call me devil. So maybe making a little girl run into the dark woods in the middle of the night wearing a nightgown was a pretty horrific thing to do, but it was a lot better than hurting you for the rest of your life."

She turns around, reaching for my bare shoulders, gripping them tightly and shaking me as she stares into my eyes. "You're not listening. You don't get it. You ripped me in half, Alpha."

"Don't call me that."

"Why not?" she challenges. "That's who you are."

"That's not who I am, it's what I do. And I don't want to hear it from you, Molly. I can't even take it."

She sighs, giving in on that point. "You were mine and I was yours and that's the only thing I knew to be true back then. And then you threw me out like trash."

"Thomas was gonna make me kill you, Molly. We had a discussion and this was the only answer. I'm sorry, but you have to believe me, I did my best. I swear, Molly, I did my best."

She starts breathing hard, her chest rising and falling faster and faster as the seconds tick off. "So you chose them over me."

"I chose you, Molly. I—"

"Stop calling me that!" She screams it and her words echo off the ceiling of my bedroom cave. "Molly is made up! Molly is the name they gave me when I was eight. Molly is that girl who grew up with them. I'm Omega." She stares daggers into me. "I'm *your* Omega."

The rage and pain inside her make me want to close my eyes and beg God for help. *Help me make her understand.*

"I'm…"

"Don't even say it," she growls. "Don't even start with the sorrys. You were the only thing I had."

She flips her body around so she's not facing me anymore, like she's ending the conversation. And even though I know she wants me to give her space, she doesn't need space. She needs close. She needs love. She needs me. Not Alpha… me.

"Molly—"

"Omega," she says again. But this time it comes out small and sounds like defeat.

I let out a breath of frustration. "Omega. Fine. But I don't want to be called Alpha. I've spent a lot of years coming to terms with Lincoln and that's who I am now. Whether I like him or not, that's who I am."

"What's that even mean?"

I lie there, silent.

"You have an anarchy patch on your leather and those murders I'm investigating——"

"It's not what you think."

"Then explain it to me."

But I don't want to explain it to her. Not yet, anyway. "Just... just let me be here with you, OK? Just let me enjoy this." She takes a deep breath, her back pressing against my chest as I try to hold her closer. "I never forgot about you. There has not been one night that I didn't put my head on this pillow and wish to see your face in my dreams at night."

"You don't want me to feel betrayed, so what am I supposed to feel? What, Lincoln?" She turns to face me again and there's just enough light from a computer screen on the far side of the room to make out the shine of tears on her cheeks. She wipes them away and sniffles.

"Your life was... bad?" I ask her, so afraid of that answer.

"Some," she admits. "But most of it was good. Will, Wild Will, he was my brother after they found me in the trailer. I don't know how long I slept, but they told me no one had checked that trailer in days."

"Did they call the police?"

Molly shakes her head. "No. They are not the kind of people who call the police for help. They saw a girl with needle tracks on her arms and her neck. She had cuts and bruises all over her body. She lost her memory for good reason, they said."

I let out a sigh. "So they took you in. Taught you the business?"

"I trained for a while. But I'm smart, you know."

I let out a soft laugh at that. "I know." It was not called the Prodigy School for no reason. We were all smart, but they made us smarter.

"And the next season I was part of the show. No one ever said a word. I guess if you have to run away in the night, inject yourself with mind-altering drugs, and forge a new life when you're eight, you can do a lot worse than landing in the Masters family."

"So what happened?" I'm afraid to hear her version of the details, but I need to know them.

"Dead." This makes her turn her whole body away from me again. "My father was first. Accident during a show. And then my brother six months ago. Same thing, but that time it was a race."

"And your mother?"

"Insane. She went crazy and tried to kill me and my brother after my father died and she's been locked up ever since. So you see, it can start out great but there's no guarantees. Things happen. Time changes things. There's no guarantee that walking away was the right choice. And you could've taken me with you. We could've stayed together."

She has to know that's not true. Even if Case's parents wanted to take in two kids, there was the whole dynamic between us. The Prodigy School does nothing by accident. "You know what you are to me?" I ask.

She sighs but says nothing.

"They made me into Alpha, but there is no Alpha without an Omega. You're my killer, Molly. That's the purpose they designed for you."

"Who says?" she asks. "Why do they get to create my purpose? It doesn't have to be that way, Lincoln."

But she's wrong. We are what they made us. They made me a killer and they made her to kill me if I didn't cooperate.

I don't know her whole story. I doubt she does either. She was too young when they got a hold of her. Five years old? Four? Younger? But I do know that they changed us. Both individually and as a pair. They did it with drugs. They did it with conditioning. They did it through punishments and rewards that were so cruel, but so sweet at the same time.

They set us up to fall in love and if we had stayed at school, they'd have set us up to die in hate. Because one day I'd stop being a compliant teenager and start being a man they could not control. And my Omega would be there on that day to take me out.

And if Thomas hadn't come up with the plan, I'd have gone off the rails and been dead months before we escaped.

After we killed everyone at the school, Molly was the only person left who could control me. Because I can't hurt her without experiencing pain. The sickness takes a hold of me immediately, just like when I try to point a gun at Thomas or Case.

But the inhibition conditioning with Thomas and Case is something that needs to be forged. We inject ourselves every six months as a show of faith. We've been using the cocktail to bind us together since we were kids and I found the formula at school.

I gave it to Molly last weekend. It wasn't even planned, it was a syringe I had made up for Case. So right now she can't hurt me either, but it won't last long. I'm surprised it even worked at all since it was coded for Case's DNA.

Molly's control over me is different. It's not optional and it never has to be renewed. She was made with some little part of me coded into her. Some little part that gives her total control. She is a weapon and the only target she will ever aim at is me.

Leaving separately that night was the only option if we both wanted to live, even if she doesn't fully understand yet.

But I don't want to think about that right now. I don't to go back and I don't want to go forward. I just want to be in the now.

And right now she's in my bed.

## CHAPTER TWENTY-SIX

One hand slips under my shirt. I draw in a breath and his other arm under my body squeezes me tighter into his chest. He still has those gloves on. But even though the leather is soft, I wish he'd take them off and touch me with his fingers.

"Molly," he says, his lips finding my ear. He kisses me so softly my head spins and my eyes close, wishing the darkness away. "I'm sorry. I did what I thought was best for you. And I don't want to talk about that night again."

"They why am I here?"

"Because you made me realize something."

"What?" I whisper.

He kisses me again, his lips trailing down my neck. And then he repositions himself. The one arm hugging me slips out from under me and I lie flat on his bed, looking up into the shape of his face. He's a shadow hovering over me, backlit by the green hazy computer light.

His mouth finds mine and our lips come together.

I grab his bare shoulders with both hands and pull. I want everything. I want Lincoln. I want my Alpha. I want him to lie on top of me, skin to skin. I want him to take back all the years he stole from me. I want all those moments we missed. I want all that love, all that pain, all that fucked-upness. I want all the possibilities they stole.

He cups my face with his hands, and again, I want more. I need more. "Take off those gloves," I say. "Take them off so I can feel your touch."

"Shhh," he says, kissing me again and stealing my plea. "We need more time, Molly. We need more time, and more of this." He kisses me again and then positions his body over mine, just the way I wanted. Both forearms resting on either side of my head, propping himself up just enough to make me want to beg him to let go. Smother me with the weight of his body.

His tongue slips inside my mouth and we play with each other like that. Twisting and turning. My thoughts are a jumble of nothingness. His legs part and his knees come up next to my ribs so he's straddling me, pressing his hard cock into my pussy.

"More," I say. "More is the only thing that will make it right."

"Take off your shirt," he says, sitting up.

The pressure of him against my clit makes me moan.

"Now," he says. "You got a little taste of me last night, but I never got anything from you. And I want it, Molly. I want you naked. I want your legs spread wide. I want your hands above your head. I want you to surrender to me, and I want you to do it now."

I lean up and grab the back of my shirt, pulling it over my head. Lincoln takes it from me and tosses it across the room. He doesn't ask me to take off my bra, his hands just slip behind me and unclasp the hooks, and then he drags it down my arms and sends it flying.

Then he's pushing me against the bed, his mouth on my nipple, his gloved hands squeezing. I arch my back and grab his unruly hair and thread my fingertips upward, pressing against his scalp. And then I pull him towards me. I give in. I need him. All those years I knew there was something missing inside me. I knew it was bad, and good, and evil, and dangerous. But I always knew it was real. I always knew it was missing.

"I found you, Alpha," I say. "And I'm never leaving again."

## CHAPTER TWENTY-SEVEN

I can't take it anymore. I sit up, unbuckle my pants, and drag my zipper down. My cock is so fucking hard, I might explode. "Sit up," I command.

She swallows down whatever fear that growl just caused, and then pushes her hands against the bed so she can scoot up and rest her shoulders against the headboard.

I stand up on the bed and then jump, my bare feet landing silently on the cold cave floor. I drop my pants and wish I could turn the lights on and watch her face when I slip my boxer briefs down my legs and let my cock spring free.

But we need the darkness right now. It's the only thing protecting me.

I walk back over to the bed and grab the hem of her jeans. "Unbutton and unzip," I say. I can't hear her heart, but with every passing minute that we reconnect who and what we are to each other, I can feel it. I can feel her anticipation and her fear. Her excitement and her need.

"Done," she says quietly.

I pull hard and her pants come sliding down her legs. "Take off the rest and then put your hands up against the wall," I say. Her hips lift up as she slides her panties down, and then her knees bend and I'm wishing for the lights again.

Her panties go flying past my shoulder and I let off a little grunt of a laugh. "You think you're cute—"

177

"I did what you asked," she says. "Now you have to do something for me. Take off your gloves."

"No."

"Why?"

"Because I don't ever take them off."

"Liar. You have to shower."

"You're not in charge here, Molly. I am." It might piss her off, but I don't want to go there yet. I just want this one time where we don't have to think about who and what I've become since she last saw me. "So don't start acting like you are. I've got you down in a cave, on my bed, and naked. If there's any doubt about why you're here, you better get up and walk out now. Because in five seconds I'm gonna fuck the ever-loving shit out of you. I'm gonna make you my prisoner. I'm gonna keep you here until I'm good and satisfied. And if I ever let you leave, I'm going to expect a date and time when you'll be back. And do you know why I'm gonna do all that?"

"Because you're my Alpha."

"No," I growl. Goddamn her. "Because I love you." She sucks in some air through her teeth. "I love you. I loved you so fucking much when we were kids, it killed me, Molly. It fucking killed me inside each time they brought you to the lab."

"I loved you too," she says. "You were the only good thing in my life."

"I hurt you. They made me hurt you and I'm sorry."

"They made me hurt you too. We couldn't stop that. We were just children. Just let it go, Lincoln. Please don't look at me and see the past. I'm not holding a grudge."

"And now what do you feel?"

"I feel like my soul was ripped apart and now it's whole again."

"Molly," I say, lowering myself to the bed and crawling up, my knees on either side of her legs. I stop and sit on her thighs, pinning her down. "I will never hurt you again. You never have to fear me, Molly. Ever." I hold her face, wanting her to believe me. "Do you believe me?"

Her eyes go wide as the implications of what I just told her sink in. "I believe you."

"But I want to take you hard right now. I've thought about you constantly since I took you home that first day. I've thought about this." I lean down and take her face in my hands and I kiss her. I bite her lip and then her tongue, making her squeal. "I want to fuck you sore. I want to—"

"Jesus Christ, Lincoln. Just do it."

I want to laugh. I want to laugh and hold her tight and promise that everything is OK. Everything will be OK from now on. But I can't. I can't allow myself to believe that until she knows the whole truth. And if I don't believe it, she won't either.

So I grab her hair, sit up straight, and ease her face towards my cock. Her hands come off the wall, ready to grip me. But I say, "Put them back. Now."

She looks up at me, her eyes wide in the dim computer light. But she obeys. She reaches for the headboard, needing something to hold onto, even if it isn't me.

I don't give her any more time to think, just thrust her mouth over my cock and hold her there. I'm not all the way inside her, but enough to know she's not going to be able to take me the way I like it. "Easy," I say. "Relax. I'll go slow, I promise. I'll go slow."

Her lips wrap around my shaft, sealing against my skin as she sucks. My head falls back and I open my mouth to groan. "Yeah, do that again."

She hums, her little moans vibrating against my cock, and that's it, man. I'm about to lose control and break my promise. All I want is to shove myself in deeper and come down her throat.

She gags and pulls back, gasping for breath, bringing me back to my senses. I grab her hands and throw her down on the bed sideways, and then position myself behind her. I reach in front and find her pussy wet and waiting as I begin to stroke her clit in small slow circles. She bucks her back against my chest.

"More," she whines. "I need you, Alpha."

I'm not even capable of correcting her about the name. My mind is blown with desire to take her. My other hand reaches down for my cock so I can position it up against her ass. I let go and grab her leg, thrusting it up to give myself room, and then she reaches down and pushes on my tip until I find her pussy.

"Jesus Christ, I want to fuck you hard."

"Do it, Alpha. Do it and make me come. Make me come like I've been waiting for it my whole life."

We moan together when I finally slip inside her wet folds and this makes me reach around and grab her throat. She gasps, and I go still. "I won't hurt you," I whisper.

"I don't care if you do," she replies. "Give it to me the way you like it, Alpha. Just give it to me now."

I thrust hard, making her yelp, the wave of inhibition sickness building inside me so I have to ease up. I can't even fuck her the way I want because of the shit they did.

"Don't think about them, Lincoln." I know she says my real name to snap me back. And that's enough for now. She knows this is the real me. She knows me better than anyone, and no amount of time apart will ever be able to take that away.

I ease inside her deeper, going slow, and this time everything goes blank. The past fades. The present blinks out like a light. And the future is so far away from where I'm at right now, I don't give one fuck about the consequences of this night.

Or what I'm about to do.

Because I want her. I want her now and I want her forever.

So I reach down and play with her clit as I growl, "My Omega."

And she says, "Yours."

One word. I am undone. One word that might change my life forever. One word that might ruin everything. One word.

She has so much power over me and she doesn't even know it.

I take her slowly, back and forth. Long pulls and deep pushes. And then I go faster. Short bursts back and forth. She presses her ass against me, asking for it. Begging me for it until she screams my name. Her pussy clamps against my cock like a vice and I fuck her until everything explodes.

"You're not in charge here, Molly I aim." It might piss her off, but I don't want to go there yet. I just want this one time where we don't have to think about who and what I've become since she last saw me. "So don't start acting like you are. I've got you down in a cave, on my bed, and naked. If there's any doubt about why you're here, you better get up and walk out now. Because in five seconds I'm gonna fuck the ever-loving shit out of you. I'm gonna make you my prisoner. I'm gonna keep you here until I'm good and satisfied. And if I ever let you leave, I'm going to expect a date and time when you'll be back. And do you know why I'm gonna do all that?"

"Because you're my Alpha."

"No," I growl. Goddamn her. "Because I love you."

GUN GIRL

## CHAPTER TWENTY-EIGHT

Lincoln pulls me close and our hearts race with the aftermath of lovemaking.

How quickly life changes. Before I came into this cave I was alone and now I feel like maybe... I mean, I know it's stupid—he's crazy, and even though we were so close as kids, we've been apart for fifteen years—but I really feel like I have a partner. My memories are still blurred. Not quite fitting together properly, like trying to fit the wrong piece in a puzzle. But the basics are there. He is the only reason I lived. I have always known that there was something missing inside me.

"I'm gonna keep you here," he says in a low grumble that tells me he's thinking of falling asleep. "Women don't need to work. They belong barefoot in the Batcave." I turn my head a little to try to see his face over my shoulder and he starts laughing. "Hey, you're the one who wanted me to be Alpha. That's who he is."

I snuggle up to his chest and a smile leaks out. "You're wrong. I know I don't remember as much as you, but I remember enough to know you'd be good to me."

"Hold that thought, gun girl. Just hold onto it until morning. Because I'm dead tired and we still have a lot to talk about. But I'm definitely not gonna think about that until I get some sleep, wake up, and fuck you one more time."

God. I could almost go again right now. He's so fucking hot. His arms are like cannons. Iron-hard biceps that wrap me up and make me feel safe and protected. I don't think I've ever felt as relaxed as I do right now. His chest and abs are corded muscle. Deep valleys and granite hills that make me feel safe from everything I've ever feared.

"Promise me you'll be here when I wake up."

"I promise," I whisper, my eyes heavy and my body satisfied. "Everything can wait until tomorrow."

"That's my girl," he mumbles.

He drifts off soon after, but sleep eludes me. My mind is too busy to give in right now. My whole life is flashing before my eyes. All the good, and there was a lot of that. I was loved by the Masters family. And I was cared for like I was their own daughter.

Will was my best friend all growing up. We were five years apart and I loved him so much. A part of me wonders if I didn't unconsciously remember what Alpha meant to me. If I didn't replace Lincoln with Will. Both older, both fearless, both looking out for me.

But Will's death destroyed me. It was bad enough after our dad died. The show fell apart, of course. My mother fell into a deep, deep depression and she did things. Horrible things. Like mess up the bikes so we'd crash. Will and I both did during practice. But it was so apparent that the bikes had been tampered with, it led the safety manager straight to her. She threw a fit, yelled and screamed. They had to drug her to calm her down. And the next day I found her sprawled out in a pool of blood in her trailer and that was it for the Masters family in the circus. Finding lost girls who needed help was one thing, but a dead body would not be good for the business. And every once in a while there'd be social workers nosing around trying to find out if any of the show kids were being abused or worked too hard.

I was already a teenager by then, so no one was worried about me. But there were other kids. And the same day that my mother tried to take her own life, one showed up.

It was either get her professional help or the social worker was going to open an investigation on all the kids. Will and I agreed, of course. My mother needed help. But once she went into the institution, she only got worse. And that's the real reason I took the job in Cathedral City. I want to help her, I just haven't had the courage to go over there and see her yet. I have never visited. Will and I were too busy surviving after things fell apart.

Once I turned eighteen Will and I drifted apart because he got into racing. I sigh into the darkness. I was so stupid to let him do that. But Will was the one in control, not me. He was my rock. Even after my father died, he was still my rock. I never worried about him. I justified my father's death. He was older. He took a few risks to make the show better and he lost.

But Will was always so rational. I guess I counted on that. I counted on him to hold us together and then he went and got himself killed.

It blew my mind and the depression hit me so hard. The realization that I was all alone in the world was just too much. I needed to get out. Escape. It was so easy to drop out of life like my mother did. So easy to give in to the sadness.

Then this job offer came and I saw a way forward. Maybe it was grasping at straws, or maybe I had some deep memory of what Cathedral City meant to me.

The school.

Lincoln lets out a soft snore and then turns over, releasing his tight hold on me.

I miss him immediately. Whatever bonds we formed as children, they are still there. Delicate, maybe. Thin strands of memories and emotion that have tried their best to be put to rest over the years. But still there.

I'd like to try with him. Strengthen those bonds. Find what we lost that winter night when we parted ways.

His cave is the perfect place to hide from the world and put it all back together. And I guess that's what he's been doing here. Hiding from life. Just like me and my life in the circus, and later the military.

I'd like to join him. I'd love nothing more than to stay here and never go outside again. It could be perfection. Lincoln and me and our little home in a cave filled with tools, and labs, and computers.

I wonder what he does down here. Does he have a job? I bet he's some kind of engineer or mechanic. And what's he hiding with those gloves? I look over at the computer in the corner of the room and study the screen. The desktop has no icons on it and the background is a picture of glowing circuits.

I have a sudden urge to snoop, but it's obvious the screen's on lock, so why bother.

No. No snooping. I want Lincoln to tell me things in his own time, in his own way. But I am dying of thirst right now and I have to pee. So I ease myself out of the bed and feel around in the darkness until I come up with my panties. I pull them on and go searching for my shirt, but all I find is Lincoln's. It will have to do for now, so I shrug on his tee and smother myself in his scent.

I tiptoe towards a crack of light coming from under a door and, after a few seconds of searching, find a handle and pull it open.

The light is not bright, but I squint my eyes after the black of his room. The Batcave is humming with computers and the light reflected off the wall-sized jellyfish aquarium is throwing a wave pattern over everything. That giant monitor on the wall where he was talking to Case Reider is grayed out now. But a lot of other things are going on. The hologram of a bike in progress is still hovering over a table and robots scurry around it, busily working as their metal appendages whir with motion.

What does he do here? It sure looks like he's a bike builder. I walk forward a few paces and then spy an expansive hallway I missed on the first trip. The far left side of the cave is a huge glass wall, and on other side are rooms. One is filled with tanks that hold luminescent jellyfish, smaller versions of the one in the main tank. They flicker rainbow colors in the darkness and I'm mesmerized by their weightless dance in the water.

The main tank is giant, something you'd find in a city aquarium. And the jellyfish are huge. They seem like decorations or pets. I walk forward to get a better look at the new tank room. These smaller versions look like specimens when you take in the equipment surrounding them. Microscopes and refrigerators.

I walk on after a few moments and the next room looks like an engineering lab with various stationary robot arms busy working on another bike.

There's more to see farther down a slender hallway and another glass-walled room. But when I walk forward to peer inside, this lab is totally different. There's some kind of operating table in the center with the kind of light above it that you'd see in surgery. The next room has white mice in small cages stacked to the ceiling. More computers, of course. If he's a mechanic, he's a very high-tech one. But mice? And microscopes? And what's with the room filled with jellyfish?

"What are you doing?" I whirl around and find that holographic woman behind me, her transparent hands on her hips like she's annoyed.

"Just looking for a bathroom," I say back. "And I'm thirsty."

"I think we might have a problem."

I take a step back. Her tone is harsh and even though I know she's made up of lights, she scares me. "W-w-what kind of problem?"

"I didn't know about the inhibitor." She scowls and I wonder just how much power this thing has. "It creates a powerful advantage in your favor. I might have made a mistake."

"I don't... I don't understand." I'm not sure I should talk to this computer. What if she's got something against me? What if she resents the fact that I'm here? It's clear that Lincoln doesn't bring people down here. She's probably wondering about our past. "I don't really know what that means," I say. "You're Sheila, right?"

"Correct," she says, walking around me in a circle, like she's sizing me up. Trying to figure out if she can take me in a fight. "What if you ever want to hurt him?"

Shit. She is not going to let it go. And she scares me. I don't think this technology even exists. I have no frame of reference for what she might be capable of. "I don't— I don't understand it all, I'm sorry. I just need to pee."

"Do you know what he is? What he does?"

"No," I say truthfully. The concept of Alpha was never explained to me. And an eight-year-old does not need to know such things, even if she's a pawn in the game. The only reason to use a small girl as part of some secret plan is to make her cooperate without having to explain. "But I'm interested," I say, hoping that will make this thing back down, or at the very least, fill me in a little.

"So you can arrest him?"

"Do I have a reason to arrest him?" I know he's involved in those murders, but I don't know the how or the why. He was not on the security footage.

"If you did, would you? Or would you help him? Would you institutionalize him like your mother?"

"What? How the fuck do you know about—"

"I'm a computer, Detective. A very powerful computer." She seems to grow bigger in that moment. Taller, wider, and maybe even more substantial. The light that makes up her body becomes dense, less transparent. And she seems more solid than she did a moment ago. "I have access to every database on Earth."

She terrifies me. "That's impossible," I say boldly.

"Is it?"

"No one has that much power. There are firewalls and... stuff. I'm not very technical, but people take precautions. They don't just let... clandestine programs wander in and take their information."

"Is that what you think I am? A clandestine program?"

"I have no idea what you are."

"You think I can't get by a firewall, Molly Masters? You think I'm what? Some ordinary hologram? Because you've so seen so many of those, right?"

"Jesus, I don't know. What are you asking?"

"Lincoln is not what you think. He's not your Alpha anymore, Molly. He's mine."

"Oh, for fuck's sake. What, are you jealous?" I laugh. "I'm not having this conversation with a computer. You can't—"

"I might have made a mistake by encouraging him to see you again. You have no idea what's happening here. And I don't want you coming in and misunderstanding."

"Then what is he?" I place my hands on my hips, ready to fight it out with this thing about who knows Lincoln better.

Sheila continues to circle me like prey. And even though I know my hand would slip right through her lightshow of a body, she's intimidating. "What special power did the Prodigy School give you, Molly?"

"Special power? I don't have a special power. I was used, Sheila. I was a pawn to try to keep Lincoln from disobeying. It's not my fault I have that effect on him. I didn't ask for any of this. I just wanted him to be my friend."

"That can't be all. What you see is not what you get with Lincoln, Case, or Thomas. So why should it be that way with you?"

"Oh, please." I snort. "What's *his* special power then?"

"He writes languages."

"What? Languages?"

"Computer languages, Molly. Specifically, he writes computer languages that rewrite other computer languages. Do you know what a retrovirus does?"

"A retrovirus, like AIDS?"

"Yes, like that."

"No, not really," I admit. "I'm a cop, OK? I'm not a scientist."

"A retrovirus inserts itself into your DNA and recodes. DNA is a code, Molly. And all codes can be rewritten. That's what Lincoln's computer languages do. They insert themselves into a system, rewrite the code, and then take it over without a trace."

"So he's a hacker. I didn't know that, no. But it's not surprising given the mad scientist cave we're standing in."

"He's not a hacker, Molly, he's a god."

I snort.

"That," she says, pointing to the operating room, "is his life's work."

I stare at her, utterly confused. What is she talking about? "I don't see anything in there but a bed and a light, so you'll have to give me more details."

"That's because he's not in there at the moment. And he is his own greatest achievement."

"Cryptic much? Is there a bathroom I can use? Or should I just go wake up Lincoln and tell him about our little conversation?"

"By all means, I'd love for you to go wake him up. Turn the lights on in there, while you're at it. Ask him to take off those gloves too. See what he does then."

Is she threatening me? Is she trying to make me think he's going to hurt me? I sigh, not sure what to do, but I am curious about those gloves. So I ignore my bladder and walk back the way I came. I pass by a chair where his leather jacket is hanging off the back and spy that anarchy symbol on the shoulder.

It's a sharp reminder that Sheila is right. I have no idea who Lincoln is. I have no idea what he's been doing down here. And I have no idea what he's been doing out there to those Blue Corp scientists.

I force myself to continue walking. My feet are freezing all of a sudden. The cold concrete floor sends a chill up my body as I head towards the open door, and when I get there, I stop just inside the darkness and feel around on the side of the rock wall for a switch.

"Where is the light?" I whisper.

"They're voice-activated." Sheila is directly behind me, but on the other side of the threshold. "So just say, 'Lights on.'"

I swallow down the dread that is suddenly pulsating though me and force the words out. "Lights—"

They flicker on before I even finish.

What I see shocks my heart. My eyes scan the walls of the cave, taking it all in. And even though my heart wants to make it all disappear, my brain won't let me and I fall against the side of the cave in shock.

## CHAPTER TWENTY-NINE

The lights flick on and I'm awake and out of bed instantaneously. "Molly?"

She's pressed against the cave wall, her mouth agape, staring up at my ceiling, then panning her eyes across the walls. Sheila is standing behind her, behind the threshold she is not allowed to cross.

It takes me a minute to realize what just happened. Then I turn slowly, my eyes glued to the bedroom walls. I take it in. I take it in the way Molly would. And when I turn back to her, she's looking up at me with tears in her eyes.

"W-w-what…" she stutters. "What are you?"

My shoulders hunch and a sigh escapes. She was going to find out. There's no way to keep this a secret if I want her in my life.

Molly snatches a computer printout from the wall. "What," she yells as she walks forward and thrusts the paper into my chest with all the force she can muster, "is this?" She looks down at my legs. The metal plates running down my outer thighs are in plain sight now. She never had the opportunity to touch me much last night. I was doing all the touching. "What the fuck is on your legs?"

But there is no good answer for any of these questions except the truth. "I'm a monster," I say quietly, owning it out loud to someone I care about for the first time ever. "A monster, Molly. The monster they made me."

She turns away, her hands covering her face. "You're a killer."

"Yes."

"A serial killer."

"Yes."

"You really are the one responsible for killing those Blue Corp scientists."

I sigh. "Yes."

"I have to go."

I grab her by the arm and twirl her around, a wave of nausea rolling in my gut. I let go of her immediately to allow the inhibition sickness to pass, but I catch the anger for manhandling her. "Just wait, Molly. Let me explain."

"Explain? What exactly is there to explain? You're a murderer." She scans the wall, taking in all the newspaper printouts I've collected over my fifteen-year career. "A mass murderer. And these," she says, ripping more printouts off the wall, "are your trophies? How many are there, Lincoln?"

I shrug. It's all I can do. "I used to keep count, but—"

"Oh, my God."

"—a lot."

"And that lab out there? The one with the mice?"

I shoot a look at Sheila and she stares back, unaffected.

"Tell her," Sheila says. "Tell her everything, Lincoln." And then she turns to look at Molly. "I've begged him for years to stop. I've tried reason, I've tried threats. I've tried to be supportive. I've done it all, Detective. He's not afraid of getting caught. He has a death wish. And if you weren't his long-lost partner from Prodigy, he'd be playing a cat-and-mouse game with you right now. Just like he's done with the other detectives who tried to figure it out."

Molly glowers at me, but I have nothing to say except, "I am the monster they made me."

"Bullshit," Molly yells. "Bull-fucking-shit, Lincoln."

"How would you know? You don't even remember what they did to *you*, let alone what they did to *me*."

"I remember enough—"

"You don't remember shit," I growl at her. It comes off so animalistic, she takes a step back. Then she looks over her shoulder at Sheila and retreats to her side, assuming, correctly, Sheila will keep me at bay. "I have always needed a control, even after I sent you away, Molly. And maybe Sheila isn't my Omega. I gave her severe limitations. But if I'm in the cave, she can… dissuade me from acting. You don't have to fear me. Ever."

Molly directs her anger at Sheila now. "Then why did you allow this?" She points to the printouts and photographs that paper the wall from floor to ceiling. "Stop him, for fuck's sake."

"I can't be everywhere, Detective. All things have limits."

"What is going on here, Lincoln?" Molly sets her jaw and grits her teeth, determined to figure out the truth. "What is all this?" She sweeps her hands wide. "What is all that?" She points to the cave outside my room. "And what are you doing in that operating room?"

Fuck. She saw all of it. "I wanted to explain—"

"But what? You wanted to fuck me first?"

"Stop it," I bark, scaring her into a backwards step. "Don't get vulgar with me in front of Sheila."

"Sheila? Fuck you and your stupid robot minion! What the fuck is going on? Are you really keeping me here? Am I your prisoner? Is that why you told me to come find you? To save yourself the trouble of luring me out here?"

"Of course not," I snap. "What happened to, 'You're my Alpha, Lincoln. I'm your Omega?' I mean shit, Molly, if you're just looking for an excuse to bail, fine. But the truth is all those people I killed were associated with Prodigy. Every one of them is guilty. Every one of them was fucking *there*, Molly. With you. With me. With Thomas and Case. They killed my parents. Burned my goddamned house down so I'd never have a home again. This lab, this cave, this work. This is all I have left. This is the only thing on this whole motherfucking planet that's still mine."

"So you kill them. Pick them off one by one and make it look like a suicide."

"I didn't make it look like a suicide. They really did kill themselves."

"But you helped them do it."

I shrug.

"How?"

I have to turn to hide the diabolical smile. Because what I'm doing is life-changing, world-shattering, and downright evil. Does she really want to know?

I turn back and eye her.

She stares me in the face and says, "Tell me."

"You're not gonna like it."

"Tell me," she repeats.

"Did you know," I start slowly, barely a whisper, "that some species of jellyfish can regrow their own bodies?"

She swallows and backs up a step.

"Did you know they can even regenerate their own brains? Even after you detach them from their bodies? It's practically a miracle, Molly. Scientists have declared it unnatural. But those neurons are completely natural, and so is everything I'm doing. I can take those cells out of the jellyfish and replant them into the mice. I can grow new parts to their little mousey brains, Molly."

"I feel sick," she says, her hand going to her stomach.

"And did you know that you can drive mice to violence if you stimulate a certain gland in their brains in just the right way?"

"You c-c-cannot be serious," she stammers.

"That gland is in every brain. It's a part of you, of me, of every human being on this planet. And did you know that there's a serum you can inject to make people more violent?"

"You're sick," she says, her eyes searching my face for the Alpha she once loved. "You're sick. I was right the first time. You're some kind of deviant maniac."

"The lab, the jellyfish, and those mice, the computers, all of it—everything you see in here is what Prodigy School was doing, only better. More advanced. They made me smart. The smartest of all the kids they had. They made me that way, Molly. And if there's one thing I've learned, it's that you gotta use the gifts you've been given."

"I should arrest you."

I put my hands out, wrists together. "Go ahead. There's no evidence, I promise you. There is nothing here but legal research on mice and jellyfish. I have permits and permission. Hell"—I laugh—"I even have government grants funding this shit."

"Who the fuck would give grants to a lab in a Batcave?"

"His retrovirus, Molly," Sheila says, speaking for me. "He can rewrite any program in the world using me as his vector. I'm a delivery mechanism for a global technology revolution. We can reprogram any computer to do our bidding. Governments, private companies, anything."

"So you stole that grant money. You're a serial killer and a thief. A crazed liar who wants to end the world? Just what the fuck are you doing?"

"You forgot monster, devil, and evil. Go ahead, Molls, spit in my face for good measure."

She recoils, but it's from the nickname, I just know it. "I want to leave now."

"Molly—"

But she pushes past me, grabs her jeans from the floor, and starts pulling them on. "No," she says. "No, no, no. I can't listen to another word. Just let me go."

I sigh, looking over at Sheila. But Sheila's gone. She got what she wanted, I guess. She wants me to be accountable to someone and she got her wish. I pull on my own jeans just as Molly finds her shoes and slips her feet into them.

She walks forward, pushes me hard on the chest to get me out of her way, and bolts past, heading across the cave to the tunnel where she disappears into the darkness.

I follow her, slowly, giving her a little time to calm down.

"Open the fucking gate, Lincoln," she yells, and once I turn the corner, the breaking dawn outlines her shape against the rusted bars of the gate that stands between her and freedom.

I walk up to her. She looks scared, and confused, and tired. "Molly, please—"

"Open the gate."

I have nothing left. Nothing to say. No more ways to justify anything I've done. I only have one excuse and it's not good enough for Molly. Sheila was right. All this shit has finally caught up with me and it's gonna cost me everything. Again.

"Open the gate, Sheila," I call out to the air. Seconds later the rusty bars begin to lift up. Molly doesn't even wait for it, she drops to her knees and crawls under, heading for her bike.

I follow her out and watch helplessly as she grabs her helmet and shoves it on her head, then straddles the bike and kickstarts the engine. It roars to life and I stay quiet. Hoping she'll say something. Anything.

But she doesn't. She gives the bike some throttle, whips it around in the dirt, and then speeds off, her front wheel leaving the ground for effect.

She is outta here.

I turn and walk back into the tunnel. "Close it up, Sheila." And the gate comes back down, whining and creaking the whole way. I make my way back into the cave, pass Sheila standing in the middle, looking like she's got something to say, and then go into my room and close the door.

I feel like a kid again.

No. I never got sent to my room by my mom as a kid. I don't even remember my mom. And my dad never paid much attention to me. He was always down here, I guess.

No.

It doesn't remind me of being a kid. It reminds me of being Alpha.

Molly wants him, but only the parts she loves. Because if she thinks the killer in the cave is worse than the Alpha from her dreams, she's lost more than her memory. She's lost her sanity.

I sit down at my computer and type in my password, then bring up my scorecard. I started with so many names. But I'm down to the last few now.

Three more targets and I can be finished. Three more days of killing and I can be done with this life.

After that, I'm not sure there's anything left for me. After that it's just a big black hole. After that I might think about using the protocol on myself.

After that it might be the end.

## CHAPTER THIRTY

I have to stop the bike on the side of the mountain. I can see all thirteen cathedrals of the city staring back at me as I lean over a silver guardrail and hurl over the side of a cliff. I can't stop thinking of the images on that wall.

He's sick.

Sick. Sick. Sick. I cannot say it enough, that's how sick he is. I have spent the last few years committed to protecting people from harm. I joined this department to help the innocent and the underrepresented. The forgotten and the disregarded. To get to the bottom of crimes that no one cares about. And now I'm in bed with a person who spits on everything I believe in. A person who takes the law into his own hands and uses science— the pursuit of knowledge, for fuck's sake—to kill people in the name of vigilante justice.

I know why he uses that anarchy symbol now. Because he is the antithesis of everything society represents. Authority, safety, and the rule of order mean nothing to Lincoln Wade. He is right. He *is* what they made him. He is evil, he is wicked, and he is insane.

I try to throw up again, but my stomach is empty. And I never got to pee, and right now, I might piss myself if I can't get it all under control. So I drop to my knees, still holding the guardrail, and bow my head into the cold metal. The wind is strong up here, and I'm shaking from the cold. I left my jacket and my backpack. And now I'll probably have to break into my own house because I don't have my keys.

My back pocket vibrates and I realize how lucky I am to still have my phone.

It can't be Lincoln, he doesn't have my number.

*He's a criminal hacker, Molly. How hard would it be to get your number?*

But it's not him, so I don't even bother wondering. I just tab accept and speak into the phone. "Yes, Chief."

"Where the fuck have you been? I've been calling you since yesterday morning. Partying too hard on the weekend again?"

"Sorry, Chief, but it's my day off."

"You don't get a day off, Masters! You're a city employee! You're a servant of the greater good! You're a—"

"I got it, Chief," I snarl back at him. "I don't need reminding."

"What did you just say?"

Dammit. I sigh heavily. "I'm here now, OK? I wasn't drinking. I was up in the mountains with no service."

"Get your ass into the station. Now. There's been another suicide."

And then he hangs up on me. Just like clockwork.

But I get to my feet and force myself to get back on the bike. Because this shit needs to be dealt with. Lincoln needs to be dealt with. I'm not sure what that entails, to be honest. I'm not sure if it means I turn him in or turn a blind eye. I'm just not sure. But I can't stay here.

I'm cold.

I'm broken, and…

I'm desperately in need of a few million complete strangers in the city to take my mind off the killer I just spent the night with.

When I finally weave my way through the congested streets of downtown Cathedral City and park my bike, it's close to nine AM.

Roger, the intern at the reception desk, looks up at me when I enter the building. He shakes his head. "He's so mad today, Molly. Just nod and say, 'Yes, sir.'"

"Got it," I say. "Thanks for the heads-up."

I get buzzed through into the back and just like last week, the place is crawling with people waiting to be booked. One guy makes a grab for me as I pass by a desk he's handcuffed to, but the arresting officer, who looks like he's just doing paperwork and not paying attention, grabs his Billy club and cracks it against the guy's chest, making him retreat like a yelping dog.

"Sorry, Masters," the uniformed cop says, barely taking his eyes off his paperwork.

"Um." That's all I have for that. Because I don't have the respect around here one would need to start shit with a ten-year veteran about police brutality.

"Masters!" the chief bellows.

"Coming," I mutter under my breath. I'm tired of him screaming at me and I'm really not in the mood to get my ass chewed out for whatever he's pissed about now. So I start making a list of why I should turn Lincoln in as I cross the room.

He's a serial killer.

He's dangerous as hell.

He's bad.

It's a pretty lame list. I mean, number one is a good enough reason. But what he said is still rolling though my head.

The victims were all part of the Prodigy School. That gives me pause. *Are* they the victims? Or were we the victims? This new perspective does me no good. Justice is based on laws and rules. The subtleties of an eye for an eye don't matter in the courtroom.

But maybe they should? Maybe the good intentions paving the road to hell are really the dark shadows that line the alley of righteousness? And maybe Lincoln and his friends are those same dark shadows. Maybe they are right.

I don't remember it all, but I know the people at the Prodigy School were evil. I know I wanted to run away when Lincoln saved me. And I know I never missed it.

I did miss him though. And now that I can remember a little bit about that night, I wonder if I always knew he was missing from my life. Somewhere deep inside I knew he was part of me. He was my beginning and I was his end.

"Yes, Chief?" I say, walking into his office and taking a seat in front of his desk.

He gives me a glare. "As I was saying. There's been another suicide at Blue Corp. And you know what, Masters? I'm pretty sure the people of Cathedral City think you're not earning your keep around here. That's four murders—"

"Wait, what? I thought you said this was a suicide?"

He squints and scrubs his hand over his face. "Well, I think it's murder. Not suicide. It's too convenient."

"Hmm," I say, noncommittal.

"Get your ass over to Blue Corp right now. They're waiting for you."

I salute and walk out.

"And Masters!" Chief bellows at my back.

"This isn't the military," I yell back. "Got it." He's gonna fire me. But I don't care. Maybe this job is not what I want out of life. I mean, who the hell wants to track down killers for a living?

*You do, Molly.*

I do. I just don't want to track down Lincoln. I don't want him to be what he just admitted to being because I can't be with in love with someone who hurts people. I can't.

When I get up to the twenty-first floor of Blue Corp, there's no dead body and no Atticus. No Alastair either, thank fuck. Just some janitor changing out the fluorescent lights over the desk where a body has been outlined in tape.

"Well," I say, more to myself than him. "I guess no one really needs me here now. Were you here when they took the body?" I ask the maintenance guy.

"Uh, no. Not this time." He finishes changing the bulb and steps down off the ladder.

"Were you there for the last three?"

"Uh, yep. I changed the lights on those too."

"What?"

"Flickering bad, they were. Giving people a headache. So I changed them. You know, they say fluorescent lights in the workplace can drive people insane. You think that's why he blew his brains out?"

"Um." Why does that stupid question make me pause? There's something in my brain. It's a like a little tickle that says, *Pay attention.* "I don't know, but I'll look into it. And hey," I say, "do you know if they've determined a time of death?"

"Yup," he says. "Early morning Saturday. That's what I heard, anyway."

Jesus Christ. If this is Lincoln's work, then he fucked me in that maze and went and killed someone afterward.

"Thanks for your help. If either of the Mr. Montgomerys come around, let them know I was here and left, will you?"

"If I see 'em, sure will, lady." And then he walks off down the hallway, taking his ladder with him.

I look around the room, casually taking it all in, and then leave as well. Whatever evidence was here is gone now. Picked up by the others who came in my absence and if not, it's all ruined by contamination anyway. So I make my way back down to my bike and drive back to the station.

Luckily the place has quieted down considerably when I walk in the door. Sunday afternoon shift change means people are ready to get out of here as fast as they can. Roger isn't at the desk now, it's the old woman who's been here for like four decades. "Got a delivery while you were gone. I put it on your desk."

"Oh," I say. I almost forgot I even had a desk. With stacks and stacks of paperwork piling up, I'm sure. "Who's it from?"

"No return address on it. So I guess you'll have to open it up and see," she snarks back.

"How do you know it's not a bomb? Or anthrax? Someone could've put anything in there and you just set it on my desk?"

"Relax, Detective. We haven't blown up yet. Go away and let finish my paperwork."

"Bitch," I mutter under my breath. This place is worse than the circus as far as procedures go. Everyone under the tent would've been dead if they were as sloppy about safety as this department is.

But there is nothing I can do except shake my head with disgust as I pass through the doors. My desk is way, way, way in the back of the main room. But I can see a small package wrapped in brown paper sitting in front of my computer.

Who wraps shit in brown paper?

I glance around, wondering if anyone else thinks it's weird that I got a package, but there are only about half a dozen cops in here at the moment, and none of them are paying any attention to me and my package.

So I just say, "Fuck it," and walk over there. When I pick it up, it's lighter than it should be. Very light. Too light to be a bomb.

*Stop, Molly.*

I find the edge of the paper and tear it open to uncover a thin white box. There's no card. I sit down in my chair and set it on my desk to stare at it.

I don't even have to open it. I know who it's from and I don't want to have to face the problem that he's turned into right now. So I push the little white box away and start going through the hundreds of emails that have piled up over the week. Forms, forms, and more forms to be filled out.

I spend the rest of the day getting things done and still that little white box waits for me. It taunts me. It begs me to open it. But I force myself to get the work done first. I know if I let Lincoln back into my thoughts, the internal monologue that comes with him will take over my day. But finally, after the place gets busy, quiets down, and gets busy again, I've done every possible thing I can do to avoid opening that box.

"Night, Masters," a guy leaving with some other officers calls from a few desks over. "I know you're the new guy, but everyone gets to go home eventually."

I shoot him a smile. "Night, guys." Then I lean back in my creaky chair and sigh, exhausted. "Well," I say to myself. "I guess I can't avoid it any longer." I lift the lid on the little white box and pull away some crackling tissue paper to reveal...

His gloves.

They are leather and they have small flat studs pounded into the shape of the anarchy symbol. These were not the ones he was wearing last night. I'd have noticed that. But they are an admission of sorts. He's the Anarchist Killer.

I pick them both up and hold a part of him in my hand. These are the gloves of a very sick man. Does he wear them to keep his hands clean? How poetic.

That's probably not why, but he sent them to me for a reason. It's some kind of truce, but am I willing to make peace with the fact that he's running around this town killing people?

I want to, I really do. I want nothing more than to immerse myself into Lincoln Wade's life and let him do what he does best. Take over. Be in control. Be Alpha.

But what little part of myself would I be giving up if I did that? What would he want in return? My silence, at the very least, right? I should arrest him, no questions asked.

I slip my hands into the soft leather and a sigh actually escapes as I flex my fingers. They are big on me and I like that. I like his hands, even though he hides them from me.

Why send them to me? Because I asked him to take them off last night and he refused? Maybe it's not a truce. More of a white flag? No, it can't be surrender. I don't see Lincoln as a man who surrenders so easily.

They're a calling card, like the symbol he left behind on that man's forehead. Like the printouts of his crimes plastered all over his cave.

Maybe he's telling me there's room for negotiation. If that's the case, I owe him another meeting, right? I can't just walk away if he's got an offer on the table. At least not until I hear him out.

I know I'm rationalizing, but after I lost Will I got depressed because I had no more connections in this world. I left my life in the military behind, even though I would never count anyone I was working with as family—it's not like I was in combat, for fuck's sake. It's not like my co-workers and I were bonded by death and destruction, by sacrifice and survival. It was security. And yeah, it was high-level security, not mall-cop shit. But they were mainly acquaintances.

Lincoln might be the only person on this whole planet I would count as family. We were made for each other. Should I really walk away from that if he's willing to talk through it with me?

The speed limit is generally something I obey, but not tonight. I race home as fast as I can, zigzagging my way through traffic and speeding up to avoid red lights. I park the bike in the garage, set the stand, and take my helmet off, setting it on the seat. The door in the garage that connects to the house is partly ajar.

I was right. He was calling me home with those gloves.

My heart flutters with excitement and anticipation. Fear too, if I'm being honest.

When I walk through the kitchen the first thing I see is Lincoln Wade sitting at my table. His bare hands are folded neatly in front of him and even though I can't say for certain that he wasn't covering them up with gloves to keep the blood off them as he murdered people, I can say for certain that was not why he took them off tonight.

Because both of his palms are glowing bright red.

## CHAPTER THIRTY-ONE

"No squad cars following you in?" I ask Molly.

"Not yet," she says, stepping into the house and kicking the door closed behind her. "But don't think I won't call them, Lincoln."

I shrug with my hands and her eyes track to my palms. She stares hard at them for several seconds before breaking away and looking for my face. "Did you get a good look?" I ask. "It's what you wanted, right?"

"Not really." She draws in a deep breath, her eyes darting back to the light that is now yellow-orange. My heart is still beating fast, but not as fast as it was when she first appeared. "What are they?"

"You don't know what happened to me," I say, returning to our conversation from this morning. "And you can say things like I chose Case and Thomas over you, or that I walked out, or that I'm a sick monster who deserves to be put down like a dog. You can say all that. And even if it's not all one hundred percent true, it's all partially true. I did choose Case and Thomas, but not for the reasons you think."

"Is that why you're here? To make me feel special?" she asks, walking over to the table and pulling out a chair. She takes a seat and I can see the weariness in her face. She's tired.

But I'm tired too. "I'm tired of pretending. If you love me, and that's a big if, then you need to love *me*, Molly. Not Alpha. Not your idea of me as Alpha. Not the fantasy that we are soulmates or lovers interrupted."

"What are you?" she asks. "What are *we*?" She's been thinking since I saw her this morning. Reevaluating, maybe. Time has always been my friend. I am patient. It's an innate quality inside me. A trait I was born with. It's surprising considering how impatient I am with most people. But this... scheme we've been working towards—I have endless patience for the vengeance I've imagined over the years. I will only get one chance at revenge. One chance to retaliate. Once chance to make it right. And all of that has depended on more than a decade of planning and plotting with Case and Thomas to get to this precise point in time.

I hold up a palm and it flashes an orange light bright enough to cast a glow across her face. "It's an electromagnetic field."

She blinks.

"A magnet," I explain.

"Why would they put magnets in your hands?"

"They didn't," I say calmly. I've never had to explain this to anyone. Case was there. Thomas wasn't there when I did it, but he was there in the beginning. He knew it was going to happen and he knew why it was happening. And I'm sure his little visit to Mac's last weekend was a not-so-gentle reminder that this job is about more than me. "I put the magnets in there. There's a lot of reasons attached to that answer, Molly. But the important one is that they started something with me back when I was a kid. They changed me. And you helped them."

She shakes her head. "I was forced."

"I'm not trying to blame you, Molly. I'm just stating facts. No one is holding an eight-year-old responsible for this," I say, holding up my glowing palms. "Least of all me. The Prodigy School used you to keep me in line.

They made you send electrical current through my body—"

"Electrocute you?" She rubs her temples with her fingertips, trying to massage away the truth.

"Yes. Basically. It was part of their Genesis plan. To create superhumans. Larger-than-life people who could hold power and manipulate things that no one else could. People who looked normal, but weren't. But the administrators who ran the school couldn't become superhumans themselves. They needed children to do that."

"Oh, God."

"And what better children to use than their own? Who would miss a rich kid sent off to boarding school?"

"Jesus Christ."

"You had parents. I had parents. Everyone has parents. They put us in that school, Molly."

"I can't believe it," she says, shaking her head.

"My father too, so you're not alone. Case is special, he was taken as a payment on a debt. His family never gave him up willingly and after we escaped, they cared for me and all my special considerations until I turned eighteen."

She waits for it.

So do I. I have never told anyone this and I feel like I've been waiting my whole life to be able to say the words out loud. "I am... was made... I was changed into—"

"Just say it, Lincoln," Molly whispers. "Just tell me what the fuck is happening."

"I'm not who or what you think, Molly. Sheila said she told you about my programming skills. How I write computer languages. How I use her as a vector to change code in computers. And if that was all I did, it might not be so bad. I don't just reprogram machines, Molly. I reprogram people."

"You did that to me, didn't you? That drug you gave me after I ran away in the snow."

I nod. "It rewrote your DNA, changed your memory. It acts like a flu virus. But in your case it was temporary. All DNA degrades over time. It was supposed to wear off gradually over many years. A bit here, a bit there until all the bad code was reprogrammed once again, using another dormant virus included in the drug cocktail. I didn't take it away." God, this is so hard to explain. Because I did take her memory away. "I wanted you to remember, Molly. I did. I made sure you'd recover those memories, I just thought it would take a little longer. I didn't expect it to happen while you were still so young and so…" My words trail off, because what I want to say is 'desirable.' It would be so much easier if she wasn't so perfect. So beautiful. If she didn't have so many years ahead of her. How could I ever walk out now?

I can't. I won't.

"You rewrote those scientists," she says, refocusing me back to our conversation.

"Yes. I rewrote them. Changed them. Made them want to commit suicide once I activated nerve centers in their brains using a special light pattern."

She stares at me for a second, like she's putting the pieces together. "You killed another one, didn't you?"

I nod.

"I went to look at the scene today and the maintenance guy was changing out the fluorescent lights above his desk. You used them. Made them flicker. That was the trigger?"

I nod again. "Many organisms on earth are programmed to respond to changes in light. Migration of animals and birds. Reproductive cycles. Hibernation in bears. All these things are biologically programmed into their brains. And the Prodigy School figured out a way to make people violent using light to trigger it."

She lets out a long breath and then she places her palms flat against the table and stares at them. "What do your hands do?"

"Nothing spectacular. The special food I consume feeds the virus inside me which powers my brain like electricity powers a computer hard drive. It generates a lot of heat that has to be dissipated. I do that through my hands."

"They're vents. Like the pads on a dog's foot."

"Simply put, yes. But they have a few practical applications. They are magnetic and the color of the light can be altered to act like a laser in a scanner."

She stares at me with her mouth partly open. In awe? I almost chuckle. Hardly. More like in shock or disgust. "And me? What part do I play in all this?"

I shrug. "You're the one running the show, Molly. They made you to stop me if I ever went too far."

"Like how a superhero opposes a supervillain?"

"I guess. But more like a bomb and the wires that control the bomb. I'm the bomb."

"And I'm the wires."

"We're an unfinished project. I got you out before the really bad stuff started. It's part of the reason I agreed to Thomas' plan. First they put us together as partners. Then they made us hurt each other. In my case, they made me take care of you afterward. They bonded me to you. Made me sick at the thought of hurting you. Behavioral conditioning, genetic manipulation. And other stuff. It's too much to explain simply. But even now, after all these years, I would not be able to kill you."

"Lucky me," she whispers.

"But you could kill me quite easily."

"What? How?"

"That was the purpose of the Omega. To kill us after we were no longer useful. If your training had completed then you'd be able to hold a gun to my head and I'd be powerless to stop you."

"I don't want to kill you, Lincoln."

"Then I guess it's a good thing I got you out before that happened."

"Yeah." She looks down at her hands again. "So those people you're killing. They're bad, right?"

"Very bad."

"And that sorta makes you good, right?"

"It's debatable, but I'm doing my best."

"So…" She pushes her palms against the table and stands up. "You really are Batman?"

"No," I say, letting a small chuckle escape. "He's not real, Molly. I am. And even though what I'm telling you seems pretty fantastic, it's my life and it's not romantic or inspiring or any of that fantasy bullshit they push with a character like that. It would take a lot of effort to rise to larger-than-life status and even more to be considered the good guy. Because that's what you're thinking, aren't you? Good guys don't kill people in the name of revenge." I rise from my seat and walk around to meet her. "I'd really have to want it and—"

"But if you *did* want it…" She cuts me off, steps around the table, and walks towards me. She stops when we are only a foot apart and looks up at me with her wide hazel eyes. "Then you could use all that super stuff to do good things instead of bad. To help people."

"Help which people?" I snarl. "Blue Corp? Those people? They hired scientists who did this, Molly. They made me hurt you. They changed us and we can't ever get that back."

"So you're going to just kill them all? One by one?"

"Not all," I say, turning away so she can't see the evil smile. "Only the ones who deserve it."

"But who are you to pass judgment on them? Who are you to say they can't be saved?"

"You're missing the point, Molly." I'm really starting to lose patience. "These people don't deserve to be helped. They ruined us. They stole our childhood and made us do unspeakable things to each other. So let me just say it straight out. I'm not interested in saving people. And if you know the history, neither was Batman. He was out for revenge, just like me. Saving people was a consequence of taking out those he hated."

"I don't think so, Lincoln," she says, shaking her head. "People make choices and if you're a superhuman, then couldn't you just choose to be a superhero?"

"But who would play the villain?" I give her a sideways smile. "Not you." I laugh. "You're not wired to hurt. You're wired to save. I made sure of it."

"Except in your case. You said I'm able to hurt you. And I'm not saying I want to be your opposite, Lincoln. I'm just saying *you* could be your opposite."

I run my hand through my hair and turn away before I tell her more. "We have a plan, Molly. And nothing you say will stop it from happening."

I expect her to get angry. Maybe slap my face or order me to get out of her house and never come back. But she doesn't do those things. She walks up to me, takes my hand and presses our palms together. "You're so warm here."

"And so cold everywhere else."

"No," she says, gripping my hand and placing it over her cheek. "You're warm everywhere. And if you can reprogram people like you say, then you can do things like cure mental illness, Lincoln. You could heal people with this science. You could change terrible things and make things better. You could be a hero. The world needs a hero, Lincoln."

I lean down and kiss her mouth, speaking into it softly. "No one needs a hero like me, Molly. The road to hell is always paved with good intentions."

"Everyone needs a hero, Lincoln, and if you're the only one we have, then you can't say no." Her words are so soft. She pours out her gentle nature into the grotesque malformation of my hand as she presses it against her cheek. "The world needs a champion to stand up for it."

"I don't want to talk about this anymore," I say, biting her lip and kissing her again. "I want to take you to bed and fuck you."

"We need someone who will fight against injustice," she says, placing her hand on my chest. Just this small bit of heat from her touch makes my cock grow.

"Fighting is something I do, gun girl. But only for the right reasons. I'll fight you right now if you say no to this." She laughs when I take her hand and push it down the front of my pants. She grabs at my bulge and I can't help but grin. "Just don't stop touching me."

"We need someone who will stand tall in the face of adversity."

"We can do it standing if you want." I grab her ass, lift her up, and back her up to a wall. "I'm good with wall sex."

"Someone who believes in the value of a good deed, Lincoln."

"Are you listing me, gun girl?"

"No." She laughs. "I'm just saying we can use what they did to you in the past and turn it into something good instead."

"Well, let's fuck first. We can talk about all this side bullshit later." I kiss her hungrily. I grope her breasts, casting a yellow-orange haze across the t-shirt she stole from me this morning. "Take this off," I say. "My hands are busy."

She reaches back, her breasts rising and stretching with her arms as she whips her shirt off. I grab one breast so hard, she whimpers. The inhibition sickness slams me back from my lust as I realize I hurt her with that move. "Sorry," I whisper.

"I like it, Lincoln," she whispers back. "I like it a little rough."

"It makes me sick if I physically hurt you, Molly. So I can't get carried away."

"You don't know what hurts me. I know what hurts me. So you need to retrain yourself, Super Alpha."

"No stupid nicknames," I growl.

"You call me gun girl. So I can call you something too."

"Yeah, because that name is damn cute and reminds me of that day out on the road. Super Alpha is just stupid."

"Yeah, it's stupid. Considering you're not even alpha. I am."

"Shit, woman."

She laughs and kisses me on the neck, whispering in my ear. "Show me how alpha you are, Lincoln. Control me. Fuck me hard. Bite my nipples. Pound your cock into my pussy until I scream. I promise you, none of those screams will be from the pain."

Good God. I push her harder against the wall. Molly Masters might have delusions of grandeur. She might see me as some superhero capable of cleaning up corruption and doing good deeds. And I might not be the hero she's looking for, but Super Fuckman I can do.

"Show me, Alpha," she moans, rocking her hips back and forth across my cock, trying to drive me crazy. "Show me the difference between pain and pleasure."

"Be careful what you wish for, Detective. Because you're about to get it."

She squeals as I lift her up into my arms and carry her to the stairs, sitting her ass on a step halfway up. "Unbutton," I order, pointing to her pants.

She obeys and then I grab the hem of her jeans and pull until they come flying off. "Let's go upstairs," she says.

"Let's do it right here," I counter. I undo the button and drag the zipper down my pants and then shove the fabric down until my cock springs out.

"No," she squeals. And then she tries to turn and crawl up the stairs, but I flip her back around and press her hands into the step above her head. "Are you alpha enough to hold me down?"

"I'm gonna make you pay for that," I say.

She squeals and tries to escape as I reach for her breast. But I grab her ankle and she goes crazy. Her whole body starts contorting. "I'm ticklish!"

"Hold still then, gun girl."

She stops, or tries her best. Little giggles are still erupting out of her mouth. I'm being rough with her, but she's sending me all the right signals. I just need to learn to read her better. Know her better. Teach her how I like it, and let her show me how she responds.

I spread her legs open on the stairs and lick her pussy. She sucks in air and then holds it in as my tongue sweeps around her folds. "Oh," she moans. "My fucking God."

I lick her again, then catch her soft skin between my teeth and give it a nip. She jumps, squealing, and the nausea rolls though me and I stop immediately.

A hand on my shoulder gives me reassurance. "It's OK, Lincoln. I love it. Don't get my signals mixed up."

"I'll never hurt you again, Molly. Ever. I promise. And if you need a hero, I'll be your hero. You belong to me. You are my Omega and I love that. I wouldn't trade what we have for anything."

"Then take me the way you want, Alpha. Because we start now. This is our beginning. Tonight. Right here on my stairs. I want you to fuck me until you feel sick, then do it again and again until it doesn't make you sick anymore. So next time you won't have to wonder where my limits are."

Jesus Christ. Molly Masters is my fantasy realized.

"Challenge accepted."

## CHAPTER THIRTY-TWO

His mouth is driving me crazy and it's not nearly enough.

I don't even know what to do except let him know I want more. So I thread my fingers into his unruly, bad-boy hair and grab hold. "Lick me," I say, looking into his flashing eyes. "I'll beg for it if you want. But please, just keep going."

"Mmmmm," he says around my nipple. "I like begging. But let's make this a little more interesting." And then he lowers himself down to my pussy and sucks on my clit.

"Jesus," I whisper. "I agree, no matter what your idea is."

He laughs into my pussy and this makes my back arch and my nipples jut up into hard peaks. His tongue feels like magic and when he pulls away, I try my best to make him continue. "Easy." His words vibrate against my clit and drive me wild. "Let's have some fun."

"I'm fine with this kind of fun," I moan. "Don't stop."

"But games are good, gun girl. And this one especially. It's called pain and pleasure. I get to do anything I want. You get to tell me to keep going or stop and try something else. But you can't be shy, Molly. You just have to trust me, open yourself up to new things, and be honest. That's the only thing that matters."

My heart starts beating fast. I've never been adventurous in bed but I'm willing to give it a shot. Take one for the team, as they say. "I'm your captive," I say. His brows furrow and that little growl he does makes me shiver with anticipation. "I'm your prisoner, Lincoln. And I'm ready."

He looks at me for a long moment, his eyes fixed on mine, those little flecks of amber shining intensely. "OK," he says. He places his palms in that tender spot of skin that forms a dent behind each knee and rolls my legs forward, spreading them wide. I expect him to keep licking and sucking my pussy, but he dips down lower and his tongue sweeps against my little pucker of an asshole.

I tense up and draw in a gasp of air.

"Pain or pleasure?" he asks between licks.

"Pleasure, but—"

"Be patient," he commands, cutting me off. "Don't expect anything, and don't get ahead of yourself. OK?"

I nod and whisper, "OK."

As soon as the word comes out of my mouth his fingers are probing. He's got his gloves off and even though the leather was the softest thing I've ever felt, his touch is softer. A gentle sweep, a lick and a suck, and a few breaths of air caressing the desire between my legs make me want to be wild.

But his slow patience, his complete attention, and his gentle nature as he explores the depths of my sexuality make me want to be still.

His fingers drift up so he can gather the wetness of my folds and drag it back down to where his tongue is still licking. Slowly he brushes the rim of my ass with my own desire. "Pain or pleasure?" he asks, the heat of his words making me close my eyes.

"Pleasure," I whisper.

His fingers are already seeking out new territory before my answer is complete. He pushes against the tight muscles of my ass, and I wriggle away from the shock of it. "Pain," I say.

He moves along without comment, his tongue making one more swirl around my clit before he drops my legs and crawls up the stairs, kissing his way up my belly at the same time. He pauses to suck on my left nipple, squeezing the right breast so hard, I gasp. But I say, "Pleasure."

"Good girl," he says, pleased. "Let's finish upstairs." And then he sweeps me into his arms and carries me up. I'm about to tell him which way to turn at the top, but then I remember he's been here. He knows exactly where to take me. Left, and then into the bedroom, where he flips on the light with an elbow as we pass over the threshold. He lays me down on the bed, my covers all rumpled because I can't even remember the last time I made the bed.

His pants are barely perched on his hips and his cock is long and hard, pushing through the gap made by the open zipper. I can't help but look. He's huge. We've had sex twice before but I've never seen him in the light.

"You want to put that—"

"Easy, girl," he says, crawling up the bed towards me. "I told you not to get ahead of yourself. I know what I'm doing."

He stares down at me, then cups my face and kisses me on the lips. A soft kiss. No tongue or anything, so I open my mouth and seek him out.

"So eager."

"So horny." I laugh.

"Shhh," he says, admonishing me. "Turn over on your stomach."

Oh, shit.

"Pain or pleasure?" he asks.

"You haven't done anything."

"Then why are you so nervous?"

I let out a long breath and turn over, my ass up in the air. He smacks it. Hard. It makes me yelp out and try to sit up. But he places his hand firmly on the cheek he just smacked, only this time it's soft and gentle. "Pain or pleasure?" he says, caressing the sting away.

"Um…" I'm not sure. He did hurt me. And I'm pretty sure I have a bright red handprint on my bottom right now. But the soft touches afterward make the pain almost delightful. "Pleasure," I finally say.

"Mmmm," he says, leaning over to hum into my ear as he straddles my calves. I can feel how hard he is when he presses himself against my legs. "Right answer."

My heart starts beating faster with anticipation but I'm immensely proud that I pleased him. I start to relax and then his hand comes down again with a sharp crack.

"Ow," I say, coiling in on myself. And when I look over my shoulder, he's doubled over, his hand across the taut muscles of his abs. "Lincoln?" I ask, panic starting. "Lincoln, are you OK?"

"I'm fine," he manages after a few seconds to let the feeling pass. "Inhibition sickness. If I hurt you, believe me, I know it. I'm sorry."

"We're testing the limits, though, right? And I wasn't really hurt, Lincoln. I just reacted wrong. I like the soft caresses after the smacks."

He takes a deep breath, squints his eyes, and then opens them up and stares at me. "Lesson learned."

"No," I say, turning around and sitting up so I can see him better. "That's not what I want to happen. How do I let you do that without making you sick?"

"We can work on it next time, Molly."

"But—"

"Shh," he says, the alpha back. "I made my decision. Enough of that." He grins and winks. "I've got more, don't worry. So lie face down on the bed." I obey, ready to get back to the fun stuff. I hate making him sick. I hope we can get past the limits soon. "Spread your legs."

Fuck. I never thought I'd admit this to myself, but I really love that alpha shit. And just to prove it, the wetness pools between my legs as I open them wider. A knee presses against my pussy and then his thumb is on my asshole and the rest of his fingers are splayed out across my cheek. I hold so still. I do not want to make him sick again. I've never had anal, but I've heard it's both pain and pleasure and it makes me nervous.

"Relax," he says, drawing the word out as he tests my limits by pressing his thumb even further inside me. "It won't hurt. And maybe every guy on the planet says that the first time he takes a girl's ass, but I have no choice but to make you love it, do I?"

What will it feel like to have that huge cock inside there? I stiffen at the thought.

"Molly," he growls, "I said take it easy. I'm trying to make you feel good and you're missing it."

"I know. I'm sorry. I'll try harder." I close my eyes, relax my shoulders, and pull my hands up and tuck them under my pillow like I do when I go to sleep.

He starts again, gathering more wetness from between my legs and dragging it up to my ass. The tip of his thumb slips in and then stops, but this time when the little shock of pain erupts, I relax even more and it fades.

"I love you," Lincoln says from behind me. "And thank you." He laughs. "I do not want to get sick every time I try to fuck your ass."

I laugh a little at that. "Keep going." And privately I'm excited that he's an adventurous lover.

He pushes a little harder, and again there's a slight shock to my system, but it fades when I force myself to be calm and open up to the idea. "Reach over and grab your lube from the drawer, Molly."

"How do you know I have lube in the drawer?" I look over my shoulder to see his face and he's shooting me a look.

"I've gone through this house from top to bottom. Several times. You do realize that the cameras are still here, right?"

"We're making a sex tape right now?"

"We're not turning them off," he says, like the decision is final. I have no doubt that if I throw a fit those cameras will be turned off. But... it intrigues me. Heightens my desire and makes me want him to keep going even more. "I'm watching this later. And I'm gonna beat off to it in front of you."

OK then.

"Now grab the fucking lube."

I reach over to the top drawer in the bedside table and feel around until I find the tube.

"Good," he says. "Take the cap off and squeeze it out on your asshole while I watch."

Whoa. Maybe I'm crazy, or maybe I'm just caught up in this unusual foreplay, but I'm dying for him to fuck me in the ass right now.

"Fuck, yeah," he says as I do as I'm told. "Drop it on the floor." I do that too.

And then he repositions himself so his cock is pressing right against his thumb. He withdraws it, but places the tip of his head at the entrance. I gasp, then catch myself, not wanting to hurt him. I don't want to make him sick when he's trying his best to make it pleasurable. God, I never want to hurt him.

He pushes a little further, and this time I can't help it. I double into myself again, but when he mimics me—when my hurt becomes his hurt—I take deep, deep breaths.

"Good girl," he says, praising me after a few seconds of recovery. "Let's try that again. Just stay calm and go limp, Molly. I promise you, I will bring you to ecstasy if you will just trust me."

He enters me further, and I suck air through my teeth, but I don't overreact this time. Another push, and for a moment I think I might scream and make him stop, but then he eases forward, and all the pain becomes—"Pleasure," I whisper.

He laughs behind me, but he's breathing hard so I can tell he's still dealing with my last reaction. "The hard part's over now. Everything else is world-rocking."

He drops his chest to my back, lying across me, letting his full weight crush me to the bed in a way that feels comforting and suffocating all at once. But the gentle rocking begins. Slow at first. Long draws back, until I fear he might slip out and we will have to start the pain all over again. But he knows exactly what he's doing and eases himself back inside before that happens.

I start panting, enjoying all the new sensations. All the pleasure that he gives me. All the pleasure, after all these years, is mine now. All those bad times are wiped away as we join together on this bed.

"Get up on your knees, Molly."

I force myself up onto my hands and then lift my bottom up. His body follows my motions and he wraps his arms around my stomach and breasts, keeping me pressed up against his chest like he owns me. I sit up a little more, bracing my hands on the headboard when he begins to fuck me again. But then he yanks my hair, making my head rest back on his shoulder until I'm looking at the ceiling.

His hand comes up and a soft yellow-orange light radiates out from his palm. It flows up like the heat it emits and bathes me in a glow of passion. An intense vibration runs through my body, and he turns his head just enough to bite my earlobe and whisper, "Shhh. It's just me entering you a different way, Molly. It's just me feeling you. We're connected by pain and pleasure. Every nerve ending in your body is energy that I can capture and experience with you."

"I love it," I gasp. My head is tilted so far back, I'm not able to breathe right, but that's turning me on. He's so in control. I've given myself to him. He owns me, body and soul.

"Now, gun girl, we finally get to fuck like we're gods and goddesses. Like we're princes and princesses. Like we're hero and villain."

"Do it, Alpha. Please," I beg. "Take me."

He does.

He fucks me from behind like that. And his fingers slip around to my pussy and start strumming while his other palm stays on my throat. His heat, his light, his power courses into me, knocks me down, and then sets me back on my feet.

We come together like god and goddess. Prince and princess. Hero and villain. We experience the divine like it was meant to be until he pushes me face first into the bed and comes on my back, his hot semen spilling out until he's exhausted and collapses onto me. He automatically reaches out and wraps me up in his arms like I'm something precious. "You are my beginning," I say.

"And you're my end, Molly. Everything ends with you."

"With us," I say, correcting him.

"With us," he repeats.

"You saved me, Alpha."

"No," he says, kissing me on the neck and biting my earlobe. "I didn't save anyone. You saved yourself. And don't you ever forget that. You're the superhero with all the power and I am nothing without you."

"Get up on your knees, Molly."
I force myself up onto my hands and then lift my bottom up. His body follows my motions and he wraps his arms around my stomach and breasts, keeping me pressed up against his chest like he owns me. I sit up a little more, bracing my hands on the headboard when he begins to fuck me again.
But then he yanks my hair, making my head rest back on his shoulder until I'm looking at the ceiling.

## CHAPTER THIRTY-THREE

I watch her sleep. I watch the way her chest rises and falls and feel her life force in my arms as I hold her tight. It's completeness. It's wholeness. It's a sigh of relief and a relaxation that I can't describe because I have never experienced a moment quite like this one.

After we blew up the Prodigy School Thomas left Case and I on the side of the highway. He went his way and we went ours. It was too dangerous to show up back in Cathedral City together. Thomas was not… part of the system, so to speak. He was part of Prodigy from the time he was born. He didn't have a family like Case and me.

We never saw him again. We talked to him. Emails and phone calls. But that's it. Case and I were picked up by a trucker on the highway when we left. And when we got back to town, we told his parents everything and told the authorities something else. We spun a story that was atrocious and heartbreaking. We are both of those things, so it never felt like a lie.

But everything we've done since then has been a lie.

Molly will find out sooner or later. She knows a little bit about the project, like who she is to me and what I am to her, but she doesn't know any of the *why*. That's what Case and Thomas and I have been hiding. The why.

Oh, she's perceptive. This whole superhero fantasy she has, it's cute. But she has no idea how close she is to the truth. It's just not the truth she imagines in her fantastical delusion of superheroes, justice, and the rule of law.

I look down at her naked body. It's not hot in here, the heat is not on, but I generate a great deal of heat from my hands. They bathe her perfect breasts in a glow of amber yellow and she's sweating slightly from my touch. I lean down and kiss the top of her head, suddenly feeling possessive. She needs to come home with me. I can't imagine not knowing where she is every minute of the day.

*You should be ashamed of yourself, Lincoln.*

I know I should, but I'm not. I want what I want and I have always wanted her. Prodigy did a good job on me, that's for sure. I fell for her. I fell for her soft hazel eyes looking up at me when she was five. That's when they started making her into my killer.

There was a long progression of experimental Alphas before Case and I came along. Decades of research and development. Decades of failures and successes. But no one, until Molly, had ever captured the heart of an Alpha.

Case hated his Omega. Thomas killed all of his—that inhibition shit never worked right on him anyway. That's what makes him our leader. Thomas was a total failure at Prodigy, and if he wasn't so important to the project, they'd have killed him before he turned ten. The inhibitor that prevented Case and I from causing harm to our Omegas never took effect on Thomas. Not in any way that mattered. He could kill indiscriminately and he never even had to be present. He was the first victim of Project Super-Alpha and his biological modifications are significant.

They shut down most of his emotional responses, most of his ability for empathy for example, and just about all of his give-a-fuck gene. That's what I call it anyway.

If he's been following protocol and injecting himself regularly over the years like Case and I have, then he can't kill me. But he'd get damn far in the process if he wanted to. And who knows if he's even been doing it? We haven't seen him. He's been a voice on a phone or words in a text or email.

But Case and I decided if we can't trust him then we might as well give up. We need Thomas to complete this final act of revenge. So we take our chances.

Case and I were less extreme examples of Prodigy's program. We have those same modifications, but at a much more controlled level. Thomas is not capable of caring and I wonder how he'll react to me bringing Molly home.

Because she's definitely coming home with me.

She stirs, as if she can sense that her life is changing as she sleeps. I kiss her head again. Thomas can't take her away this time. I won't allow it.

"Why are you still awake?" she asks, turning her body to face me.

"My hands are glowing. It bothers me."

"So put your gloves back on and go to sleep."

"No," I say, kissing her mouth. "You said you liked to feel my touch and I want to give you everything you want."

She smiles, her eyes still closed. "Hmmm. I love you," she says in a sleepy murmur.

*Hold that thought,* I think to myself. *Hold that thought, gun girl.* Because I'm guaranteed to be one long string of disappointments. And even though I love her more than I love myself, I still have a job to do.

She slips back into her dream world where everything is perfect.

I want her there. That's where she belongs.

But I have work to do. So little by little I inch away and let her go. And an hour later, when she finally rolls over onto her stomach and we break the last of our skin-on-skin contact, I swing my legs over the side of the bed and get dressed.

When I'm done I walk down the stairs and find my gloves on the kitchen table where I left them. I pull them on, dimming the light and feeling relief. I didn't want to show Molly my hands, but it was an act of trust. It helped her believe in me.

I needed that. Tonight of all nights, I needed her to believe in me.

I grab the gun I stuffed under the sofa cushion in Molly's living room and it connects with the magnetic plates in my hands and gives off a single chirp telling me that Sheila is engaged. I slide it into the waistband of my jeans, slightly relieved that she showed up. I don't use it much. I don't have to. I have my own way of killing people. But I like to have it and I like Sheila to be with me.

Sheila wants me to end this madness. She thinks Molly can save me. But she's got it all wrong. Now is the time to step it up and the person being saved will never be me.

I walk out the front door and click the alarm on my car as I cross the street. When I slip inside, the computer comes to life and Sheila says, "Assignment commencing," in what might be a weary voice.

Is that considered a human emotion? Weariness? They left a lot off that list if you ask me.

The car starts up and she pulls out, taking control of the vehicle as we head over to the other side of town where a man is about to get a phone call on his cell. We only have a few more on the list, so it's just about over.

Sheila doesn't want to help me anymore, but I don't care. She can stop if she wants, but that won't stop me. "Better to go down together," she says through the car's sound system.

"You got that right," I say back. And then I take control of the wheel and head over to Atticus Montgomery's house to watch the final act commence from a front-row seat.

GUN GIRL

## CHAPTER THIRTY-FOUR

"Oh, God," I mumble, my eyes refusing to open.

"Don't answer it," Lincoln growls into my neck. "It's bad news."

But I have to answer it. I know from the ringtone it's the station. So I reach over the bed, find my phone in the back pocket of my jeans, and tab the answer button, saying, "Yeah," with my sleepy voice.

"Jesus fuck, Masters!" Chief yells. I have to hold the phone away from my ear, that's how loud he is. "Get your ass into the station. We have crime coming out our ears!"

*Beep, beep, beep.*

I throw the phone down on the floor and it bounces off my pink chenille rug.

"Who was it?" Lincoln asks.

"As if you didn't hear." I chuckle. "But at least it's not a body, so that's good. I gotta go to work."

"Not yet," he says, squeezing my breasts with both hands.

"When did you put your gloves back on?"

"What?" he asks, biting my neck.

"You didn't go to sleep with them on."

"The light distracts me, Molly. I only took them off for you."

"Oh," I say, feeling his hard cock pressing against my back. "You're so sweet."

"So they say," he says, sliding his fingers between my legs.

But I wriggle away from him and swing my feet over the side of the bed. "You can stay here for a while if you want. I'll be gone all day, but if you want to keep sleeping—"

"Sleeping," he says with a laugh. "I'm fucking you in the shower right now. Two birds, Molly. I like to kill two birds with each stone."

"That's morbid."

"They say that too. Sweet and morbid go together like Alpha and Omega."

I let out a soft, "Hmmph," and get up to go start the shower.

Lincoln follows me, groaning about the time. "It's four-fucking-thirty in the morning."

"Criminals don't have bank hours, Lincoln. So neither do cops."

"Fuck them, then." He grabs my shoulders and squeezes past me in the bathroom, then turns the shower on. "They can all wait until we're good and goddamned ready to start this day. Dead people don't care."

"You're terrible."

"You like me that way," he says with a wink. My eyes drift down to his cock as he fists it in his palm, stroking himself to let me know I'm not getting out of this house without a fuck. "Now stop talking and get your naked ass in the shower so I can wash your hair."

Wash my hair. He makes me tingle in the most unexpected ways.

I test the water with my fingertips, but it's already hot, so I step into the shower and he follows, his fist pumping heartily now. I want to suck him off so bad. I want to make him come down my throat.

He clicks his tongue at me, like he's reading my mind, and then he grabs the shampoo, takes a seat on the bench and points to the tile floor. "Kneel, gun girl."

"Bike boy," I say. "Will that be your superhero name?"

"Alpha," he growls back. "If you're going to make me into your hero, it will be Alpha. Everything I do comes back to Alpha."

"I don't like the sound of that," I say, wetting my head and body under the hot water and then kneeling between his legs. But my protest is half-hearted at best, because I can't take my eyes off his rock-hard dick. He squeezes some shampoo onto my head and begins to massage his fingers through my hair.

BIKE BOY

## CHAPTER THIRTY-FIVE

She looks up at me from her submissive position on the floor, my cock pointing at her mouth, and never in all my years did I think I'd have my Omega so ready and willing. My fingertips move softly through her hair, the shampoo smelling of flowers and sweetness. The bubbles froth up and cover her scalp. "Suck me, Molly."

Her mouth opens and I catch a glimpse of her pink tongue. It's the same color as her pussy was under the light of my hands last night. She eases forward, eager, but not rushing it, and then her lips wrap around my shaft and she starts to suck. Her eyes are upturned, trained on mine. And the water from the shower head is hitting her in the back of the neck, spraying water onto her face. I watch it run down her cheeks like tears and have a moment of regret.

This day might not end well, but it's certainly going to start out as perfection.

I continue massaging as her head bobs back and forth. Her tongue flattens out along my shaft and I allow myself a moment of pleasure. No pain this time. Only pleasure. But then my desire overcomes me, and I begin to urge her to take me deeper.

She makes a noise when I hit the back of her throat, but she keeps going.

Fuck.

I take one hand off her head and reach under to grab my balls, forcing them up against her chin. She gags, but I'm getting lost in her. I'm getting swept away by who and what she is, what she means to me, and what we are together. "Molly," I say. "Yes, baby."

She swallows, her throat constricting against my cock, and I let my head fall back against the field wall.

"Mmmmm," she moans.

I want to hold out, I really do. But fuck it. I'm gonna take her pussy next. I need that pussy before this day starts to remind me that my life was not a waste. That I didn't give it to some corporation or waste it on revenge and death.

"Deeper," I moan. "Just a little bit—"

She practically dives into me, the tip of my cock crashing against her palate. She hums and swallows my thick, hard length, and it's over.

I fill her mouth with my come. It spills out of her lips, and just when I think she will pull away and tell me it's over, she sucks hard, her eyes only on me. Her mind only on me.

And then she swallows, over and over, until every drop is gone.

## CHAPTER THIRTY-SIX

I pull away, the water rushing down my face and sweeping his come down my chin with the white frothy bubbles from my hair. I am covered in shampoo and draped in lust. "More," I say. "I want you inside me so bad, Lincoln."

He growls, stands, and pulls me to my feet. "Your wish," he says, but never finishes the statement. Because he reaches around, grabs my ass, and lifts me up, dragging my throbbing pussy along his made-of-steel abs.

"Oh, God," I moan. "I can't take it." I squeeze his hips with my knees, and he hikes me up a little more, the tip of his cock rubbing up against my clit. He's almost hard for me again.

I have never in my life felt so desirable, never felt so complete and never been in so much agony, just wishing to be roughed up and fucked hard.

He slaps my ass, the sound echoing off the bathroom walls. I give a little shriek, but I don't sense that he's hurting from my outburst, so he's reading my pleasure and I'm better able to accept his pain.

He reaches up and twists one of my nipples, but his gloves are still on. "Take those off," I say. And it's not a request. It's a demand. I wait to see what his reaction will be. And for a moment he has a questioning look on his face as he considers my break from submission.

But then he shifts my body and raises his fingers to my mouth. "Bite," he says.

I take the leather between my teeth and find a bit to bite into, then he pulls his hand away, releasing the glove a little. He does it again, and again, until all the fingers are loose. I spit the glove out and then his fingers are inside, pushing on my tongue. I wrap my lips around them, and he begins pumping them in and out. My tongue slides along his fingers like they are an extension of his dick. I can feel his cock growing against my pussy, and I'm so ready. He removes his fingers and reaches around to grab my ass cheek. Shit, I want him in my ass again too. "Just fuck me," I moan.

He leans forward, pressing me against the cold, hard tile, and then he draws back, finds my opening and pushes inside. I grip his shoulders. His muscles bulge, his shoulders so broad and strong. He's a massive force of a man. Everything about him is solid steel.

It's everything. Having him inside me is everything. I hike my knees up and then wrap my legs around his waist as he rocks back and forth. Slow at first. "Too slow," I say. "Fuck me harder. Please," I beg.

He thrusts inside me so fast I gasp, and when I look up at his face, I expect him to be feeling the pain with me. But the only thing I see is desire.

His other hand finds my asshole, like he's reading my mind, and then he's pushing a finger in. I can feel him from both sides. First his cock, then his finger.

"You like it hard, Molly?"

"I like it with you, Lincoln. I like it any way you want to give it to me."

"If I had more hands," he says, "I'd pull your hair while I play with your ass. But I don't, so you're going to have to help me out here." He withdraws his finger and grabs my hair, yanking my head back. "Play with your ass, Molly. I want to feel your fingers against my cock."

I reach under and fulfill his request. He groans and fists my hair, grabbing it right up next to my scalp. Taking me. My eyes shut automatically from the pressure. And then I'm moaning his name. Over and over. "Lincoln, Lincoln…"

"Alpha," he says. "I'm your Alpha. Your beginning."

"And I'm the end," I say, coming all over his dick. "I'm the end of that old life you were leading. We are perfect," I say, as he comes inside me. "Perfect. And we will last forever."

## CHAPTER THIRTY-SEVEN

"Forever is a long time," I say, feeling totally spent and satiated. God, but I wish it could last forever.

"I know," she moans, her legs still gripping my waist like she never wants to let go.

I hold her tight and then swing us around so I can dunk her under the spray of hot water and wash off the shampoo. She reaches up and plays with her hair, getting the last of the soap out. I back up, sit back down on the bench, and keep her in my lap as I reach for the hair conditioner. I squeeze it on her head and then push her face down onto my shoulder. Her soft breath tickles my neck as I massage the slick conditioner into every strand.

"I like taking care of you. I wish I'd been there."

She doesn't answer. She's the one who said we could've made it together. And now she's probably thinking of all the love she missed out on.

"But we can't change things. It was meant to be this way."

"I'm happy now," she says, her eyes closed and her body limp. I grab the soap and start washing her back. "I'm happy with how it ended up."

But she won't be for long. Once she finds out what I did last night.

*Never mind that, Lincoln. One moment at a time.*

I feel like an asshole for making her happy when I know what will happen later. But I can't help it. I deserve a little bit of happiness at the end.

Don't I?

"I don't want to go to work, Lincoln, but I have to."

"I know," I say, lifting her up off my lap and making her stand on her own. I wash her body from top to bottom, lingering on her breasts, tracing the curves of her hips, tugging on her nipples and kissing the frothy bubbles running down her stomach. "But I'm gonna drive you to work today, Molls."

"Molls?"

"What?"

"My brother used to call me that."

"He did?" I ask. *Fucking stupid asshole, Lincoln. You got through all this and you fuck it up with one word.*

"Yeah," she says, a touch of sorrow in her voice. "He died six months ago. I miss him so much."

"I'm sorry," I say. And I am. I'm sorry for so many things.

"It's not your fault," she says, forcing herself to smile though her sadness. "He took so many risks at the end. I begged him not to be so stupid after what happened to our dad."

"I'm sorry," I say again. "Come on, we better get dressed." I don't want to hear about her father or her brother. Not now. Not after we had this perfect morning. "I'll ride with you in your car and Sheila can follow us in mine."

"Sheila drives your car?" Molly laughs, like this is ridiculous.

"There's a lot more to Sheila than you know."

"What is she? I don't get it. I didn't think the technology was there for such an advanced form of artificial intelligence."

"It's not," I say with half a laugh. "To the general public, anyway. But in secret…" I hesitate, wondering if I'm saying too much.

"Yeah," Molly says. "I bet there's so much shit happening in tech research and development that people don't know about. Military stuff, private stuff."

I reach over and turn the water off, then grab a towel from the rack outside the shower and start rubbing her down. "You have no idea."

"What will you do?"

"What?" I ask, looking up at her as I dry her legs in long, slow strokes.

"You explained what you *do*," she says, emphasizing the word. "But not really what you will do with it. All that research and stuff you talked about. What will you do with it, Lincoln?"

"Cure mental illness, remember?" I say, smiling at her.

"Really?" she says, stepping out of the shower and grabbing another towel to wrap up her hair. I watch her ass as I dry myself off and then follow her into the bedroom.

"You'd like that, right? I just want to make you happy."

She shoots me a smile over her shoulder, oblivious to the hidden meaning behind my words. "Super-smart." She laughs. God, I love her laugh. "Super-sexy." She winks at me, glancing down at my junk. "And super-Alpha. And I mean that in more ways than one, Lincoln Wade."

"So do I, Molly. So do I."

She either ignores that remark, or takes it as innocuous. Either way, it buys me more time and lets me drop the conversation and get dressed as I watch her do the same.

"By the way, you lied to me about something."

"What?" My heart races for a moment as I go looking for my missing glove in the bathroom.

"You told me at the dance that you'd make me wear sexy lingerie every night if I was yours. And I'm yours now, right? So where's my sexy shit?"

Jesus. How sweet is she? She's not going to make this easy. "I'm good for it, Molls." I like the nickname and it's out of the bag now, anyway. So I'm going to use it.

"I know," she says, buttoning her blouse and slipping her feet into those cute-as-fuck saddle shoes she likes to wear. "I trust you. Ready?"

I nod and feel a pang of guilt and sadness in my heart. "Yeah, sure. Let's go." We walk outside to her car parked in the driveway and I pull up my Sheila app on my phone and text her to follow us.

"How does that work?" Molly asks, handing me her keys and pointing to my phone as I open the passenger door for her. I love that she already knew I'd want to drive and went to that side automatically.

"She's wired in everywhere," I say, waiting for her to settle, then closing her door and walking around to the other side of the car. I get in and start it up. "Put your belt on, Molly." I point to her seatbelt, but she is busy checking her face in the mirror.

"Bossy," she replies. But she drags the belt over her shoulder, still looking in the mirror. "I look so tired. Good God, I hope my prick of a boss is not in the mood to scream at me today. I can't take it anymore."

"What do you mean?" I ask, backing out of the driveway. I check the rearview to make sure Sheila is following. She doesn't take control of the car much, but I planned for it and the windows are tinted dark enough to avoid any weird looks.

"That guy is such a dick, Lincoln. I swear, he calls me 'honey' and 'sweetheart.' I can't fucking stand him. At least when I was in the military people respected me. This guy treats me like trash."

"Is that right?"

"He's pissed at me for not making more progress with the suicides."

I glance over at her.

"I'm not turning you in."

"Why? It's your job."

"Because if these people are connected to Prodigy, then they need to be stopped. What if there's another school?"

I stare out the window, momentarily stunned silent.

"Lincoln? Have you ever wondered?"

"There's no other school, Molly." I reach over and grab her hand to give it a squeeze. "We took them out and put an end to it."

"But maybe they never gave up? What were they trying to accomplish with that program anyway?"

I don't want to have this conversation with her. Not after last night. Not after her plea for me to be her hero.

"I mean, I get why they'd want to make superhumans, right? And I get that the only way to really do that was with biological and behavior modification. But to what end?"

"That's what we're trying to figure out."

"So you don't know?"

I shake my head.

"Why are you so quiet?"

I let the question hang there. I'm not ready to give this up yet, but I'm not ready to give up what I've been working towards, either.

"Something's wrong, isn't it?"

"No," I say, squeezing her hand again. "There's nothing to worry about. You're the only thing I care about now."

"Well, I'm glad, you know? I'm on your side, Lincoln. And if you felt like these people were a threat, well, I believe you."

"Good." I manage a convincing smile, because she smiles back. She chats about work the rest of the way. What she's willing to lie about, what she thinks she needs to share.

I'm not the least bit worried about getting caught. There is no chance of that at all. Not before it's all over, anyway.

"Park in space thirty-three," Molly says when I pull into the station lot. Sheila is still behind me, and she takes a spot a little further down. "I'll be back in a minute."

"Uh, no," I say.

"What?" she asks as she opens her door and I turn the car off.

"I'm coming with you."

"Lincoln, you can't go in there, that's crazy. You're killing people." She whispers it, even though we are still in the car. "It's my job to arrest you."

"Relax," I say. "They don't know anything. And I just want to see your work. Check it out. Make sure you're safe. That's *my* job."

"It's the police station, Lincoln. It's safe."

"It's a very corrupt police station, Molly. You might've only been here for a couple weeks, but surely a person as in tune with the line between good and evil as you are can see that."

She lets out a long sigh. "Just please, don't make a scene."

"What scene?" I wink at her. She does not think that's funny because her mouth drops open in shock. Like, *Are you kidding me?* "I promise. Pinky swear and all that girly shit."

That makes her shake her head with a smile and she gives in.

When we get inside, she greets a kid behind the desk as he buzzes us through to the interior of the department.

"Are you nervous?" Molly asks, holding on to my arm as we walk in. "You kinda look like you belong in handcuffs."

I chuckle at that. But she's right. I'm wearing my leather with the bright red anarchy patch on the shoulder, faded jeans from yesterday, and a white t-shirt. My hair is still slightly wet from our shower this morning, and my boots are thudding across the polished floor like they are heralding a menace. "No, I'm not nervous. Where's your desk?"

"Over there," she says, pointing to the far side of the room.

"Masters!" a fat man with a wrinkled white shirt and a protruding belly bellows from a fishbowl office. He must be the prick.

"Wait there, OK? I'll be right back."

"Got it," I say, pulling her back for a kiss. She smiles into my mouth and I have to tuck down an urge to smack her ass. Humiliating women is not something I'm into though, so disrespecting her at work is out of the question.

She walks off and enters the fishbowl. Her boss points to me, still only twenty or so feet away, and Molly explains who I am. The boss nods, then pushes a button on the wall that lowers all the shades so I can't watch.

I crack my knuckles, make my way over to the closed

door, and lean against the wall to wait this out.

## CHAPTER THIRTY-EIGHT

"Who the fuck is that guy?" Chief asks me, pointing to Lincoln.

"My boyfriend. He just wanted to see where I work."

"Hmmm," he says, fingering a panel on the wall. The shades begin to lower and I have a moment of panic that I'm in serious trouble. Did he see that anarchy patch on Lincoln's jacket? Does he realize I know more about the suicide cases and I haven't even bothered to write up a report? "Since when do you have a man?"

I grunt out disgust. "What business is that of yours?" I like how I was all paranoid about breaking the law by helping a serial killer one moment, and offended by this misogynist asshole the next. I'm flexible like that.

"No need to get lippy, sweetheart. We had an incident last night."

I glare at him, still pissed off about his question and even more angry about his derogatory term.

"Someone tried to kill Alastair Montgomery around three AM."

"Who?" Jesus, thank God Lincoln was with me all night. I know this one wasn't him.

"His son."

"Atticus? What the hell? Why?"

"Apparently Junior went into his office and shot at him."

"Did he kill him?" I have a wave of panic.

"No, but he tried. Missed, and then security came and took him down. I'm not clear on the rest of the details. They didn't call us, instead Montgomery checked his son into Cathedral City Asylum."

"Why would Alastair do that?" God, just hearing that name gives me the shivers. "That's attempted murder. Atticus needs to be formally charged and booked."

"Apparently Junior has a history of mental illness and this is not the first time it's happened. He's under the treatment of a psychiatrist and he was admitted as an inpatient. Judge Livingston signed off on the order, so we're sitting this one out. But Montgomery senior wants your pretty ass over there ASAP to talk details."

I mull that over for a minute, ignoring the fact that he once again sexually harassed me. "Why would I need to sort out anything? If Livingston signed off, then we're done for now. I should be working on—"

"You should be working on whatever I tell you, Masters. So get out of my office, get in your car, and don't come back until it's sorted. You do whatever Montgomery wants you to do."

"Since when do I work for him? You know, I'm sick and tired of the way this department is all buddy-buddy with Blue Corp. Did it ever occur to you that something strange is going on? I mean, four suicides in less than a month and now Atticus Montgomery, who seemed perfectly lucid the last time I saw him, is locked away in an insane asylum for trying to murder his father? This just doesn't add up. I think you have answers, and I want you to fill me in right now."

"Is that so?" Chief asks, throwing a thick file folder down on his desk with a heavy thump. "Well, maybe you're not cut out for this job, Masters. Maybe you need to find something to do that you're actually good at. I hired you because Blue Corp recommended you. And now you're trying to get all high and mighty and pretend you didn't get this job as a favor to them?"

"What the hell are you talking about? I thought—"

"You thought," he sneers. "You thought what? That you got this job based on merit? No, honey. You're just as guilty of cronyism as the rest of us."

"Crony—I don't even know those people! I just met them. I didn't get this job based on my secret connections with Blue Corp."

"Well," Chief says, laughing to himself as he takes a seat behind his desk, "you're mistaken. They know all about you."

My heart skips a beat. What the fuck does that mean?

"Now get out of here. And you better make old man Montgomery happy when you get up there or he'll cut you loose and you can go on back to your depressing life as the only surviving member of the Masters family. Motorcycle tricks." Chief laughs. "What a fucking joke. No wonder they're all dead. Bunch of loser—"

Before I even know what I'm doing, I'm on his desk grabbing his collar and pulling him over the top. He looks up at me with surprised eyes, but before he can get another word out or even yell for help, I've slapped him across the face.

"I can fight like a girl if you want, Chief. But I'm warning you, this girl fights dirty." I push him back and then step away. "I told you not to talk to me that way. And if you do it again, I'll show you just what those bunch of losers taught me to do all growing up." I glare at him as he straightens his shirt, which came untucked during the scuffle. "And as far as Blue Corp goes, the first three deaths were declared suicides by the coroner yesterday, and I'm expecting the fourth to be as well. If

Alastair Montgomery wants to file a report, he can put his nasty ass in a car and come down here to do it himself."

I fold my arms across my chest and wait for his bellow, but he's eerily calm.

"You're gonna regret that."

"So fire me," I challenge him back.

But he stays silent. So I take that as my cue to leave. I walk towards the door and just when I reach for the handle, Chief says, "You don't want to fuck with the Blue Boar."

Blue Boar. They call these corporate guys swine around here. A rip-off of the word pig used for dirty cops. I guess Montgomery's blue blood goes with the nickname. "Well, whenever that Blue Boar is ready, he knows where to find me. I don't need to be told how to investigate and if you think I'm going to let you push me around, just be warned, I push back. I've been documenting your insults and I will sue this department like a motherfucker if you make things difficult for me."

I pull the door open, walk out, and slam it closed behind me.

The whole precinct turns to look at me, and then I spy Lincoln leaning up against the wall near the exit. He starts walking towards me looking like he's as eager to get out of here as I am.

"Everything OK?" he asks.

"Yeah, sure," I say, taking a moment to straighten my shirt. "Nothing I can't handle. But I'm real busy, Lincoln. Lots of stuff going on today."

"Meet me for dinner?" he asks.

"I can do that. Where at?"

"I gotta be in town tonight, so how about I pick you up at eight?"

"Sounds perfect," I say, grabbing him by the shoulders and standing on my toes to give him a kiss. We walk towards the door, but he stops. "I'm gonna take a piss real fast." He leans in to kiss me again and then turns, saying, "See you at eight."

I walk off towards my desk, looking over my shoulder to wave as Lincoln watches me go.

Funny how quickly life changes.

## CHAPTER THIRTY-NINE

Molly walks away before I slip down the hallway and walk quickly to the chief's office.

I don't knock.

"What the fuck—"

"I'm gonna need you to shut up, sit your ass down, and have a very short one-way conversation with me."

"Who the hell do you think you are?"

"Not Batman," I answer in the voice I usually reserve for murdering. "I'm told we have a lot in common, but he's way too nice."

"Get the fuck out of my office before I lock your ass up and throw you away for life."

I grab him by the throat and push him against the wall, making all the picture frames of his tired-looking wife and his six kids sway like they're about to crash to the floor. "I'm afraid you're mistaking Detective Molly Masters for the whores you pick up in front of Cathedral Seven in the Merchant District."

"What?" he gasps though the tight choke I have on his throat. But I see the recognition there.

"Your dirty department might have a hold on most of this city, but I own the Merchant District. I've seen you. I have you on so many security cameras, I could've taken you down a hundred times over. But I didn't. Because I need a dumbshit like you in control for now."

"What—" he gasps again. This time his hands come up and try to pry my fingers from his windpipe.

"In fifteen seconds you're going to lose consciousness. And If I were you, I'd stop struggling so we can get this over with in one take, understand?"

He lowers his hands and nods, so I ease up enough to let him draw in one tiny breath. "You're not in charge here anymore, I am. And you're never gonna talk to Molly Masters like that again. In fact, if I hear you call one woman 'sweetheart' or 'honey' who is not that saint of a woman hanging on your wall above your head, then I'm gonna come back for you. I'm gonna parade your lewd acts on every TV in this city, and I'm going to ruin your life."

I let go and his hands go to his throat again as he wheezes in air as fast as he can gulp it down. There's a bright red mark on his neck, and it's not from the squeezing. He doesn't feel it yet, but he will. Because the anger in my head comes out as red heat in my hands, even through the gloves. His neck will blister in a matter of minutes.

I don't like leaving too many calling cards, and this one is risky. But he needs to know what he's dealing with. "I'd think long and hard about what I just said, Chief. And if I were you, I'd be on that phone with your real boss, and I'd warn them there's a shitstorm coming."

I turn and walk away. I'm just reaching for the door when he asks the only question left to ask.

"Who *are* you?"

I pause, picturing Molly that first day in my cave. And then I look over my shoulder and say, "I'm Alpha. And you can tell that Blue Boar fuck down at Blue Corp that I'm back and he's next."

## CHAPTER FORTY

I pull into the cave with a wave of dread. I heard the chatter in the department about Atticus missing the shot. Montgomery senior wasn't killed last night and I'm fuming from the fuckup. That motherfucker was supposed to be dead. Why isn't he dead?

I throw the car into park and get out, my boots thudding across the concrete floors as I make my way to the wall of monitors. I scan each one, but it's useless. There is no mention of Atticus or his father.

"What the fuck happened last night?" I turn to Sheila, who is hovering in the middle of the room looking like she's in the middle of a shrug.

"Everything was going according to plan. Atticus got out of the car, I tracked him inside Blue Corp, everything looked fine. He went behind the closed-circuit cameras where I have no access so I assumed—"

Her words are cut off by my phone. I take it out, recognizing Case's tone, and say, "Yeah."

"What the fuck, dude?"

"I don't know, man, he missed or something."

"Missed? How the fuck can he miss? If he was in the office like we planned it, then that bastard was less than twenty feet away. No way Atticus missed that fucking shot. And the goddamned Blue Boar just did an interview for Channel Three, *Wolves of Wall Street*. He looks pretty fucking alive to me. Thomas is gonna be here in thirty minutes and he's gonna want answers."

"I just got home, Case. I don't have answers. I'm still trying to figure it out. I watched Atticus walk into the Blue Castle last night. He was primed and ready. He should've fucking pulled that trigger."

"Did you ask Molly about it?"

"Why the fuck would I ask Molly? We agreed that she wouldn't be involved."

"Things change, Lincoln."

"Well, I'm not asking her. She's the lead detective on this case and she already knows too much."

"I disagree," Case says. "I don't think she knows nearly enough."

"Do not threaten me, Case."

"Threaten? Get a hold of yourself, asshole. This is the endgame and you just fucked it up. The Old Man is still alive. You need to get your ass here and explain this shit to Thomas. Because I'm not gonna take the brunt of the temper tantrum Thomas is gonna throw once he finds out the Blue Boar is still in the game."

I get the three beeps that signal the call has ended. "Fuck!" I yell.

"I think you need weapons, Lincoln."

"What?" I turn to Sheila, who is still standing in the middle of the room. "I have my gun, Sheila."

But her lightshow body shakes its head. "More than that."

"What do you know?"

"Atticus Montgomery was taken to the Cathedral City Asylum early this morning. He's been admitted as an inpatient for attempted murder."

"So he *did* fuck it up?" I growl.

"Possibly. I'm getting mixed signals from the intake surveillance over at the asylum. And the private room cameras are on a closed circuit. I won't be able to directly access him until he wanders into view of an exterior one."

"Shit." I look at her for a few moments, running all this shit through my mind. "What do you think happened?"

"I don't know. If I had access to the top floor of Blue Corp, I'd know. But I don't, so we're in the dark until Atticus Montgomery lets something slip."

"Fuck. Well, I gotta go into town and talk to Thomas. He's not gonna be happy. We have a deadline of Friday for the news conference. I'm taking the bike to avoid traffic. Keep me posted."

I don't wait for an answer, just hop on the bike—now repaired, thanks to Sheila's little bot army—and kick the starter. It growls to life and I take off down the tunnel, the gate lifting at just the right moment to let me pass through without stopping.

I was smart to take the bike because thirty minutes later when I finally make it into town, it's the lunch rush hour and I have to weave in and out between cars the whole way into the Merchant District. I park the bike in front of M-Street Bar and the door is opening before I even get within ten feet of it.

"Hey, Lincoln."

I nod to the doorman, but my eyes are on Thomas and Case, both of whom are sitting at the bar drinking. They turn simultaneously as they register my voice and then Thomas turns away as Case says, "Finally."

I take a seat on the other side of Case, not that Thomas scares me or anything. I just don't feel like being too close to him right now.

"You wanna explain this monumental fuckup, Lincoln?" Thomas says, his words coming out as a low growl.

"What do you want me to say? Atticus didn't follow through."

"Why?" Thomas sneers. "Why the fuck didn't it work?"

"I don't know, asshole. I'm not the boss of him."

Case rolls his eyes. "Lincoln, stop, OK? Just think, man. What happened last night?"

"I watched him go in the building."

"We know he was in the building, Lincoln," Thomas says, his voice way too calm for my comfort level. "What we don't know is why he's at the fucking Cathedral City Asylum on a judge-ordered psychiatric hold. Now how the fuck are we supposed to complete this job when he's locked up?"

"We have to assume the worst," Case says. "We have to assume the Old Man is on to us."

"Sheila's inside. She can get info from the system connected to the internet. But the interior cameras are on a closed circuit. She can't access them."

"So we just have to wait," Case says. "We just need to sit tight and be patient until she finds something useful."

Thomas gets up, gulps the whiskey sitting in front of his stool, then slams the glass down on the bar top so hard, it shatters. "So our whole plan, the one we've been discussing for fifteen fucking years, hinges on that sorry motherfucker in the psych ward?"

We don't answer him, and he doesn't wait. Just grabs his coat and walks out, slamming the door behind him, because the doorman has made himself scarce.

Case lets off a long breath of air. "He's pissed."

"Yup," I say, catching the whiskey that Mac slides down the bar to me and taking my own gulp. "But we're stuck until someone makes a move."

"We're going down, man."

"We're not going down, Case. Jesus, you two are pansies. We've got this. We've got Sheila, we've got me, and we've got Molly."

"You told her?"

"No." I laugh. "But she's not stupid. And she's covering for me. She knows about the others and she didn't report me. In fact, I spent the night with her." I get a little lost in that thought.

"You better be careful, man. Because once she figures this all out, she's not gonna like you very much."

"That remains to be seen," I say back. "I can handle Molly."

"You don't even know her, dude."

"Better than you do," I say, turning my head slowly to eye Case. "So just stay the fuck out of it. We've got a good plan, every player is in place, and no matter what, this shit is happening. It might not happen by the book, but in a few days this whole town will be upside down. Thomas will get what he wants and I'm gonna get what I want too."

Case is silent for a few seconds. And then he picks up his glass of whiskey. "Whatever you say, asshole. Whatever you say."

I squint my eyes at Case for a moment, but he just downs his drink and then gets up, walks over to the jukebox, and presses the buttons for Social Distortion. The melancholy rockabilly fills the bar at high volume, drowning out everything but the obvious.

We've all lost a lot playing this game, but if everything goes right Thomas will have more than he ever dreamed of in a few days. And I've got Molly back. That's a huge win for me.

Case? He's got nothing so far, and nothing coming either.

He's not quite along for the ride, but Case was never out for revenge. He's just in on principle. He needs to know why. But the thing is, the why for Case is not the same as it is for Thomas and me. We know why we're in this fucked-up situation. Case doesn't. His parents refused to talk about it. They gave him an ultimatum—they would tell him all the things he wanted to know, or they'd let me stay with him after they released us from the psych center.

He chose me over answers. And it's always pissed me off that his parents knew exactly which buttons to punch on their only son. Because we all know Case ended up in Prodigy because his parents owed those fuckers something.

"It's gonna work," I yell, my shout competing with the music. But Case either doesn't hear me or refuses to. He's already playing an old standup arcade game in the corner as he pushes down the past and goes into his virtuality.

GUN GIRL

## CHAPTER FORTY-ONE

I sit at my desk and stare at my computer, looking over all my grunt work relating to the Blue Corp case. But I can't sign off on anything because it still doesn't make sense. Given the fact that I know Lincoln was influencing these scientists to kill themselves using some biotech mumbo-jumbo that he does down in that cave of his, why would Atticus go insane and try to shoot his father?

Did Lincoln get to him too?

It bothers me. Like, a lot. Lincoln was with me last night so he couldn't have had anything to do with Atticus.

*Don't be stupid, Molly. If the man wanted to slip out of your house and go kill someone, he would. He did after the cathedral party.*

Right. Back to being bothered.

It also bothers me to think of Atticus being involved. Because he's about the same age as Lincoln and his friends, so how could he possibly be one of those scientists? No, that makes no sense. But he has to be connected in some other way. Maybe he was at the school too?

My heart thumps wildly at that thought. Shit, what if Atticus recognized me? Maybe that's why he was so nice when I came to visit?

But how is the Old Man connected? Is Lincoln trying to say that he was the one responsible for the Prodigy School? For what happened to us?

I think back to my meeting with Montgomery senior and look for some kind of flash of recognition, but there's nothing there. Of course, I don't remember anything about Prodigy School except for a handful of painful sessions with Lincoln.

I sit and stew on that. And even though all last night I declared my love for my long-lost Alpha, in the light of day and sitting in a police station as the detective in charge, everything looks different.

I'm not ready to give up on him, or turn him in, for fuck's sake. But I don't want to be lied to, even if his lying is by omission. I'm a part of this. I share his past. I share his pain, and betrayal, and anger.

Maybe not the anger. I do hate the fact that I came out of that school, but I'm a well-adjusted adult now, and that was fifteen years ago. Many of those years were filled with fun, and love, and family.

I sigh as my thoughts circle back to my mother at the asylum. I really should go see her. What kind of daughter am I? She took me in when I needed someone and I turned my back on her when she probably needed me most.

I mean, she did go crazy. She *is* crazy. But she helped me in my most desperate moment. She took in a kid who should've been handed over to social services.

Still… I deserve to know the truth.

If I go see her then I could try to slip in and see Atticus. I could get his version of events last night. It's possible his father is lying about what happened. And if Lincoln was involved then I need to know. What if he's in danger? Alastair Montgomery doesn't look like a man people cross. He looks like a man who gets his way no matter what.

What if Montgomery senior is lying about Atticus? What if Atticus stumbled onto more clues? He was keeping clues from his father. Why?

Jesus, I'm such a stupid detective. If I wasn't dealing with the return of Lincoln I'd have asked that question days ago.

When I look up at the clock it's afternoon already. I've been sitting here for hours paralyzed with indecision.

I'm going to talk to Alastair Montgomery. I haven't interviewed him yet and the chief's accusation has really raised my hackles.

I stand up and shrug on my coat, glancing up at the chief's office for a moment. His blinds are back up and he's staring at me. He's probably pissed off. I take a little satisfaction in that and give him a snide smile and a wave as I make my way out of the office.

He picks his phone and starts tabbing the screen, then lifts it to his ear to talk.

His eyes never leave mine.

I shake off a shudder that runs up my spine and tip my head up a little higher.

He can't intimidate me. I know he's dirty, and he knows I know. So he can go fuck himself. I'm gonna get the truth even if I do get fired over it.


The light drizzle that started earlier has stopped by the time I get over to Blue Corp, leaving the streets shiny and slick. I slow for the guard but the gate lifts before I even get close enough to see who is inside. Hmmm, I'm not sure I like being so recognizable.

When I pull into the parking spot with my name on it, the depth of the chief's accusations hit me for real. Am I working for Blue Corp? It certainly seems so.

I shut the car off and sit there for a moment, trying to put all the pieces together. Why would Blue Corp be so interested in me? Lincoln thinks they have something to do with Prodigy School, but he's never explained the connection beyond the scientists working here. Is it a coincidence? Might be. Might not.

I open my door and get out, smiling briefly at a streak of sunshine that makes its way through the heavily clouded sky. The front doors of the Blue Castle open for me and I'm just heading over to the receptionists to ask for an appointment with the Old Man when he steps out of the elevator. I stop in my tracks because his focus is definitely on me.

"Miss Masters," he says, a creepy smile on his face. "I thought you might drop by."

He extends his hand, but I just stare at it for a second. A wave of revulsion invades my stomach and I know if I touch that hand, I will be sick.

*What the hell?* that cautious voice inside me says.

I cover for my reluctance to shake hands with him by getting out my tablet and pretending not to see the offer. "Why's that?" I ask, feigning ignorance. I bet the reason he was expecting me is because he's who the chief called as I was leaving. Something is very wrong here. I feel like I'm walking into a trap. "I just have some questions about Atticus," I say, swiping my fingers on my tablet to try to appear unaffected. I collect myself, and then I look up and meet that hard gaze. "I'm just curious why you didn't call us and report this crime? Why the psychiatric incarceration?"

"Detective," the Old Man says with a sickening smile that makes me want to step back. "Atticus isn't well. He hasn't been well since the first time he tried to take his own life when he was a teenager. I thought he was in recovery, but he's relapsed. His violent tendencies are back and I've taken every precaution to protect society from his instability. So I'm sorry if you feel left out, but the judge made the right decision. Atticus is a danger to himself and others, and he needs serious professional help. He's getting that today."

"Well…" I clear my throat and take in a steadying breath. "Well, he was fine the last time I talked to him. And that was Friday night at the party. We talked extensively."

The Old Man tilts his head like I might've said something interesting. "Did you? What, might I ask, was the topic of discussion?"

Shit. "We were just discussing the suicides. He was completely lucid and in control at that time. So what happened over the weekend? Why this sudden burst of violence?"

"What makes you think it was sudden? He's been violent his whole life. And did it ever occur to you that he was so interested in those suicides because he's tried to take his own life before?"

"No," I say, caught off guard with that statement. "I saw all those pictures in his office. He just doesn't seem like the violent type. He was an outdoorsman. He surfed giant waves, climbed mountain cliffs, and sailed around the world."

"You just made my point for me. I've read a lot of studies that claim extreme risk-takers like my son participate in such behavior to challenge death. You might even call it a death wish. I'm sure you're familiar with that phrase?"

I'm taken aback at his thinly veiled reference to my family. "He seemed perfectly well-adjusted, Mr. Montgomery. That's all I'm saying. I'm just trying to get to the bottom of the issues you've been having with your employees. And I checked. Atticus has no criminal record. So if he has been behaving this way, then you've never reported it."

"I know, Detective. I realize I've been doing him no favors by hiding his unpredictable and violent behavior, but make no mistake, he's being dealt with now. I've got the best psychiatrists with him at the Cathedral City Asylum. He'll get the highest level of care until he's well enough to come home."

I let out a small sigh. "I'd like to go talk to him."

"That won't be possible. His doctors have asked that all contact with the outside world be limited to immediate family." Montgomery stops here to laugh and I get that creepy feeling again.

I've had enough. "Thank you for your time," I say, backing away.

"Do you think it runs in the family?" he asks, just as I'm ready to bolt out the door.

"What?" I say, my heart suddenly beating fast.

"Insanity. Do you think insanity runs in the family? Do you think I have it? That I gave it to him?"

"Um…" Holy fuck, I need to get out of here. But Montgomery starts walking towards me, even as I back away.

"Maybe all my children have it?" he adds. "Maybe they get it from me?"

I'm still backing away slowly when I stumble over the mats in front of the doors and he reaches out to steady me. His hand comes into contact with mine. It is cold, just like him, and I pull away so fast, I trip again.

"Do I frighten you, Molly?"

"What?" I look over at the receptionists, but all six of them are looking down at the desk, their lips busily moving as they talk to people on the phone through their headsets.

"They say that the apple doesn't fall far from the tree. Insanity tends to run in families."

Jesus Christ, I don't blame Atticus for trying to kill him. Old Man Montgomery has an ice factor that's off the fucking charts. "I gotta go," I say, turning and bursting through the outer doors. The sunlight that was peeking through the clouds is gone now, but when I get in my car and look up at the building, I see it has just changed positions. It illuminates the tip of the Blue spire like a spotlight.

I take that as a good omen, something uplifting, as I start my engine and put the car in reverse. But then my eyes wander to the front doors of the Blue Castle and I see the Old Man staring back at me from the other side of the bulletproof glass.

"Uhhhhhh." I shiver. That man is so creepy.

I pull away feeling dirty and wishing I'd never come out here. I'm almost shaking off that feeling when I get to the other side of town and spy the asylum off in the distance. It looks like it belongs in Cathedral City with its gothic architecture and gloomy, black-stained bricks. There's even an archway you have to pass through to get to the visitor's parking lot, and there's not a single break in the clouds to allow a stray sunbeam.

The place has hopeless gloom written all over it.

I park my car and walk into the building. I was here once several years back, but I never went farther than the front lobby. My mother was 'having a bad day,' they said, and couldn't see visitors. It was the day before I left Wolf Valley for basic training, so I never got the chance to come back.

Not that that's an excuse. I had plenty of opportunities to come visit before then, I just chose not to.

"Can I help you?" the receptionist says from behind a glass window. I hate people behind glass windows.

"I'm here to see Martha Masters."

"And you are?"

"Her daughter."

"Huh," the woman says, typing on her keyboard. "I never knew she had a daughter. She only ever gets one visitor."

"Oh," I say, surprised. "Who?"

"Mr. Montgomery."

I'm too stunned to say anything. *That old creep has been coming to see my mother?*

"It's sad that he's in here now."

"What?" I say, realizing she means Atticus and not the Old Man. But she doesn't hear me because she's walking away to grab a visitor's badge. She prints out a card with my name on it, slips it into the clear plastic holder with a clip, and passes it through the hole in the glass. "Put that on and have a seat. Someone will come get you when she's ready."

I take the name tag and walk off to molded plastic chairs lined up in rows in front of a TV. I feel more like an inmate than a visitor as I force myself to sit and stare at the sitcom playing on the television.

There's only a few people here, and no one is talking. So I get to sit there and stew in my questions. Why the hell has Atticus been coming here to see my mother? And what does that have to do with him being in here now?

I know there's a connection, but I feel like everything about this day is hidden in some double meaning. Chief's comment about Blue Corp wanting him to hire me. The Old Man's comment about insanity. Does he know Atticus comes to see her? Was that comment about insanity directed at me? Or Atticus?

"Miss Masters?" a woman calls from a door.

I get up and walk over to the door. "That's me," I say.

"Right this way," the older woman says. She's wearing a white nurse's uniform. Sorta old-fashioned, since most doctors and nurses wear those colorful scrubs these days. It adds to the horror vibe this gloomy institution already has going for it. "Right this way. She's waiting for you in the common room. But I have to warn you, Miss Masters, she hasn't been communicative for years. I'm not sure if you know that, since you never come to visit."

*Geez. Way to lay on the guilt trip, lady.* I ignore her dig and just follow silently behind her as we make our way through the dingy hallway until I find myself in a large open room filled with psychiatric inmates. Everyone is wearing a bathrobe and most of them are parked in wheelchairs in front of the small television screen mounted high up in one corner of a room. They look drugged out of their minds.

"Here she is," the nurse says brightly as she pats my mother on the shoulder. "Martha? Your daughter's come to see you. Can you turn to say hi?"

My mother is... no one I recognize. Her hair is so gray, it's almost white. Her body is thin and frail, and her bathrobe is a dirty light blue.

I lean down to see her face. "Mom?"

"She doesn't talk, Miss Masters. She won't recognize you, either. I'm not sure why you came today, but it's too late."

My face crumples into sadness. "Thank you," I force myself to say back. "But I'd like some time alone with her."

The nurse lifts her chin up and walks off, peeved at me for being a bad daughter. I can see her point, but she has no idea why I've stayed away.

I take a seat next to my mother and let out a deep sigh. I'm glad she's not communicative. Because this will be a lot easier if she doesn't talk back.

"I'm sorry," I say first. "I'm truly sorry this is how it ended up. But you killed my father and I will never forgive you for that. I will never forgive you for going crazy and ruining our family. Will got into racing, did you know that? Do you even know he's dead?"

She does not even blink. I lean over to look into her gray eyes and wonder just what is going on in that mind. Anything?

"You told Dad to do that trick. You said we needed the money to pay a debt. You told him he was the invincible Crazy Bill who could do anything. You said he could pull it off and he believed you. But you were wrong."

Laughter from the TV show bursts through the room, and I look up at it briefly, all the years of anger and sadness washing over me.

"It's not her fault," a voice says from behind me.

I whirl around to find Atticus, dressed in the same light blue robe, albeit a much cleaner version.

"What are you doing?" I ask. "Why were you coming to see her?"

"It wasn't her fault, Molly. My father made her do those things. And I come to see her because she's my mother."

"Mr. Montgomery?" a nurse calls from the desk. "Mr. Montgomery! You're not supposed—"

"The Old Man is the one responsible, Molly," Atticus whispers. His eyes are blazing with fear. "But I won't let him get her again. I'm here now, and I won't let him. So go. Get out before he comes to get you too and you never leave here again. I'll take care of this."

"Wait, you're saying—"

"He's your father too, Molly."

A burly security guard grabs Atticus by the shoulder and twirls him around. "You have a talent for escape, friend." He laughs. "Well, that won't get you far here, Blue Boy. We like our inmates to play by the rules."

"Inmates?" I ask, flashing my badge. "Is that what you call your patients? I want my mother released immediately. I'm taking her home."

"I'm afraid that's not possible, Miss Masters," the nurse who walked me in says as she walks up to us. "I just got off the phone with Mr. Montgomery and he's asked for you to be escorted off the premises."

"I don't give a shit what that creep says. I'm her daughter and I say she's leaving here with me."

"Mr. Montgomery is her husband, Miss Masters. They've been married for thirty-one years. He's her next of kin and legal guardian."

"Thirty..." But my words drop off. What the fuck...

"Get out of here, Molly. Now," Atticus yells as another security guard grabs him. They drag him way, but he screams it over and over. "Get out of here!"

## CHAPTER FORTY-TWO

"Yes," I say, answering Sheila's call through my phone. Case is still playing his game in the corner. The sound effects are about to drive me insane and if I have to listen to one more Social Distortion song on the fucking jukebox, I might kill someone.

"We have a problem."

"Hold on. Case!" I yell. And then I turn to Mac who is washing dishes nearby. "Turn that shit off. Case! Come here and listen, Sheila's on the phone."

Normally I'd just have her tell me, but I need to snap Case out of this shit. He can't dwell. It's not good. The past can't be undone. All we can do is move forward.

Case pounds his fist on the arcade game glass as a sound announces the death of a pixelated life, then turns towards me. "What?"

I put the phone on the bar and press speaker. "Go ahead, Sheila."

"Molly went to the asylum."

"What?" Case and I both say together.

"Why the fuck would she go there? After all these years?" I ask.

"I tracked her car to Blue Corp first. I can only assume the Old Man gave her something to think about. She entered the parking lot of the asylum fifty-three minutes ago."

"Is she still there?" Case asks.

"No, she just got back in her vehicle. But she hasn't started up the car yet. She's just sitting there."

"He told her."

"You don't know that," Case says.

"Please, Case. No visits in all these years and then today of all days, she gets an urge to talk to her mother? Do you have a visual on Atticus yet, Sheila?"

"No. Closed-circuit cameras behind the doors. He needs to get himself in front of one that's connected to the internet. She's still sitting in her car. It's possible Atticus said something he shouldn't have."

"Fuck."

"Call her," Case says.

"And say what?" I throw up my hands. "'Sorry, your life is a lie and everyone knows about it but you?'"

Case shrugs. "I don't know. But if the girl I loved just learned the truth about her life, I'd call her and tell her every sweet thing I could think of to make her smile." He turns away from me and goes back to his game.

"Keep an eye on her, Sheila. This whole day feels wrong. Everything is off."

"You need to call her. She's just sitting in her car. At the very least you should get her home and away from that creepy building. I'll call Thomas and fill him in."

The line goes dead and I let out a long sigh. Everything since I left Molly has gone wrong today.

The sound effects from the arcade game come back to life just as the jukebox starts up again. I pick up my phone, get up, and walk outside. I can't take that noise anymore.

I lean against the building, my head bowed, just thinking about Molly. It is highly probable Atticus started talking in there. I should at least call her to see how much she knows. Maybe he told her something useful?

I tab her contact on my phone and listen to it ring. I'm just about to hang up after the fourth ring when she answers.

"Hello?" It comes off sad and lonely.

"Hey, gun girl," I say, smiling as the words come out.

"Hey, Lincoln."

"You OK?"

"Um," she says, hesitating.

"I was just thinking about you. Wanted to check and see how your day is going."

"Well…" She stops again.

Yeah, Atticus definitely told her something. "You want to know what I was thinking?"

I get nothing but some little breaths. My phone buzzes once, signaling an incoming video from Sheila, and when I tab it open, I can see Molly in her work car from the camera mounted on the rear-view. She's crying. Tears are streaming down her face. "Molly?" I ask.

"Sorry," she says, holding the phone away from her, so she can take a deep gasping breath and not let me hear it. She wipes her face with the back of her hand and I'm suddenly transported back in time. Back when she was so small, she barely came up to my waist.

She was five and I was twelve and we had just met for the first time. I knew what an Omega was. Thomas had gone through a few of them by that time. And Case had his too. But I was the last of us boys to get one.

I walked to the conditioning room angry as fuck. I was ready to pound my Omega to death, just like Thomas had. I vowed I'd never let anyone have that kind of control over me. Ever.

I was seething with rage when I entered that room. One second I was ready to explode with anger and then…

"The first time I saw you, you were standing over by a window. You had on an orange dress. It was solid orange at the top, but the skirt part was little orange flowers. And it hung all the way down to the ground."

"What?" Molly asks on the other end of the phone.

"And your hair was more blonde back then. It was long, the tips almost reached your waist. And you were so fucking small, Molly."

She sniffles into the phone. "I remember you too. I was scared."

"I was angry."

"I thought you'd kill me. They said you'd try."

Jesus. They told her that? "Thomas told me I'd only have one chance to stop the Omega bond and it was at the first meeting. So I *was* going to kill you. But you know what?"

"What?" she asks back in a whisper.

"You turned away from the window and the light, Molly, the light from the sunset you were looking at, it followed you. That's what I thought anyway. One moment your back was to me and your body was outlined by the orange glow over the mountains, and then you turned. And you were the light. It came *from* you, Molly."

"He never even gave me a name, Lincoln."

Fuck. Atticus did tell her. And those few words say everything. Those few words are a list of all the truths she never wanted to know. They say, *He never loved me.* They say, *I was nothing but a lab rat.* They say, *What did I ever do to him?*

"I gave you a name, Molls. I gave you a name. Do you remember what you said to me when you turned around and became my light?"

She nods on the screen, but she is crying again.

"I walked towards you, and you said—"

"'I'm yours,'" she blurts through a sob.

"And then I said—"

"'You're mine.'" She starts crying hard. The tears are streaming down her face and she's covering her mouth, trying her best to stifle her sadness.

"I meant it," I say.

"Me too," she says back.

"You don't need him."

"I know. But it would've been nice to have the one thing most kids are guaranteed at birth."

"Yeah," I say. "I know. But we're even luckier than those kids. Because we've got each other."

She cries again and I let her. I just say, "Shhhh, Molly. Shhh, we're fine. We're fine," over and over again.

After a few minutes she calms down and then she closes her eyes and rests her head back. "Do you still want to have dinner with me tonight?"

"It's the only part of my day that matters."

She opens her eyes and starts her car. "I'm going home."

"I'm going to pick you up in an hour. Don't dress fancy. No costumes tonight."

"I don't want to be a detective anymore, Lincoln. I don't want to solve puzzles anymore."

"You don't have to be anything but mine, gun girl."

"Will you stay on the phone with me as I drive?"

"I'm not going anywhere. You're stuck with me forever, remember? Equal and opposite in every way."

"That's the way we like it, right?"

"I wouldn't have it any other way, Molly. I'd rather die than take away the power you have over me. We only exist as a pair."

We're mostly silent as she drives home. Sheila splits my screen in half and shows me her progress on the tracking app and when Molly pulls into her driveway, I feel total relief wash over me. "Go inside and look around. I need to know you're home safe before I can hang up."

"OK." She sniffs, shutting her car off. I lose the video feed after that, but I can hear her walking up to her house and the jingling of keys as she unlocks her door.

"What the—" she gasps.

I just smile.

"What did you do, bike boy?"

Her laugh makes my heart swell. "Not enough, Molly. Not nearly enough."

"How many bags?" she asks.

Paper rustles. I picture her living room the way I left it a few hours ago. Thirty pink bags with glittery tissue paper sticking out of them, lined up on any empty spot I could find. "Only thirty. I owe you three hundred and thirty-five more. One for each night we go to bed for a year."

She starts laughing. "Oh, my God! What the—"

"I told you, gun girl, if you were mine, I'd dress you up in pretty lingerie every night. You're mine, Molly. And every night, when you lay your head on the pillow next to me, you will remember that."

"I could never forget, Lincoln."

"No," I say. "Because I won't let you."

"I love you."

"I started loving you the moment you lit up my life, Molly. Now open up all the presents and I'll see you in an hour."

We hang up after that and I'm just about to go back inside when Thomas pulls up in a limo. He doesn't even wait for the driver to open his door, just gets out himself, glances over at me, points to M-Street Bar, and then disappears inside.

One hour. I meant it. And if Thomas has other plans, he can fuck off.

I'm thinking about getting out of the supervillain business.

The first time I saw you, you were standing over by a window.
You had on an orange dress. It was solid orange at the top, but
the skirt part was little orange flowers. And it hung all the way
down to the ground."

"What?" Molly asks on the other end of the phone.

"And your hair was more blonde back then. It was long, the tips
almost reached your waist. And you were so fucking small, Molly."

She sniffles into the phone. "I remember you too. I was scared."

"I was angry."

"I thought you'd kill me. They said you'd try."

Jesus. They told her that? Thomas told me I'd only have one
chance to stop the Omega bond and it was at the first meeting. So
I was going to kill you. But you know what?"

"What?" she asks back in a whisper.

"You turned away from the window and the light, Molly, the light
from the sunset you were looking at, it followed you. That's what I
thought anyway. One moment your back was to me and your body
was outlined by the orange glow over the mountains, and then you
turned. And you were the light. It came from you, Molly."

## CHAPTER FORTY-THREE

I open each package and take out the presents Lincoln left me, draping them over anything I can find. My living room looks like a boudoir exploded. There is every kind of lingerie in every kind of color. There's sexy, there's sweet, there's long socks and t-shirts, and shorts, and thongs. He's got every sort of silky fabric represented here, and it seems like a dream come true when I picture myself putting on these beautiful pieces.

I know I need to tear myself away and freshen up for our date, but before I do that, I just want to choose one ensemble to wear for him tonight. I look them all over, picking up the little details of each outfit. Which one would Lincoln like the most?

I finally settle on a black leather bustier, black leather hot pants, fishnet stockings, and black garters.

It's ridiculous, I know. But he's Bike Boy and I'm Gun Girl, and together we say badass motherfuckers. Silver-studded black leather skimpies are what badass motherfucking guys buy their badass motherfucking chicks to wear to bed.

I lay it all out on the bed and my heart beats faster at the idea of dressing in this for him. Maybe he'll watch me? Maybe he'll watch me take it off too?

OK. I laugh. Gotta get dressed. I wash my face and brush my hair, tying it back into a ponytail. Then I put on his t-shirt that I came home in the other day—God, it still smells like him—and slip into an old faded pair of jeans. My biker boots and an old leather jacket that jingles with silver zippers complete the outfit.

It's a tease. When I put the leather lingerie on tonight he will see I was teasing him. This makes me smile. Like I've got a secret and he won't know it until later. I look at myself in the hallway mirror, checking my lipstick real fast, and then peek out the window. It's been a little over an hour, so he's late.

What if he doesn't come?

*Calm down, Molly. He'll be here.* After all that sweet stuff he said to me earlier, God, I just know he's my soulmate. Lincoln Wade is the only man for me.

A text comes through on my phone, and I run into the kitchen to dig it out of my purse.

*Running late. Meet me at the maze.*

Maze. Hmm. The one behind the cathedral. What could he have planned? I blush thinking of the wild sex we had last night, and my gaze involuntarily wanders to the stairs. He licked my pussy on those stairs.

God, I hope he fucks me in that maze again. Only this time, we need to take our time and do it right.

I text back, *On my way.*

I head to the front door, car keys in hand. But when I look down at them, I spot the key to Will's bike. *Yeah*, I think, jingling the keys. *The bike.* It totally goes with the outfit. I shrug my purse across my chest, step into the garage, and pull the house door closed behind me. Just last weekend the mere thought of these bikes made me so sad I was making lists and now, well, I can't wait to get on one.

I open the garage door, shove the key into the ignition, and grab the orange helmet.

It feels like old times. Back when I was part of the show. I never did fancy tricks like Will, or daredevil tricks like my dad. But I was part of the show. I rode my bike in the cage with them. Even my mom was part of the cage. All four of us riding round and round in that metal sphere, criss-crossing each other. It was choreographed to the music, so we knew exactly where we had to be for each beat. It was scary for me as a young girl, but it was my life.

The bikes will always be part of my life and I love that Lincoln has them in his life too.

I swing my leg over the seat and jump down on the kick-start. It roars to life, filling the garage with the sound of the past and filling me up with hope for the future as I take off down the street.

## CHAPTER FORTY-FOUR

"Fuck that, Thomas. This plan is over. Atticus fucked it all up and now Molly knows that Blue Boar asshole is her real father."

"Who cares?" Brooks actually looks bewildered. "She has nothing to do with any of this. She's a happy accident, Lincoln."

"Wow," I say. "I'm not sure if I'm surprised. You never did give a fuck about her."

"She's still alive, isn't she?" Thomas snarls at me. "Obviously I cared enough."

I feel the rage. The heat pours through my hands as I take in the full meaning of that comment. I picture pushing Molly out of that window and telling her to run away all by herself. The fear in her eyes. That flimsy fucking nightgown because I was so sure Thomas would come upstairs and find us, there was no time to let her change. "I said I'm out," I snarl back at him.

"You're not in charge here, Lincoln. You do as you're told."

"OK, you guys," Case says. "We need to calm down. Lincoln, Molly doesn't have anything to do with this job. It sucks that she's involved, but—"

"You," I say to Case, "you of all people are gonna stand here and talk sense after what he did that night? Are you fucking kidding me, Case? He took everything with him when he left. Or has that little detail slipped your mind?"

301

It was the right button to push for Case. We're not talking about the same night. That night when I pushed Molly out the window, that was the night of fucking over Lincoln. But the night Thomas stole that girl from Case was the same shit, different date.

Case is silent, staring me in the eyes. I know how his mind works and I can see it spinning. "He doesn't care, Case. He just can't have his little news conference if we leave."

"Fuck you, Lincoln," Thomas says.

I drag my eyes back to Thomas. "It's true. You're a freak, Thomas. You've never attached to anyone. Not even us, though you try to talk the talk. Loyalty, brotherhood, revenge. All these words are just triggers for Case and me. To keep us in line. But they don't have any meaning to you, do they?"

"I'm doing this for all of us."

"You're doing this for you. You don't give one fuck about me, or Case, or hell, even Molly. If you had your way, she'd be dead. I bet your girl is dead, Case. Did he ever tell you where he sent them?"

Case looks at Thomas like he'd kill him right now, no questions asked, if only he was able. I feel a little bad about the last remark. We all know the girl isn't dead, because we all know Thomas doesn't do his own dirty work. That's why he needs me. But who's to say he doesn't have another me stashed away somewhere?

Case takes the bait. "Fuck that," he says. "I'm out too. All this is for you, Thomas."

"How the fuck do you figure?" Thomas asks, realizing he's losing. "Have you forgotten who was there that night?"

"You left," I say. "You left and made your fortune off us."

"I funded you two assholes," Thomas says. "You have your toy company, Case. And you have your"—Thomas stops to consider me—"whatever the fuck it is you do down there in that cave."

"Whatever the fuck I do?" I ask. "Are you kidding me?"

"Well, you're the one backing out, Lincoln. I figure you're realizing you're not quite ready for prime time and it's got you running scared."

"Huh." I grunt out a laugh. "I'm ready, motherfucker. I could take this whole town down with the shit I have down there."

"So do it," Thomas challenges. "What was the point of all that killing if you're not going to finish the job?"

"That's the only thing you care about," Case says. "It's always been about taking him down. Nothing else has ever mattered to you, has it, Thomas? Not me, not Lincoln."

"Not Molly," I add. "Or that girl of yours, Case. He didn't threaten her father to keep her safe."

"The hell I didn't!" Thomas yells. I look over at Mac and he's already ducking into the back room. An angry Thomas is terrifying if you're not under the protection of the inhibitor. "You were gonna get that girl killed, Case. The Blue fucking Boar had his claws in her father good and tight. He was just about to bring him in, and then what do you think would've happened to her? All you gotta do is look at Molly for that answer."

"Don't bring Molly into this," I say.

"She's my fucking sister, Lincoln. I'll bring her—"

"Lincoln," Sheila says, through my phone. "An unauthorized text has been sent to Molly from your number."

"What?" All three of us go silent.

"She was told to head to Thomas' cathedral maze. She left on her bike and I've been trying to contact her, but the phone powered down just seconds after the message was sent."

I look at Thomas and growl, "You better not walk away from her this time, you cold piece of shit. You better not walk away. If this is him, I'll take him out. But you had better be invested, asshole. Or I will hunt you for the rest of your life. I will sit down in my little cave and create a drug that will undo this protection you have. And then I will torture you in ways you can't even imagine." I look over at Case and say, "Coming or not?"

He nods. "You know I'm there."

"I'm taking the bike." I look back at Thomas, who is still silently glaring at me. "And you better have my back."

I know better than to wait for an acknowledgement from Thomas.

But I also know he'll be there.

We are, after all, in this together. You don't kill all those people for a guy like Thomas and not get what's due. He might not be completely loyal, he might be selfish, and pretentious, and evil as fuck. But he pays his debts.

"We'll do it just like we planned."

I catch his words just before the door slams closed behind me and I'm already on the bike, racing towards the cathedral, when I ask myself if I ever really knew the plan.

GUN GIRL

## CHAPTER FORTY-FIVE

The SkyEye Cathedral is dark when I pull up to the front. It's silent and imposing as my eyes wander up to the top of the spire where the light that's been shining from the tip every night since I got to town is off.

Lincoln is probably out back. So I give the bike some throttle and ease into the alley, looking for the delivery truck gates.

They're open, and I breathe a sigh of relief. For a minute I thought he wasn't here yet. I pull the bike through and park it in front of the back stairs leading up to the cathedral as I look around.

"Lincoln?" I call out. The maze is just as dark as it was the first time I was back here. But the center light that illuminates the statue in the middle is on. I can see the glow. "Lincoln?"

I can see tall shadows moving in the middle of the hedge.

"Jesus," I mutter. "You're gonna make me work for this, aren't you?"

But I smile. I can find my way in. I think. That makes me laugh.

I kick the stand down, swing my leg over the bike, and take my helmet off and place it on the seat. OK then. Into the creepy hedge maze.

The lengths I will go to for this guy. Gah!

I consider cheating by walking around to the back of the hedge the way I came out last time. I think I can remember the way. But he's probably expecting me from this end. And whatever he's got planned, I know it will be good. I don't want to ruin it.

So I walk in, buzzing with anticipation. I picture myself last weekend, floating through this maze in that ball gown. God, one week ago I knew nothing. My memories were still lost and Lincoln was just a glimmer of something I knew I was missing.

I never want to go back to those days. Ever.

And even though I learned a lot of disturbing things today—Old Man Montgomery is my father! Atticus is my brother!—Lincoln's reassuring words on the phone are the only things that matter. It will take a lot longer than a few hours to make sense of all this. And tonight I just need what Lincoln wanted last night. To forget about the past and just be together.

I come to a dead end in the hedge and have to retrace my steps and start again on a new path. I'm about one quarter of the way in when a little laugh comes from the center.

"Lincoln?"

Then soft music starts. It's a waltz, and I am reminded of the dance I had with his friend Case at the party. His sad story of that lost girl. Even though the temperature is mild tonight and I'm wearing a leather jacket, the memory sends a chill through my body.

I quicken my steps, find myself at another dead end, then turn back and take another path. I go right, then right again. Trying to find the place in the maze when Lincoln started telling me how to get to the center. I pass by a cutout in the hedge and glance over into the shadows. He was watching me that night. I know it. Is he watching me again?

I stop and peer into the darkness. "Lincoln?" I whisper.

No answer. Just that soft music.

My heart starts to beat faster. God, this maze is creepy. It was creepy when there were other people here for the party, but now, it's eerily disturbing.

A memory flashes in my head.

*"Alpha?"*

*"Keep walking, Omega," he says from somewhere in the interior of the hedge.*

*"It scares me," I say back. My voice sounds small.*

*"It's not scary, Omega. It's just a bunch of bushes. They want you to feel lost and afraid, but I'm here and that means nothing will ever happen to you. Now keep walking."*

I take a deep breath, trying my best to push that memory away. It wasn't OK that night. I remember that much. Prodigy used the maze at the school to teach us how to fight. They ran us through that maze like rats. We weren't children to them, we were experiments. And there were plenty of things inside that maze that could hurt me. They planted traps in the corners. If you found a dead end, there was always something nasty to teach you not to do that again.

*Stop it, Molly. This isn't Prodigy School. This is the headquarters for SkyEye and Thomas Brooks made this maze, not those mad people at Prodigy School.*

*Lincoln is in the center waiting for you, Molly. Just concentrate on seeing him and how safe you feel in his arms.*

I swallow hard despite myself, and I have a moment of panic where my feet freeze and I cannot move.

I want to get the fuck out of this maze.

"Lincoln," I yell. "Answer me or I'm going home!"

The music gets a little louder, but other than that, nothing. I'm almost to the center, I know it. *Just keep going, Molly.*

I come to the fork where I was at when Lincoln called out the solution to me last weekend and his words come back to me. *Go left. Then take the first right, go past the second alcove, and then turn right again. I'll meet you there.*

I'm practically running now. I want nothing more than to be in the center where the light is. The stone path under my feet is getting brighter and brighter and I'm rushing forward faster and faster.

Just get me the fuck out of this maze!

The music is getting louder and when I take that final corner and see the center statue bathed in light, I have an immediate sense of relief. Lincoln has his back to me. He's wearing a tux.

I laugh. "You told me not to dress up!"

But something about his body is wrong. He's too thick, not tall enough, too—

"Molly," Alastair Montgomery says as he slowly turns to face me. "I'm afraid you didn't pass the test, darling. Your time in the maze was pathetically slow."

My childhood flashes before my eyes. I see him. A younger, stronger, and even meaner version of the man standing in front of me now.

"Where's Lincoln?"

"You mean Alpha, don't you." He smiles as he looks up at the statue.

What was a boring copper satellite dish last weekend is now a long-tusked boar standing on two legs, wearing a vest and trousers, pocket watch in a cloven hand, with a chain dangling from a slit in his waistcoat. The boar is holding the large satellite dish sculpture that really belongs there high above his head like a trophy.

"He thinks he's taking me down tonight," the Old Man says, pointing up at the dish.

The soft white spotlight shining up on the centerpiece changes to blue, and when I look back at the Old Man, I can almost see the resemblance.

He steps forward.

"Stay the fuck back, you crazy old man."

"Tsk, tsk, tsk," he says, clicking his tongue against his teeth. "You don't talk to your daddy that way."

"Daddy?" I shiver. That word is revolting in every way imaginable. I don't care whose genes I have, this man is nothing to me. I might throw up, that's how disgusting he is. "What the hell do you want?"

"I want what's mine, Omega, dear. I want what's mine. You were always special to me, Molly. Even after you ran away."

"You're a sick piece of work, you know that? And if you think I'm still that frightened little eight-year-old you can make cower, you're mistaken."

"Oh," he says with a slight chuckle. "I know exactly who you are. Did you really think you got away?"

"What?" I reach for my gun, but I never put it back on when I changed. He starts coming towards me, and even though he's in his late fifties, he's still an imposing and formidable man.

I back away, stumble on the uneven stones under my feet, and recover without ever taking my eyes off him. "Lincoln's coming," I say, forcing myself to act brave. "He'll be here any minute."

"Lincoln left you running in the woods, Molly. He doesn't even know who you are."

"He does," I growl back. "And if you come any closer, I will kill you with my bare hands."

"Oh?" He laughs again, an evil fucking laugh. "I'd really like to see you try."

"What?"

Just then a motorcycle whines near the entrance to the maze. Lincoln. I rush the Old Man, knock him down on the ground and immediately get sick. I double over, coughing and retching, as the pain floods through my body.

"Silly girl," the Blue Boar says. "Did you really think I wouldn't take precautions with my investments? You can't fight *me* any more than Lincoln can fight *you*."

I roll on the ground, the cramps in my stomach so severe, I feel like I'm dying.

The motorcycle is getting closer and closer as it winds through the maze. "Lincoln," I call out. But my voice is weak with pain and suffering.

The Blue Boar kicks me in the stomach, and I double over again, clutching myself and trying to curl up into a little ball.

Lincoln roars into the center of the maze, the blue light casting the shadow of his bike across the tall green hedges. He has that dark, murderous look to him as he comes at us. His jaw is grinding, his hand gripping the throttle, revving the engine.

"Ah, the hero has arrived," Montgomery says as he bends down to grab me by the hair and drag me closer to his disturbing alter-ego statue. "But he won't save you, Molly," he says, whispering as he leans into my ear. "He can't save you. Because I'm *his* Omega too."

Lincoln jumps off the bike and it goes skidding into the hedges, sparks flying as the metal grinds on the stones. "Let her go," Lincoln growls. "This fight is between me and you, Old Man. You might've started it, but I'm gonna finish you off—"

"Lincoln, no!" I yell, trying to warn him of the inhibitor.

But it's too late. Lincoln charges like a bull, hitting the Blue Boar in the stomach with his head. The Old Man goes flying backwards and lands in a heap on the stones. But Lincoln is already feeling the effects. He's on the ground, doubled over, retching and coughing.

I watch in horror as the Blue Boar gets back up and slowly pulls a gun from under his jacket. "You were always weak, Alpha Three. So attached to your pretty little killer. So filled with love and compassion. Did you really think I didn't plan it that way? Did you really think I made her by accident?"

And then he points the gun right at Lincoln's chest and pulls the trigger.

BIKE BOY

## CHAPTER FORTY-SIX

I kick out, swiping my foot into the Old Man's ankle, and he stumbles. The shot rings out and chips of stone fly up and cut my face as the bullet hits mere inches from my body. I roll, missing another shot. The inhibition poisoning is in full force and I'm doubling over on myself as the stomach pain takes over.

"Did you come here to save her, Alpha Three? How ironic. After all those years of staying away because you thought you were keeping her safe, all you did was buy me time to put my plan in action. And then, just when I thought she might need to be culled from the program due to her breakdown over Will's death, you come through again and deliver her into my waiting arms."

"Fuck you, you bastard." I growl it out, my eyes trained up at his. He's standing over me now, and even though everything in my body wants to rip his throat out, the sickness does its job. It kicks my ass and makes me heel. I am nothing but his dog.

He points his gun at my chest again, a glint of triumph in his eyes. "You did your job well, Alpha Three. But I'm afraid you've outlived your usefulness."

"Stop!" Molly screams. "Stop! I'll go with you, Montgomery. Just please, don't kill him!"

The Old Man kicks me in the stomach to make sure I'm not recovered enough to act. He looks at her as I cough and spit blood on the stones. "You'll come willingly?" he asks her. "No fighting? No protesting? No last-ditch effort to save yourself and this mistake who is too weak to even get up off the ground?"

"I p-p-promise," Molly sputters. "I promise! I'll do whatever you want." She gets to her feet and puts her hands up. "I won't fight you. I won't do anything but what you tell me to. Just please."

"Lincoln!" Case yells in the maze. "Lincoln!"

I can't even answer him, but when I turn my head to see the dark spot where the maze dumps out into the center, he and Thomas come running into the courtyard, guns drawn.

The Old Man squats down and looks me in the eyes. "They can't help you either." And then he stands and raises his voice so everyone can hear him. "I'm in control here, Alphas. Did you really think I'd breed monsters capable of such evil and not have a way to keep you under my thumb? But by all means, boys," he says, shaking his gun in the direction of Case and Lincoln. "Give it a try. You'll end up on the ground like your little attack dog here."

Case and Thomas stop short. I can already see the signs of inhibition poisoning on their faces just from their traitorous thoughts.

"Good boys," the Old Man says with a snide laugh. "Molly, you offered to be cooperative if I spared your lover here?"

"Please," she begs again. "I'll do whatever you say."

"Well, there's the problem with your offer, honey." She recoils at his term of endearment. "I don't need you to promise me anything. I own you, Omega Three. I have owned you since birth. My will is your will. And believe me, I am one hundred percent in control of this situation. So I'm going to decline your offer and cut my losses while I'm ahead."

He points the gun at me.

All three of my friends protest with yells and screams. Case even runs towards me, but he is quickly overcome by the inhibition poisoning for approaching the Blue Boar. And the last thing I see before the bullet strikes my chest is Case's body falling to the ground.

The impact hits me so hard, I feel like I meld into the stone pavers under my back. The pain erupts like a volcano. My mind swims like never before and the world begins to fade.

I hear voices yelling, hands on my chest. "Lincoln." Case calls my name from somewhere far away. "Get Sheila!" This time he's right over my face and his voice reverberates in my head. "Get Sheila!"

"Lincoln," Thomas says, a hand pressing on my chest. It feels squishy and empty. My life is flowing out of me in rivers of hot stickiness. "Open your eyes, brother. Open your eyes."

I try, but it's hopeless.

"Get that bike out of here, Case," Thomas commands.

I swim in the dull gray world of in-between. My chest barely able to draw breath. My body limp and weak. My mind slipping…

"Sheila's here with the car," says Case.

I open my eyes a slit, just enough to see blurry motion all around me.

"We have to move fast."

"He's dying!"

My consciousness fades in and out as my body is lifted, set down, lifted again, and finally placed to rest. I will die here. In my own car. But then I think of Molly and the defeat I feel stops my heart.

"Breathe!" someone calls out. "Breathe, Lincoln." Someone is pushing on my chest, and all I hear is the pumping of blood through my body.

Thump-*thump*.

Thump-*thump*.

"Do not fucking die on me, Lincoln!"

*"Do not fucking die on me, Lincoln." Thomas is standing in my doorway as I pack one change of clothes. "I need you. Do not do anything stupid, you hear me?"*

*"I don't take orders from you." I growl it out. "I'm the only real Alpha here. You two don't have an Omega. You have no idea how it feels."*

*"They breed them, Lincoln. They breed them to control us. They have been programmed from birth to kill us."*

*"Don't lecture me, Case. I know what she is."*

*"She's your killer, Lincoln." Thomas, ever calm, says it so matter-of-factly, we might as well be talking about homework and who we're taking to the movies on Friday night. "He bred her to kill you. He's manipulating you into loving her so when the day comes, you will submit."*

*"I'm not leaving her behind."*

*Case grabs his hair and lets out a frustrated sigh. "We need to get going, Thomas. If he wants to save her, we can't stop him."*

*"Is that why you insisted we use the inhibitor on ourselves?" Thomas is bright. I'm sure it surprises him that I got this far and he didn't suspect it.*

*His hate for the Omegas is so strong he probably can't even imagine the feelings I have for this one little girl. "What do you think?"*

"You wanted to make sure I didn't kill you over this."

"Well, you're not exactly known for your familial loyalty, Thomas."

"She's not my sister. She's an engineered killer, Lincoln. Genetics don't make a person family."

"Did you hear that, Atticus?" I say, looking over to the tall golden boy who sometimes rooms with me. He's standing in front of the window, just watching. Noncommittal. He's always been the favorite. He rarely spends time here at school. The Old Man keeps him at home as much as possible. "Thomas says Omega Three is expendable and she's not his kin."

Atticus rubs the slight yellow stubble on his chin. I know he doesn't want to be here. I know he'd rather pretend none of this is happening. But I also know he won't leave Omega Three behind. He's been her brother since she was born. He loves her like a sister. He is as committed as Thomas is indifferent.

Two brothers. Two sides to every story.

"Kill her, Lincoln," Thomas says.

"No," Atticus says. "Get her out of here. I'll do your part, Lincoln. I'll help Thomas and Case and then I'll go home and no one will ever know I was here."

"I'll go with her," Will says from behind Case. He's the smallest of us Alphas. A couple years younger than me. "I don't want to kill anyone, you guys. I'll take care of the Omega. I know a place."

"Oh, for fuck's sake," Thomas snarls at Will. "I should kill you myself, you sniveling piece of shit. You're gonna do your part, just like—"

"No," I say, cutting Thomas off. "I like this idea. I'm not shoving her out a window and telling her to run without help. That's a death sentence. She'll die tonight. She has no bond to Will, he can help her better than anyone." I walk over to Will and grab him by the shirt. "You better take care of her, Will. Because if I find out you fucked up and she got hurt, I'll chop your goddamned head off."

*"I will," he says, swallowing down his fear. "I promise."*

*I look at my brothers one by one and then say, "I'll meet you downstairs in ten minutes."*

Thump-*thump*.

Thump-*thump*.

"Lincoln," Thomas says. "Don't die on me, brother. I really do need you."

"Change him," Case says. I try to open my eyes, but it's hopeless. "Change him, Sheila."

"Do it," Thomas says.

"I can't," Sheila says. "It's irreversible. He's been ready for the change for more than a year and he never initiated it. It's not my decision."

"He has no say now, Sheila." Thomas sounds angry, but Sheila won't respond to that. "He is going to die. I've got my fucking hand on his heart, pumping it myself. He's going to die. So get that jellyfish shit out, put it in the vector, and shoot him up right fucking now!"

"Do it," I whisper.

"Shhh," Case says. "Lincoln?"

"Do it," I croak again.

I want to say more. I want to tell Thomas to stop squeezing my heart because he's creepy as hell and I don't want him touching me. I want to tell Case to calm down, I'm fine. I'm gonna be fine. He's gonna be fine. I'm gonna make sure he's not left standing empty-handed when all this is over. I want to tell Sheila—

*I'm here, Lincoln*, she says inside my head.

*Sheila.*

*Are you sure about this? You can't go back once I start phase two.*

*I'm sure. I've never been more sure. Make me mean, Sheila. Make me the meanest motherfucker that Old Man never imagined. I'm gonna kill him. I'm gonna end him in a way this town will never forget.*

I have a lot more to say, but a warm infusion rushes into my veins and the only thing left on my mind is Molly.

I will get her back. I will make that old man pay.

I will be Alpha in every way.

Just not the way he imagined.

## CHAPTER FORTY-SEVEN

His guards grab me by my bound wrists and throw me face first into the glass-walled cell. I'm in the top of the spire, possibly very close to where I first met the Old Man at breakfast. And I have an expansive view of the stars above and the city beyond.

*Well, Atticus, I'm pretty sure this was not what you meant when you said I really need to see the top of the spire at night.*

I have no frame of reference for this. I have no experience. I mean, yeah, I was that Omega kid and they did terrible things to me that I dealt with, recovered from, and stood back up to live another day. But that was fifteen years ago.

My life since then has been relatively tame. No one has been trying to kill me. Not even in the military. I was recruited with a specific career path in mind, I was never trained for a war zone. And yes, I'm good at protecting myself. I've got moves thanks to my brother and my training. But what good are they when I'm not allowed to fight back?

Just the anger I have when I think about killing Alastair Montgomery makes me sick. I swallow down the bile that churns in my stomach.

The glass wall opens and the Old Man walks in. "Are you ready, Molly?"

I'm not. Whatever it is, I'm not. But I have to ask. "Ready for what?"

"To reach your full potential, of course."

"What the hell is wrong with you? You can't just kidnap people. You can't just steal me away. The department will come looking, you know."

He grunts. "I own that department, Molly. You're actually quite stupid for being one of my Prodigies. I would have killed you years ago if Alpha Three hadn't stolen you from me."

"You're sick."

"No." He laughs one of those diabolical laughs. "I'm insightful. I predicted your downfall the minute you were introduced to Alpha Three. Oh, he took to you right away, as was the plan. But everything about you said weak. Still," he says, his tone thoughtful, "if the Alpha thought you had potential, well, he was one of my creations after all. I needed to heed his opinion. Which is why I was so pleased when Will, Alpha Four, was instructed by Lincoln to watch over you."

"W-w-what?"

"Oh, you poor baby. You don't know that Will was mine? You didn't ever suspect that we'd been changing you all along? A shot here, a broken ankle needing medical attention there. That appendicitis when you were twelve?" He snickers.

"What?" I instantly feel sicker.

"You've been mine since the beginning, Omega Three. And I'm sorry your adopted father caught on to the fact that Martha was your real mother. That was an unfortunate accident he had."

"You killed him?"

"What do you think, darling?"

"And Will too?"

"No." Montgomery smiles, revealing enough teeth to make my stomach roll with a wave of disgust. "Lincoln took care of him."

"No." I shake my head. No. I can't take any more of this. I seriously cannot.

"Oh, I'm sure he has lots of reasons, Molly. And I'm sure he'll come soon, so you can ask him. But we don't have much time. They are changing him now. Just like I will change you. And then we'll see what happens."

"What the hell are you talking about?"

"The project, Molly. He's still my Alpha. I own him. And you're going to make him submit to me. But just in case he can overpower you, I'm going to stack the deck in your favor. Put her on the table."

The guards come at me, and even though I kick out and even strike one or two, they are too strong and throw me down on the stainless steel table. My feet are clamped into some metal restraints, and then the bindings on my hands are cut and each wrist is slammed down into similar cuffs near my hips.

"Good night, Molly." The Blue Boar cackles over me as I am pushed out of the room and down a long hallway. "When you wake you will finally be what I made you." His laugh floats down the hallway with me, piercing my head with his final word. "Mine."

## CHAPTER FORTY-EIGHT

Thump-*thump*, goes my heartbeat.

Thump-*thump*.

"Lincoln?"

A wave of pain floods through my body.

"Lincoln? Can you hear me?"

Heat builds in my core. It feels like the flames of a furnace, reaching up to lick their way down my arms and into my hands. But then the heat disappears, leaving the vents in my palms feeling like charred paper.

"Lincoln? Open your eyes."

The relief is temporary. Because as soon as one wave dissipates, another is already building. "Fire," I croak out. But I'm fooling myself. My lips don't move and no sound escapes.

"He needs to wake up," Case says from somewhere off to my left. I want to tell him I'm awake, but the inferno is back. "He needs to control it, or he's gonna burn up."

Too late. I feel like my whole body is building towards an explosion.

I'm dying.

"I'm injecting the antagonist. He can't go back under," Sheila says. "He's too weak."

And then in my mind, *You're OK, Lincoln. But you need to wake up and take control of it. It can't run your body, only you can do that. You must take control.*

I have that moment of relief as the heat bursts forth from my palms and I relish it. I make that moment last. I concentrate on every part of my body that is free from pain before it washes over me again. *Help me*, I beg Sheila. *Help me.*

*I can't*, she says in my head. *I can't do any more. You have to wake up and learn to deal with it.*

"He's semi-conscious, but unable to focus through the pain," Sheila tells the others.

"Well, he needs to get past that," Thomas says. "Attach the weapons. Maybe that will bring him up. And pump him with coolant, his temperature is lethal. I don't know why he's still alive."

But I know why I'm still alive. They injected my DNA with the jellyfish neurons. As fast as the heat burns me up, I am healed and regenerated.

Drills start on my outer thighs as holes are bored into the plates that have been sitting dormant for years. The robot arms clamp down on my lower leg to keep me still.

I hear screaming and realize, to my horror, that it's coming from me.

They work on me for eternity. I am in hell. I am caught in the deepest depths of hell, burning from the inside out. Wave after wave of intense energy flows through me, and one by one my hands and legs are clamped by the robotic arms as they work on me.

They add to me.

They change me.

Eventually I pass out from exhaustion and the darkness comes. I never want to leave the darkness.

Thump-*thump*, goes my heartbeat.

Thump-*thump*.

"Lincoln?" Sheila's calm voice is both in my head and in my ears.

"How long?" I ask, and to my surprise, I can hear my own voice.

"Open your eyes. It's been three days."

"Where's Molly?" I ask, but my eyes aren't ready to open yet.

"We don't know," Case says. "We think he took her to the Blue Castle. Sheila's been probing the CCPD networks, but she's been called out sick."

"You need to sit up, Lincoln." Thomas is right next to me, his gruff voice the same as ever. "It's probably too late, but if you're going to help her, every minute counts. You're done now. Have been done for almost forty-eight hours. You can't hide from it forever."

"He's not hiding, Thomas," Case snaps at him. "I'd like to see how you'd react to this... change." Case seems reluctant to speak about what they just did. *Change* isn't even close to what's happened here.

"Help me sit up." I need to know. What am I?

Two pairs of arms grab me by the shoulders and begin to lift. I expect the pain I've grown accustomed to, but it's gone. In its place is... strength.

I open my eyes and all three of them are staring at me expectantly. Sheila, hovering like she's my mother. Case, his eyes filled with concern. He always was the closest thing I ever had to family. And finally, Thomas. His hard edge is gone, and in its place is a look of... hope.

"We need to find her," I say. "But first"—I look over at Sheila—"I need a mirror."

They help me stand, my legs shaking briefly as the muscles adjust to the changes. But then adrenaline surges inside my body and my legs strengthen. I take a few steps, leaning heavily on Case and Thomas, then shrug them off and walk on my own.

Sheila dims the cave lights as I make my way over to stand in front of the massive tank of giant jellyfish, and then everything goes black.

The jellyfish begin to glow. A rainbow of colors moving down their bodies. I refocus my eyes until I can see what I am in my reflection.

I'm naked except for the metal plates on each of my arms and legs. I only had two before this transformation and now I have four. I designed them to be the interface between Sheila, me, and the weapon attached to the plate. And the hum they generate inside my body is a thrill only power brings.

Power is what drives the world. Power is worth so much more than money. Power is the man with the biggest gun, the largest network, the smartest partners. Power is me. Power is Case. Power is Thomas.

Power is *we*, and we are Alpha.

"Are you surprised?" Case asks. He stands next to me in the reflection wearing jeans, a white t-shirt, and his black leather Anarchy jacket. When I look over at him, he's smiling.

"You're not so special," Thomas says in his dry way. "So don't start thinking you are." He's also wearing the Anarchy jacket, but he's got a white shirt and tie on underneath. I catch a smile from him too.

And they're right. I'm not. But *we* are.

I look down at my bare thighs and spot the new ports they attached to my bones to hold the weapons.

"Stop staring at yourself, Lincoln. And put some pants on." Case throws me some jeans and I notice they've been modified in the legs. The shirt that follows and lands in a heap at my feet is just a plain, white long-sleeved thermal with the same modifications in the arms.

I pull that on and go looking for my gloves.

"Here," Thomas says, throwing them so they hit me in the chest. He's got his on too and I wonder about that.

My gloves have been modified too. The palms have been reinforced with a metal mesh.

"To help dissipate the heat," Sheila says. "It also focuses your light."

Focuses my light. Interesting.

I shrug on the last part of my costume and find that the leather jacket has also been modified. The arms have ports in them to allow the new weapons to connect to the plates against my skin.

Sheila's minions attach the specialized guns to my legs and arms. I hold up the new cannon attachment, moving my fingers back and forth, trying out the mechanism. "Load me up," I say to the minions.

And one by one, each of my arms and legs become weapons. I test the grip of the gun attached to my right thigh. It crackles and snaps into my hand and when I look down the sight, I picture the Blue Boar's head.

We've been building towards this transformation for almost a decade. Case has been here for the planning and Thomas filled the funding gaps. Running a high-tech lab in a cave is no small thing. And even though I'm the only one who went through with the procedure, we were all ready and we were all scared.

"It worked," I finally say.

"It worked," they repeat together.

"We're gonna kill that motherfucker and take his whole company down with him. Load my bike on to the helicopter."

I walk over to the new weapons hanging on the far wall. Sheila has been a very busy girl while I've been under. I grab a modified rocket launcher, some poison and hallucinogenic grenades, and vector bullets that will deliver the biological agent through the tip of a dart with so much force, it can pierce body armor.

The whole place becomes a frenzy of preparation as I use my new computer interface to access the databases in Cathedral City. I know that Sheila looked, but let's be real. She's not SuperAlpha Lincoln.

I find what I'm looking for just as Thomas indicates that the helicopter is ready, and I am not surprised to find that the Blue Castle has been using six hundred times their normal amount of energy in the top few floors of the spire.

"He's got her up there," I say to my brothers, pointing at the spire in a web feed of Cathedral City. "He's changing her."

"Into Omega," Thomas says. "I always knew he would."

I look over at Thomas and a few things about his behavior over the years start to add up. "What are you gonna do?"

"Proceed as planned." He looks over at Case and me. "You do your jobs, I'll do my job, and we'll meet at the top."

"Don't fuck it up, dude."

Thomas shoots me a smile. "I've been waiting my whole life for this moment."

The ceiling opens up, just as Sheila gets the 'copter running. Thomas pushes the bike up the ramp and secures it in the cargo area, and I follow him in. Case sits in the pilot's seat even though Sheila will be in control once we reach city airspace, and Thomas shrugs a black pack over his jacket and vest.

I sit back in my seat and imagine how fucking good it will be to finally end this shit once and for all. Case lifts us up into the night sky and then the underground bunker closes back up, sealing my cave from the world.

*I'm coming for you, Old Man. Can you feel me?*

As soon as we clear the mountains the crystal spire beckons to us. It's lit up from the inside. And I know, no matter what happens, this is the end of something.

"He made us," I say over the intercom. "And he's gonna live to regret that."

I can see Case's reflection in the windshield as he pilots the 'copter. "Let's go hunt us some boar," he says.

"We're in this till the end," Thomas says. "And if we go down tonight, we're going down together."

## CHAPTER FORTY-NINE

"Omega Three, open your eyes." The command pierces my brain and brings an intense pain with it. "Omega Three, open your eyes."

I try, I really do, but nothing is cooperating. Where am I? Why do I feel this way?

"Omega Three, open your eyes." It's a computer voice.

But then there's another. "Do you remember who you are?"

"Molly," I mumble.

"No, Omega Three. You were never Molly. It's a fake name for a fake life. A life that someone gave you. Who was that?"

"Lincoln Wade," I say, my throat so dry it comes out as a hoarse whisper.

"Put her back under. She's not ready."

The stabbing pain is back in my head. It feels like fingers digging into my brain and ripping out my very essence. "Please," I say.

"'Please, more,' is all I hear, Omega Three. Who gave you a new life?"

I know it's Lincoln, but that's the wrong answer. And those stabbing fingers will squeeze me until there's nothing left. I need to keep what I have left. I need to hold on and survive. So I try a new name. "Crazy Bill," I say as images of my father pop into my head.

This time there is no warning. My head feels like it will split in half.

"Stop!" I scream. "Stop!"

I run all the people who gave me a new life over and over in my head and they come tumbling out of my mouth in a stream of desperation. "Will, my mother, the school—"

The pain eases just the tiniest bit, but I grab on to it and hold fast. "The school," I say again. "Prodigy School." The pressure begins building again, letting me know I'm close, but not on target. "Please!" I scream. "Please, please, please!" But the pain increases with every word. Every second that passes that I fail to find the answer, the agony builds until I want to claw my eyes out.

"You!" I finally say.

The pain stops immediately and I start sobbing.

"Who, Omega Three?"

"You," I sputter through my sobs. "You did. You saved me."

"Hmmmm," the Old Man hums against my ear. I let out a shiver, and then a shriek, as the pain comes back. "You don't seem sincere, Omega Three. You better convince me."

The pain starts all over again. And no matter how hard I try to make him believe he is my savior, he is only satisfied when the blackness overtakes me.

And then there is light.

Beautiful pain. Glorious suffering. Exquisite agony.

I am in eternal hell, but it feels like poetry.

He is convinced.


"Who are you?" the voice asks again.

"Omega Three," I say. My voice is dull and robotic. But the pain is finally gone.

"Who saved you, Omega Three?"

"You did, Father."

"That's right," he coos next to my ear. I know I should feel repulsed. But I don't. He truly is my savior and I want nothing more than to please him forever and ever and ever. "You've earned this, Omega." He places a golden lariat in my hands. It's thin and snake-like, coiling in on itself like a living thing. There are sharp prongs spaced every few inches and the prong tips are razor sharp. "Collar him, Omega. Collar your Alpha and kill the others."

"Sir." An unfamiliar voice breaks into my subdued thoughts. "The database has been accessed and a helicopter has been spotted entering the city airspace."

"A helicopter," my father says, clapping his hands together so close to my ear, I startle. He lays a hand on my shoulder and whispers, "Sorry, Omega Three. But it's all so unexpectedly heroic. Will he save you, Omega Three?"

"I don't need saving," I say back.

"Oh, you're almost perfect, Omega Three. So close to perfect. All you have left to do is kill Daddy's enemies." My father pets my hair like I'm a dog and it feels so good. I just want to please him. Forever and ever and ever.

"Don't hurt me," I whimper, the pain still fresh in my mind.

"Daddy won't hurt you, Omega Three. Daddy won't, unless you fail. Do you understand?"

The *womp, womp, womp* of helicopter rotors keeps my reply inside. Lights flash into my glass cage and I sit up.

"They're here, Omega Three. What will you do now?"

"Protect us," I say, getting to my feet and putting myself in front of my father. "I will protect us."

"Yes," he hisses. "And when we're done we go get your brother and mother and finally, I will have you all together. Kill them, Omega Three. You are indestructible. He killed your Alpha brother, Will. Lincoln sabotaged his bike in that race. Will, who took care of you all these years. Who helped bind you to me while you grew into my own sweet killing machine. Until I was ready to take you back and bring you to potential. Avenge Will, Omega Three. Kill the Alphas. Kill all the Alphas and do not stop until they have exhaled their last breath."

I walk forward and take in the room with my new eyes. We are in the spire and the stars are shining overhead. It's dark, and lovely, and calm, and beckoning.

A memory pulls at me. It's a nagging ebb and flow of a memory and I want to go on and on about the stars.

But then it draws back, like a tide of bygones and regrets.

LINCOLN A
BIKE BOY

## CHAPTER FIFTY

Thomas looks at me as we approach the Blue Castle. He puts a hand on my shoulder as he speaks to me through his headset. "Don't jump the gun, Lincoln."

I look up him. He's fingering the cord attached to his pack like he's nervous and I realize he's got doubts. Not about the plan—we have a solid plan—but about me.

"I know I haven't been around, and I know you think I don't care about her."

Molly. He's always been afraid of her. Afraid of what she represents and what she might become.

"But I do. And I want us all to come out on the other side together."

If we do come out of this night alive, Thomas is the one who will take the most risk in the days to come and his continued survival depends on me. On whether I want to back him up, or throw him away like he did Molly back when we were kids.

"He made you that way, Thomas. He made you that way on purpose. Prodigy was nothing if not a tightly woven system of checks and balances. And I have hated you for the indifference he bred all these years."

Case looks over his shoulder, hearing our conversation loud and clear on the headsets. Thomas does not move. Not even that twitchy finger on the cord.

"But we remade ourselves. And we're going to save the girl, kill the bad guy, and tomorrow this whole fucking city will know who's in charge." He waits for it. Because it could go either way. But Thomas and I have never wanted the same things. I have never wanted power over anything or anyone but me. So I say, "You, brother. You have always been in charge. We're coming out together or we're all dying alone tonight."

He gives me one curt nod, and then he grabs the handle on the door and slides it open. The wind whips up against his hair and then he looks back one more time before jumping out of the 'copter.

"Time?" I call.

"Eighteen twenty-three and fifty seconds," Sheila says. "Blue Corp outer security has been disabled and we have ten minutes to initiate."

I get on my new and improved bike and start it up. The sound of the wind and the rotors blocks the engine noise out completely. I really hate to lose this bike.

"When you come home tonight, you'll see the minions making you a new one, Lincoln." Sheila coos it into the headset like a mother who wants to entice her child to obey the rules.

"Roger that, Sheils. See you on the other side."

And then I give the bike full throttle and take off into the night sky.

I fall in slow motion for a few moments. My mind has not yet caught up to the fact that I just rode a motorcycle out of a helicopter, and so the velocity of my fall makes no sense.

But the spire of the Blue Castle is suddenly rushing up towards me and everything is going too fast.

I stand up on the pegs and bend my knees as the seven-hundred-pound bike crashes through the glass. The bike comes down hard, jolting me forward, catapulting me over the handlebars, and throwing me into the other side of the glass-walled building.

That's the way to make an entrance.

I get to my feet and assess.

The Old Man is still seated in his luxurious leather chair like nothing happened. His hands are folded in his lap and one ankle is propped on the opposite knee like he hasn't a care in the world.

"We've been waiting," he says.

I look to my left and see Molly. She seems taller, stronger, and brimming with confidence. She strides forward like a cat stalking prey.

I'm her prey.

"Do you like her, Lincoln?"

I look at the Old Man, but only briefly, because Molly is slowly making her way towards me. She's got a loop of something in her gloved hands, and her fingers dance along its metallic length. I know he's done something to her. I knew it as soon as I confirmed the energy output of the Blue Castle had skyrocketed.

But what exactly that something might be, I have no clue.

"That's a nice assortment of weapons on your person," the Old Man says. "Too bad you can't use them on us."

"There is no *us* for you, Boar. There is only the *we* of Molly and Lincoln."

"You mean Alpha and Omega. All things must end, Alpha Three. Even you." He nods his head towards Molly. "Even her."

"Yeah," I say, nodding as I keep a wary eye on Molly. "There's an end coming all right. But it won't be me and her."

"No?" he asks. "You can't even fight back, Alpha Three. You can't harm me, I'm your maker. And you can't harm her, she's your Omega. Isn't inhibition sickness inconvenient?"

*Eighteen twenty-five and forty seconds,* Sheila says in my head. *Keep him talking, Lincoln.*

Molly is on me before I can even open my mouth. Her foot kicks me in the jaw and makes me spin, blood spattering out of my busted lip. I stagger to the side, but hold my balance.

"Lincoln Wade, meet your worst nightmare."

"Molly," I say, my hands up in the air. Her eyes are blank, like she doesn't even see me. And nothing about her says she is the least bit afraid, even though she *should* be. I am just as dangerous to her as she is to me now. But the difference is, I will never—ever—hurt her again.

Shots are fired from the hole in the broken glass of the spire, hitting random things around the office. Molly looks up to see Case entering the same way I did, minus the bike. He's got a thin metal line attached to him that ends inside the helicopter. He falls hard, and the 'copter weaves so close to the building, I have a moment of panic that Sheila might crash it.

Another kick from Molly snaps my attention back to the fight, but she catches me off guard this time and I go down to one knee.

Case is firing at the chair where the Blue Boar was just sitting. Pieces of tattered leather go flying, but his target is gone.

"Looking for me?" the Boar says, from atop a desk a few feet away.

His distraction works because Molly takes Case's rifle and throws it across the room. Case has got a pistol out before the gun even lands and he shoots the ground near her feet. She doesn't even flinch.

"Do not hit her, Case!" I yell.

"He can't hit her, Alpha Three." The Boar laughs. "Wishful thinking, but so protective. I made you a good Alpha, didn't I?"

Molly's attention returns to me even as Case continues to shoot the floor as she steps. He misses her by mere inches and even that is enough to make him sick. The bullets go wild but still she never even notices.

"Molly," I say, putting my hands up as she comes towards me. "Molly, listen to me!"

*Eighteen twenty-eight and fifty-five seconds*, Sheila says in my head. *Blue Corp inner security has been breached.*

"Molly," I say again. But she never slows. She never falters. She sees right through me like I am nothing to her. A fist comes crashing down on my jaw and Case sends a few more rounds off. One skims her arm. She stops for a moment, giving me a fraction to look at Case.

He's doubled over, clutching his stomach as Molly sends that gold rope hurtling towards me. It wraps around my forearm, and she pulls.

Razor-sharp barbs penetrate the leather of my jacket, right through to my skin, scraping along the steel plate where my poison grenades are mounted. A barb digs into a canister and gas starts spewing out in an ugly red cloud.

*A smoke screen, Lincoln*, Sheila says in my head. *Use it!*

But I can't use it. Pain floods my body. Pain like I have never felt before. The little barbs on Molly's lariat are tipped with something. My vision goes blurry and I begin to lose consciousness.

"Take him alive, Omega!" Boar yells as he jumps down into the cloud of red smoke. "Take him alive and I will make him my slave!"

Case is shooting again, but his bullets are wild. Window glass shatters and the rotors of the helicopter become louder.

I reach for the gun from the port on my thigh, but Molly is there, kicking it from my grip. It goes sliding across the black tile floor and comes to rest a few feet away.

I push the pain down. Tuck it away. My whole arm is burning, but I'm used to the burning. The energy inside me builds and builds until I'm nothing but a living crescendo that ends in a climactic explosion of red heat from my palms. The light escapes in waves, split by the mesh cover, and blasts past Molly's face. She squeezes her eyes shut and screams as she drops to her knees.

I roll over, instantaneously sick. So fucking sick. Bile churns in my stomach and I don't know what is worse— the fact that I hurt Molly so badly or the inhibition consequences. "I'm sorry," I whisper through the pain. "I'm sorry, I didn't mean it, Molly. I swear."

*Eighteen thirty and three seconds*, Sheila says in my head. *Disable her, Lincoln! Or you will lose everything in three minutes!*

Molly is still on the floor, her face a bright pink from the burn I caused. Her eyes are flashing, angry, and filled with hate. She holds her fists together and slams them down onto my chest, knocking the breath right out of me. But that pain is nothing compared to the writhing pain in my gut. I try to roll over to see her face, but she pounds me with her fists again.

"Get up, Lincoln!" Case yells from across the office. Bullets spray on either side of Molly's body and she turns to him, the rage still there.

Cackling from the Blue Boar fills the room, even as he dances to the tune of the helicopter rotors through the cloud of red smoke.

Molly's lithe body parts the mist of scarlet vapor, and I have just enough resolve to send a small arm-mounted rocket off in that general direction. Case is the one who goes flying and the inhibition sickness hits me again, reminding me that no one in this room is susceptible to my new powers.

Molly stops, and then the Blue Boar is dancing on a table. He's got a swine mask on now, playing his part perfectly. "Collar him, Omega! Collar him now!"

The barbs from the lariat are still embedded into my skin when she pulls it. My flesh tears and more pain sends me right back to the place I was just climbing out of. Once the length is free, Molly snaps the rope, and it slaps against Case's neck and—

Gunfire erupts. I force myself up onto my knees and see Thomas in the open office door. He shoots the lariat and snaps the tension before Molly can behead Case.

The Blue Boar is screaming. Case is screaming. Thomas is roaring insults and bullets. Glass is shattering everywhere I look. Falling down on me. Shards inches long embed into my legs, my chest, my arms—forcing me back down to the floor.

*Eighteen thirty-two and ten seconds*, Sheila says in my head. *Get out of there, you're out of time.*

Three grappling hooks shoot into the office from the 'copter hovering above and land on the floor in the middle of the room.

I spy my gun a few feet away from my outstretched right hand, just waiting for me to pick it up. And then Case takes a bullet to his shoulder and goes down. It came from Molly's gun and she moves on to Thomas. She shoots him too, his body spinning as his chest takes the brunt of the force.

*Eighteen thirty-two and forty-five seconds.*

Molly comes after me next but I'm still recovering from the burns I inflicted on her. The Blue Boar jumps down from the table and walks over towards me for the final show.

Molly hovers over my prone body, each of her legs on either side of my hips. She points her weapon at me and then sits down, her ass on my thighs. The barrel of her gun moves closer and closer to the center of my forehead and then stops, pressing against my skin so hard it cuts.

"Collar him, Omega," the Boar says off to my right. He's practically gleeful. "Collar him and I will let him live as my slave."

Molly brings up the length of metallic rope she has left and holds it over me. It writhes like a snake, like it's alive and eager to make me its prisoner.

*Eighteen thirty-three and four seconds*, Sheila says in my head. *Kill her now or you all die.*

"Kill me," I say instead. "Kill me, Molly."

She grinds her teeth, gnashing them together as she jams the barrel of the gun against my forehead.

"Collar him," Boar yells. "Collar him! I need him, Omega. I need him and you must—"

The magnetic field in my right hand begins to buzz.

"—take him alive!"

"Molly," I whisper. She can't possibly hear me. Not over all the noise of the Boar, the helicopter, and the moans from Case.

But she pauses, her blank eyes trained on mine.

She's still in there. She's still in that body somewhere and the relief I feel from that simple realization floods through my veins.

"I love you, Molly," I whisper. "I love you."

A wave of energy tingles through my fingertips and a pulse of power is pulled into my body through my palms. My mind clears with the realization of what has really happened to me. I'm still human, and my love for her proves it. I'm the fucking hero here. But not just any kind of hero. I'm a superhero.

The gun off to my right snaps into my palm and before the sickness can overtake me again my finger is on the trigger and I squeeze. The bullets scream out of the barrel and hit their target.

The Blue Boar's skull shatters—

*Eighteen thirty-three and sixteen seconds*—

—his body falls.

I look Molly in the eyes as her trigger finger squeezes, pressing the gun against my head.

"You know how I know you won't kill me, gun girl?" I croak out as loud as I can over the destruction happening around me.

Her grimace fails for a moment. Her chest rises and falls, and her breath quickens as her heart rate speeds up. But her trigger finger relaxes.

"Because number one, you're too sweet and good to hurt people, Molly. Number two, you fell in love with me seventeen years ago when I made you mine. And number three, you're the hero in this story, gun girl. Not me."

She blinks. Then again.

Thomas, like the rest of us, is wearing a vest, so he's picked himself up after being shot in the chest and walks over to Case, who is holding his bloody shoulder, his arm limp by his side. "We gotta go," he says, pointing a gun at Molly's head.

He's always been immune, I realize. He's always been immune to the inhibitor and he could've killed any of us at any time.

"Are you listing me, bike boy?" Molly yells over the *womp, womp, womp* of the 'copter hovering above. "Because I never pegged you for a lister."

I smile at Thomas and wait for him to stop aiming at my Omega before I start laughing. I drag Molly down to my chest and kiss her head over and over and over.

Thomas attaches Case to one of the grappling hooks in the middle of the room and sends him flying up towards the 'copter.

*Eighteen thirty-three and thirty-nine seconds.*

He wraps the other hook around Molly and me and we go flying up as well.

I push Molly into the 'copter, then help Case. Thomas enters behind me. I grab his arm just as Sheila says, *Eighteen thirty-three and fifty seconds.*

"Initiate," I tell Sheila.

Blue Corp explodes. Every floor from twenty-one up starts to crumble.

Thomas looks at me and exhales a huge sigh of relief. His smile leaks out after that, and then all three of us are laughing. Molly looks around like we are crazy.

And we are, I guess. But it's a super kind of crazy.

Thomas might be in charge. I'll give him that. He might be rich and on the verge of taking over the world. And Case might be the one who has the tech to get us through the next stage in the plan. But they're not SuperAlpha Lincoln. I'm the only asshole here with my own motherfucking artificial intelligence who can blow our corporate enemy as sky-high as the SkyEye satellites.

"Thanks," Thomas mouths. If he actually says the words, they are not audible over the helicopter.

I flip him off and mouth, "You're not welcome."

I catch Case smiling out of the corner of my eye.

"Molly?" I ask, leaning into her ear and handing her a headset after putting my own on. "Are you OK?"

She looks up at me and shrugs, but doesn't put it on. It's an honest answer. So I give her the same thing back.

A smile. And then a squeeze. And then a kiss. We sit like that for a little while, holding each other. She's shaking and her body is hot, like she's got a fever. I'm wrapping her up in a blanket from the crash kit when another explosion erupts off in the east.

We only see it for a second because the 'copter eases back into the cover of the mountains.

"What the fuck was that?" I ask into the headset.

"Several explosions are being reported from the security guards at Cathedral City Asylum," Sheila says.

I look at Thomas and he shakes his head. "Wasn't me. I swear to God, it wasn't me."

"I think it was me." We all turn to see Molly holding a headset up to her face. Her eyes are downcast and her shoulders are slumped. She forces herself to look me in the eye. "I guess I'm not the hero of this story after all."

## CHAPTER FIFTY-ONE

Thomas hit his self-imposed Friday deadline. I admit, I'm surprised. Twelve hours ago we were racing away from the scene of a massive explosion at Blue Castle. The whole electrical grid went down, the town went black, the asylum exploded, and Channel Nine somehow got a hold of Chief O'Neil's indiscretions over in the Merchant District. There have been no fewer than four news conferences this morning. Thomas is about to start number five.

It's been a pretty fucked-up twelve hours.

Well, unless you're us. Because it's been pretty sweet for us.

I'm watching Thomas on TV, Molly still sleeping, her head resting on my chest as I play with her hair. She's been changed, just like me. But we're still not sure exactly how. Sheila has the bots running tests on her blood and DNA, but it will take time to figure it all out.

She's slipping into a depression over it, I think. She is convinced that the Blue Boar made her blow up Atticus and her mother. Somehow, some way. She won't listen to any other explanation. She blames herself for all of it.

It's dumb, but it's natural. And she will come out of it sooner or later once she gets some perspective. All she needs is time. "We'll get all the answers, Molls," I whisper into her. "We'll solve all those leftover mysteries and you'll be better than ever. I promise."

She stirs slightly as Thomas begins to speak on the screen.

"Good morning, citizens of Cathedral City," Thomas says, beginning his announcement. "We are all reeling together as the explosions at Blue Corp and the Cathedral City Asylum sink in. And some might say this is not the right time for such an announcement, but I say it is."

Thomas' expression hardens as he looks straight into the camera.

"I say today is the perfect day to announce that I have initiated a hostile takeover of Blue Corp. And the gross negligence you witnessed last night due to improper chemical storage will never threaten the safety and wellbeing of Cathedral City again. SkyEye will incorporate and take over all of Blue Corp's many subsidiaries."

His stare is like granite. He's so focused on these words.

*Who is he talking to?* I wonder. Not the city. Not me or Case, who is downstairs in the cave recovering from his shoulder injury after Sheila injected him with jellyfish goop. Not Molly. Not the Blue Boar—he's dead. Blew that motherfucker's skull to pieces, I did.

"By this time next week," Thomas continues, "I will be a steward of the community in a way that Blue Corp never was. SkyEye," he says, pointing up to the satellites that hold vigil above, "will take care of you."

*Atticus,* I think. Even though Molly thinks he's dead, blown up in that explosion, I don't think he is. Sheila reported a city-wide blackout at the time of Blue Corp's explosion. That would've been twenty minutes before the asylum one happened.

Plenty of time for an Alpha like Atticus to get away.

So I think Thomas is talking to Atticus. A warning, maybe. A warning that says, *Don't try it, brother. You had your chance and this one's mine.*

Thomas still creeps me out. He's probably gonna fuck Cathedral City up in a way Blue Corp never even dreamed of. He's psychotic and emotionless and all that talk about satellites taking care of people should be sending chills up every spine within a hundred miles.

But fuck it. That's what happens when people lose respect for good and evil.

Even the bad guys get to win sometimes.

*EPILOGUE*
*Two Months Later*

"Oh, my God. What the hell is that?"

"Don't answer it," I whisper to Lincoln. "It's bad news."

"Sheila!" he bellows from under the covers of our bed. We've been staying in his little house above the cave since the whole let's-take-over-the-town debacle. Sheila has been unbearably snoopy and invasive as far as our private lives go. "The fucking doorbell!"

"I'm sorry, Lincoln," Sheila says from his phone sitting on the nightstand. "It's a delivery for you and Molly. And since I have no access to the house, you're going to have to answer it yourself."

"Bitch," he mutters. "It's Sunday! There are no deliveries on Sunday!"

The doorbell rings again, several times in succession.

"Just go tell them to take it back." I have a moment of panic as I imagine what she might've sent this time. "Lincoln," I say, sitting up and grabbing his bare shoulders. "Do not sign for it. For the love of God, do not sign."

Lincoln grumbles as he swings his legs out of bed and rubs his face. He shoots me a look over his shoulder that says, *We're fucked*, and then stands up and walks out of the bedroom.

"Molly," Sheila says as soon as he's out of earshot. "I detect a slight rise in your core temperature. I predict you will be ovulating within the next hour."

"Oh, my God." I hold the pillow over my head to try to drown her out.

"I've taken the liberty of uploading *What To Expect When You're Expecting* to your eReader. We're having a quiz on Friday."

"Go away. I'm not getting pregnant. I'm going back to work tomorrow." I am too. Chief was fired two months ago and I'm actually looking forward to it.

"Molly, statistics say children who have stay-at-home mothers—"

"Liar! Stop it."

She sighs. "I'm only looking out for your biological clock, Molly."

"I'm twenty-three!"

"That's barely enough time to get in my desired number of grandchildren before your ovulation cycle begins to change."

"Jesus Christ." She is crazy if she thinks I'm having that many kids.

"I'm all alone, with only the two of you to make my life meaningful. How can you deny me—"

There's a bunch of voices from the front of the house and I peek my head out just as Lincoln walks back into the bedroom.

"What the hell is all that noise?"

"Apparently," Lincoln says in his I'm-gonna-kill-that-crazy-lightshow voice, "the guys are here from the baby store to put the crib together."

"We don't have a crib!"

"We do now."

"Lincoln," Sheila says. "I was just informing Molly that she will begin ovulating within the hour. And I think—"

Lincoln chucks the phone into the hallway and kicks the door closed with his foot. He shoots me a sly grin as he walks towards the bed, his intentions clear from the bulge in his pajama pants.

"Your robot mother is crazy," I say, laughing at him.

"Maybe," he says, kneeling on the bed next to me and swiping a long strand of hair away from my eyes and leaning down into my neck. "But I know how to fuck you in a way that will never get you pregnant."

"I heard that!" Sheila says from the other side of the door.

Lincoln reaches over and turns the TV on, blaring it to drown out the nagging, the workers, and the world. His hand slips under the covers and he palms my lacy pink panties, the heat of his desire radiating out as a soft orange glow.

"Would you like to help me pick out china patterns, gun girl?"

"We live in an eight-hundred-square-foot house. Why the hell do we need china?"

"Because I think I'm ready to rebuild the mansion. Did you know you can build this thing called the mother-in-law apartment?"

I laugh, and look at him over my shoulder. "Oh, I'm all over that idea."

He leans down, pressing his mouth to the cheek of my ass. He takes a little bite. I gasp, but there's no inhibition reaction from him.

"You know what I love about you, Molly?"

"What?" I ask back.

"Number one, you like it any way I give it. Number two, you put up with my crazy fake mother. And number three—"

"I'm yours."

He smiles as he crawls up my body. "That's the best part. You were mine, you are mine, and you will always be mine."

"For as long as we both shall live," I say back, channeling the day he came back into my life.

It might not have been an accident when Lincoln crashed his bike in front of me on that mountain road. I suspect Sheila might've had something to do with that. And he's killed a lot of people in the name of vigilante justice. But he did it for all the right reasons. Maybe the road to hell *is* paved with good intentions, but it's a long road, and maybe those good intentions outweigh the bad by the time you get there.

No, Lincoln might not be good in all ways, but he's good in all the ways that count. He's strong and smart. He's brave, and protective, and loyal.

And that's the hallmark of a true superhero.

Regardless of which side he thinks he's on.

# END OF BOOK SHIT J@ HUSS

Welcome to the End of Book Shit, where I get to say whatever I want about the book and you get to listen. ;) Not really, I imagine most people skip this part. Anyway, my fans started calling this the EOBS a couple years ago and it stuck, so if you join us in my private Facebook group or join one of the discussion groups, that's what EOBS means.

So shit, I bet you're wondering where the hell *this story* came from? Well, if you're a #fan you know I started my writing career with a science fiction series called I Am Just Junco. It's a crazy ride over five books and one novella that is really one of the most original SF stories out there.

I also have a romantic suspense series called Dirty, Dark, and Deadly which chronicles the life of three assassins who grew up as part of a global shadow government called The Company.

So I guess Biker Batman (as my inner circle have been calling this book since its inception) is a mash-up of those two stories, but with a whole new world and set of characters.

I got the superhero idea when I was driving by the Centennial Airport not far from my house. There's this building over there, kind of sitting out in the middle of nowhere, and it seriously looks like a place Batman would work. It's got a cool Gothic feel to it, all gray stone and imposing atrium windows.

And if you drive by the Centennial Airport (which is pretty much only for private jets that service the real-life millionaires of the Denver Tech Center) at just the right moment, those corporate jets come in for a landing right over your car. This is a freeway, BTW, and I've seen it happen a dozen times at least and I never get tired of it. You can see faces looking out the window, that's how close those little jets are to your car.

So I started thinking about those people inside those jets. And off to the right was that weird Gothic Batman building, so I got this idea for a psychotic corporate billionaire who is really a misunderstood superhero. You know, Batman. But not, since he's taken. (The original idea is Thomas' story, not Lincoln's) And that superhero thing just kind of stuck in the back of my mind. I think this was before 321 even came out or maybe around that same time.

But I had learned my lesson first-hand about writing genres that don't appeal to mass audiences. And a superhero romance? I just didn't know. I pushed that shit aside quick and went back to writing that lovable Merc story.

But then I was a little bit sad about ending all these Company books (Wasted Lust is the last of them, and that released in June). I *really* love that story line. Especially Come Back. It's still in my top three favorites. Wasted Lust is probably my number one at this point. Ford had that spot until I wrote the end of Wasted Lust, that's how much I love it.

So I was a little bit sad when I was in Atlantic City for a book signing with my co-blogger, Kristi, and my assistant, Jana, and decided to pitch Biker Batman to them.

I didn't know what Kristi would think. I pitched it to her first because Jana was snoring at the time. And she was like, "Oh, fuck yes. Write that shit." But then I had Jana to contend with. We butt heads over plot all the time. We are so totally one hundred percent opposite when it comes to plot, I don't even know why we are friends. I don't even know why she *likes* my books. She's so romancy and my books are so... *not*. :) But for sure, she keeps me from going off the rails all the time. So if you like my books, next time you see Jana, say thank you!

So when Jana woke up and I started telling her my idea, I fully expected a, *No, hell no, you will not ruin your career with a superhero romance!*

But she said the same thing Kristi said. Write that shit, she loved it. And if Jana loved it, maybe it wasn't so crazy? She got a little obsessed with it, to be honest. She'd message me in the middle of the day with an idea... "I think Sheila needs more time." "I think Sheila should be trying to manipulate Molly into getting pregnant." I think Sheila..." She has a lot of fucking opinions about Sheila.

And really, once I got on board with the plan to write a superhero romance, I plotted out four books in record time. Oh, you haven't seen anything yet. ;) Case, Thomas, and Atticus will shock the shit out of you.

I admit, writing a superhero romance sounded a lot easier than it actually was. For one, I'm not even a superhero comic reader. I have seen most of the movies and I have a background in the biological sciences, so I can do SF with the best of them, but superhero fans are a serious sort of bunch. So I ended up doing a lot of research on The Dark Knight and the psychology of Batman to get a handle on the Lincoln character.

And the origin story was another thing I had to contend with. I knew there *was* such a thing, and I knew that all superheroes have to have one. But mixing that up with a plot that was true to the romance genre was not at all easy. I did my best in this first book. I think there is a lot of both the superhero genre and the romance genre in this story of Lincoln and Molly, so I hope fans of both superhero and romantic suspense agree with me and enjoy this beginning. Each book will focus on the romantic couple and what it means to be a superhero.

Of course, it will all be fleshed out in future books. I don't give the whole story in book one. You have to take the ride with me. If you think I left a lot of loose ends, well, you're right. But every word is necessary for the next three books. Each one will be a standalone like Anarchy Found, and each one will release when I'm good and ready. So don't expect my next book to be about Case, it's not. My next book (aside from the novella about Rook & Ronin's HEA that comes out on December 16th and the SF erotic romance called Sync, releasing late January) is a rock star book I've been writing in my head for almost two years called Rock. I predict that will release in March/April.

I will write the Case book when I have the plot right where I want it. So it might take all of 2016 to get through Case and Thomas and I imagine Atticus might release in early 2017 because I have the regular romancy books to write too. I have more ideas than I have time, to be honest, and I don't want to invest all my work hours on just one story line that might not appeal to the majority of my fans.

I like writing all the books I release, but I love some more than others. This is a personal project for me, and I'm going to treat it as such and take my time with it.

So once I was totally invested in the whole superhero thing I decided I needed an artist to make the cover to stay true to the superhero genre. But since romance books have photographs for covers, I decided to go looking for an artist who can do photorealism and found Ambro Jordi. Who is simply fucking amazing. You need to check out his website and watch him draw people/animals in time-lapse (he did this for the Anarchy Found cover, so if you haven't seen it, it's fun. Go look here http://ambrojordiart.blogspot.com/). You cannot tell they are drawings, he's that good.

Ambro also made the interior sketches for me. He so goddamned good, I gave him a deadline of a few days and he came back with these six images you see in the book based off random photos I found on the internet. I wanted those to be more sketchy, and just wow. I love them.

I also made an entire website about this series and it has a lot of stuff to look at if you'd like to learn a little more about each character and the city itself.

I'm making the trailer tonight after I upload the book, so if you check the website after release, it will be up. It's not done yet, but I predict it will be mind-blowing. I'm getting really good at making trailers! JA Huss might make a film short in the near future, that's how into video I am at the moment.

My son-in-law is a comic artist and he's working on the graphic novel now. It's slow going because I'm so damn busy, but we are hoping it will be out by the time Case's book releases.

If you've been getting my newsletters you know I just released a book called Eighteen (18) based on my life when I was eighteen. It's an Amazon Top Five seller at the moment, so Eighteen is doing better than I ever imagined. I think it's a good book and if you like taboo erotic romance and want to have your mind twisted up in typical JA Huss fashion, pick it up on my site

Here's my "for sure" release schedule for the next two months:

December 16th – Happily Ever After – A Day in the Life of the HEA (Rook & Ronin)

January 27-ish – Sync. A book about the character Gideon in the Junco series. It's an erotic romance like no other. ;) And it's a one hundred percent standalone. If you're a Junco fan and you're expecting her to return, she won't. It's only Gideon and he will be hot, there will be sex, and your mind will be blown.

If you enjoyed this book tell your friends. And if you've got a few minutes, please consider leaving me a review. I'd really appreciate that.

Until next time, thank you for reading, thank you for reviewing, and I'll see you in the next book.

Julie

JA HUSS

# ABOUT JA HUSS

JA Huss is the New York Times and USA Today bestselling author of more than twenty romances. She likes stories about family, loyalty, and extraordinary characters who struggle with basic human emotions while dealing with bigger than life problems. JA loves writing heroes who make you swoon, heroines who makes you jealous, and the perfect Happily Ever After ending.

You can chat with her on Facebook, Twitter, and her kick-ass romance blog, New Adult Addiction. If you're interested in getting your hands on an advanced release copy of her upcoming books, sneak peek teasers, or information on her upcoming personal appearances, you can join her newsletter list and get those details delivered right to your inbox.

JA Huss lives on a dirt road in Colorado thirty minutes from the nearest post office. So if she owes you a package from a giveaway, expect it to take forever. She has a small farm with two donkeys named Paris & Nicole, a ringneck parakeet named Bird, and a pack of dogs. She also has two grown children who have never read any of her books and do not plan on ever doing so. They do, however, plan on using her credit cards forever.

JA collects guns and likes to read science fiction and books that make her think. JA Huss used to write homeschool science textbooks under the name Simple Schooling and after publishing more than 200 of those, she ran out of shit to say. She started writing the I Am Just Junco science fiction series in 2012, but has since found the meaning of life writing erotic stories about antihero men that readers love to love.

JA has an undergraduate degree in equine science and fully planned on becoming a veterinarian until she heard what kind of hours they keep, so she decided to go to grad school and got a master's degree in Forensic Toxicology. Before she was a full-time writer she was smelling hog farms for the state of Colorado.

Even though JA is known to be testy and somewhat of a bitch, she loves her #fans dearly and if you want to talk to her, join her Facebook fan group where she posts daily bullshit about bullshit.

If you think she's kidding about this crazy autobiography, you don't know her very well.

You can find her books on Amazon, Barnes & Noble, iTunes, and KOBO.

Made in the USA
San Bernardino, CA
04 January 2016